P9-DOE-555

*Praise for*
# Norwegian by Night

"*Norwegian by Night* shifts along like an inquisitive wind, with a voice so confident you would follow it into a leaning house. Generous with its wit, dazzling in its cultural and historical reach, it is the kind of sweep-you-up tale a reader always wants but rarely finds, the kind where you stand in the bookstore reading the opening pages and whisper, *This is the one.*" —**Leif Enger, author of** *Peace Like a River*

"An unusual hybrid: part memory novel, part police procedural, part sociopolitical tract, and part existential meditation."
—*Kirkus Reviews*

"Have you ever lucked into one of those novels so taut and suspenseful that you can't turn the pages fast enough, yet, at the same time, so magnificently written and psychologically incisive that you find yourself unable to turn those same pages *slowly* enough? Such novels are as rare as great comets. *Norwegian by Night*, I'm happy to report, is one." —**Jonathan Miles, author of** *Dear American Airlines*

"Both an exciting chase thriller and a poignant story about a man who comes into his own again in his dotage . . . The many admirers of Scandinavian crime novels will enjoy this bighearted first novel." —*Library Journal*

"No brief plot outline can do justice to a book that deserves to find a place on a few best-of-the-year lists. Sheldon is a brilliantly imagined character, a true mensch, made of Greatest Generation stuff . . . Miller joins the ranks of Stieg Larsson, Henning Mankell, and Jo Nesbø, the holy trinity of Scandinavian crime novelists."
—*Booklist*, **starred review**

"An outrageously intelligent thriller, and its philosopher-sniper hero, Sheldon Horowitz, is a character who'll stay in your brain for decades. You might come for the guns and the ruckus, but by the last page, you'll be crying at all the goddamned beauty and love in the world." — **Patrick Somerville, author of *This Bright River***

"Truly a page-turner . . . *Norwegian by Night* is about past wars and present-day ethnic strife, family, grief, guilt, and, ultimately, redemption. Korea (and phantom Koreans), Vietnam, the Holocaust, ethnic identity — Serb, Norwegian, Muslim, and yes, Jewish — these are the true characters of the novel . . . Funny, moving, and thoroughly gripping." — ***Jewish Week***

"One of the most surprising and unusual novels to emerge in recent years . . . Miller takes readers down many paths, commenting thoughtfully on war, family, country, identity, and the personal as political, yet never loses the tension or propulsion of his story. Thought-provoking, evocative, and wry in the best way, *Norwegian by Night* is a remarkable novel." — ***Shelf Awareness***

"Ostensibly a Scandinavian thriller yet recalls Saul Bellow and Philip Roth's more cerebral creations . . . At once a rich psychological study, a political parable . . . and a moving story of an old man's last chance to slay his demons." — ***Sunday Times***

"A stunning examination of how our lives shape our character, and how our allegiances shape our destiny."
                                    — ***AARP*, "12 Summer Reads for 2013"**

"A rare comedic gem that is so special . . . Dark, moving, meaningful, absolute fun to read, and a thriller to boot." — ***Psychology Today***

# Norwegian by Night

# Norwegian by Night

Derek B. Miller

Mariner Books
Houghton Mifflin Harcourt
BOSTON   NEW YORK

First Mariner Books edition 2014

First U.S. edition 2013

Copyright © 2012 by Derek B. Miller

All rights reserved

For information about permission to reproduce selections from this book, write to Permissions, Houghton Mifflin Harcourt Publishing Company, 215 Park Avenue South, New York, New York 10003.

Published in Australia by Scribe in 2012

www.hmhco.com

*Library of Congress Cataloging-in-Publication Data is available.*
ISBN 978-0-547-93487-7   ISBN 978-0-544-29266-6 (pbk.)

Printed in the United States of America
DOC 10 9 8 7 6 5

*For my son*

# Contents

PART I

# The 59th Parallel

# CHAPTER 1

I T IS SUMMER AND luminous. Sheldon Horowitz sits on a
folding director's chair, high above the picnic and out of reach
of the food, in a shaded enclave in Oslo's Frogner Park. There
is a half-eaten *karbonade* sandwich that he doesn't like on the paper plate cradled in his lap. With his right index finger, he's playing
with the condensation on a bottle of beer that he started to drink
but lost interest in some time ago. His feet twitch back and forth
like a schoolboy's, but they twitch slower now at the age of eighty-
two. They achieve a smaller arc. Sheldon will not admit it to Rhea
and Lars—never, of course not—but he can't help wondering what
he's doing here and what he's going to do about it before the won-
derment passes.

Sheldon is an arm's length from his granddaughter, Rhea, and
her new husband, Lars, who is just now taking a long pull on his
own beer and is looking so cheerful, so kind, so *peppy*, that Sheldon
wants to take the hot dog from his hand and insert it up his nose.
Rhea, who looks oddly pale today, would not respond well to this,
and it might condemn Sheldon to further *socializing excursions* ("so

you can adjust"), and in a world filled with fairness Sheldon would not deserve them—nor Lars the hot-dog maneuver. But it had been Rhea's idea to move them from New York to Norway, and Sheldon—widowed, old, impatient, impertinent—saw in Lars's countenance a suppressed desire to gloat.

None of which was fair.

"Do you know why hot dogs are called hot dogs?"

Sheldon says this aloud from his commanding position. If he had a cane he would wave it, but he walks without one.

Lars looks up in attention. Rhea, however, silently sighs.

"World War I. We were angry at the Germans, so we punished them by renaming their food. Better than the War on Terror," he continued. "We're angry at the terrorists, so we punish the French by renaming our own food."

"What do you mean?" asks Lars.

Sheldon sees Rhea tap Lars on the leg and raise her eyebrows, implying—with the intensity of a hot poker—that he is not supposed to be encouraging these sorts of rants, these outbursts, these diversions from the here and now. Anything that might contribute to the hotly debated dementia.

Sheldon was not supposed to see this poke, but does, and redoubles his conviction.

"Freedom fries! I'm talking about Freedom fries. Goodbye French fry, hello Freedom fry. An act of Congress actually concocted this harebrained idea. And my granddaughter thinks I'm the one losing my mind. Let me tell you something, young lady. I'm not crossing the aisle of sanity. The aisle is crossing me."

Sheldon looks around the park. There is not the ebb and flow of random strangers one finds in any American metropolis, the kind who are not only strangers to us but to each other as well. He is among tall, homogeneous, acquainted, well-meaning, smiling people all dressed in the same transgenerational clothing, and no matter how hard he tries, he just can't draw a bead on them.

Rhea. The name of a Titan. The daughter of Uranus and Gaia, heaven and earth, Cronos's wife, mother of the gods. Zeus himself suckled at her breast, and from her body came the known world. Sheldon's son—Saul, dead now—named her that to raise her above the banality that he steamed through in Vietnam with the Navy in 1973 and '74. He came home from the Riverine Force for one month of rest and relaxation before heading out for a second tour. It was a September. The leaves were out on the Hudson and in the Berkshires. According to his Mabel—vanished now, but once privy to such things—Saul and his girlfriend made love only one time on that return visit, and Rhea was conceived. The next morning, Saul had a conversation with Sheldon that transformed them both, and then he went back to Vietnam where, two months after he landed, a Vietcong booby trap blew off his legs while he was looking for a downed pilot on a routine search-and-rescue. Saul bled to death on the boat before reaching the hospital.

"Name her *Rhea*," Saul wrote in his last letter from Saigon, when Saigon was still Saigon, and Saul was still Saul. Maybe he remembered his mythology from high school, and chose her name for all the right reasons. Or maybe he fell in love with that doomed character from Stanislaw Lem's book, which he read under his woolen blanket when the other soldiers had faded off to sleep.

It took a Polish author to inspire this American Jew, who named his daughter for a Greek Titan before being killed by a Vietnamese mine in an effort to please his Marine father, who was once a sniper in Korea—and was undoubtedly still being pursued by the North Koreans across the wilderness of Scandinavia. Yes, even here, amid the green of Frogner Park on a sunny day in July, with so little time left to atone for all that he has done.

"Rhea." It means nothing here. It is the Swedish word for a sale at the department store. And, so easily, all is undone.

"Papa?" says Rhea.

"What?"

"So what do you think?"

"Of what?"

"You know. The area. The park. The neighborhood. This is

where we're moving to when we sell the place in Tøyen. I realize it isn't Gramercy Park."

Sheldon doesn't answer, so she raises her eyebrows and opens her palms as if to conjure up a response. "Oslo," she summarizes. "Norway. The light. This life."

"This life? You want my views on this life?"

Lars is silent. Sheldon looks to him for camaraderie, but Lars is away. There is eye contact, but no engagement of his mental faculties in the moment. Lars is captive to an alien cultural performance between grandfather and granddaughter—a verbal duel for which he is ill equipped, and which he knows it would be rude to interrupt.

And yet there is pity here, too. On Lars's face is one of the few universal expressions known to men everywhere. It reads, *I-just-married-into-this-conversation-so-don't-look-at-me.* In this Sheldon finds a hint of the familiar in him. But Sheldon senses something distinctly Norwegian about it, too. Something so *non*judgmental that it immediately grates on his nerves.

Sheldon looks back to Rhea, to this woman whom Lars managed to marry. Her hair is raven black and pulled into a silky ponytail. Her blue eyes sparkle like the Sea of Japan before battle.

Sheldon thinks her gaze has grown deeper because of the pregnancy.

*This life?* If he were to reach out to touch her face at this moment, run his fingers over her cheekbones, and rub his thumb over her lower lip to wipe off an errant tear from a strong breeze, he would surely break into sobs and grab her, hold her next to him, and press her head against his shoulder. There is life *on the way.* That is all that matters.

She is waiting for an answer to her question, and it isn't coming. He is staring at her. Perhaps he has forgotten the question. She becomes disappointed.

The sun will not set until after ten o'clock. Children are out everywhere, and people have come home early from work to enjoy the stretch of summer that lies before them as the reward for the darkness of the winter months. Parents order open-faced sandwiches, and feed little bits to their kids as fathers return plastic baby bottles to expensive prams with exotic names.

Quinny. Stokke. Bugaboo. Peg Perego. Maxi-Cosi.

*This life?* She should already know that this life is the product of so many deaths. Mario. Bill. Rhea's grandmother Mabel, who died eight months ago, prompting Sheldon's move here.

There is no calculating the trajectory caused by Saul's death.

Mabel's funeral was held in New York, though originally she and Sheldon came from different parts of the country. He was born in New England and she in Chicago. Eventually, both settled in New York, first as visitors, then as residents, and possibly, after many years, as New Yorkers.

After the funeral service and reception, Sheldon went alone to a coffee shop in Gramercy, close to their home. It was midafternoon. The lunch hour was over. The mourners had dispersed. Sheldon should have been sitting *shiva*, allowing his community to care for him, feed him, and keep him company for seven days, as was the custom. Instead he sat at the 71 Irving Place Coffee and Tea Bar, near 19th Street, eating a blueberry muffin and sipping black coffee. Rhea had flown in for the service without Lars, and noticed Sheldon's escape from the reception. She found him a few blocks away, and took the seat across from him.

She was wearing a fine black suit, and her hair was down to her shoulders. She was thirty-two years old and had a determined look on her face. Sheldon misread its cause, thinking she was going to reprimand him for skipping out on *shiva*. When she spoke her mind, he nearly spit a blueberry across the table.

"Come with us to Norway," she said.

"Get stuffed," said Sheldon.

"I'm serious."

"Me too."

"The area is called Frogner. It's wonderful. The building has a separate entrance to the basement apartment. You'd have complete autonomy. We're not in it yet, but we will be by winter."

"You should rent it to trolls. They have trolls there, right? Or is that Iceland?"

"We don't want to rent it out. It feels weird knowing strange people are under your feet all the time."

"That's because you don't have kids. You get used to that feeling."

"I think you should come. What's here for you?"

"Other than the blueberry muffins?"

"For example."

"One wonders how much more there needs to be at my age."

"Don't dismiss this."

"What am I going to do there? I'm an American. I'm a Jew. I'm eighty-two. I'm a retired widower. A Marine. A watch repairman. It takes me an hour to pee. Is there a club there I'm unaware of?"

"I don't want you to die alone."

"For heaven's sake, Rhea."

"I'm pregnant. It's very early, but it's true."

At this, on this day of days, Sheldon took her hand and touched it to his lips, closed his eyes, and tried to feel a new life in her pulse.

Rhea and Lars had been living in Oslo for almost a year by the time Mabel died and Sheldon decided to go. Lars had a good job designing video games, and Rhea was settling into life as an architect. Her degree from Cooper Union in New York was already coming in handy, and, as the population of Oslo pushed ever outward and into mountain cabins, she decided to stay.

Lars, being Lars, was overjoyed and encouraging and optimistic about her ability to adapt and join the pod. Norwegians, true to their nature, prefer to spawn in their native waters. Consequently Oslo is peopled by Norwegians married to a shadow population of displaced souls who all carry the look of tourists being led like children through the House of Wax.

With his parents' help, Lars had bought a split-level three-bedroom flat in Tøyen back in 1992 that was now worth almost three and a half million kroner. This was rather a lot for the part of town that Sheldon associated with the Bronx. Together they'd saved up five hundred thousand in cash, and with the necessary mortgage — which was a stretch, but not a terrible stretch — they were looking at a three-bedroom place in Frogner, which to Sheldon was the local Central Park West. It was a slightly stuffy area, but Lars and Rhea were growing tired of waiting for Tøyen to gentrify, and the influx of immigrants was moving the money out to other areas and affecting the quality of the schools. There was a growing population from Pakistan and the Balkans. Somalis had moved into the local park for khat-chewing sessions, the local council in its wisdom had moved a methadone treatment facility into the shopping center across the road that attracted heroin addicts, and all the while Rhea and Lars tried to explain that the area had "character." But Sheldon saw only menace.

Luckily, though, there were no North Koreans, those slanty-eyed little bastards. And if there were any, they would stand out. Hiding a North Korean in Norway is hard. Hiding one in New York is like hiding a tree in a forest. They're on every street corner, selling flowers and running grocery stores, their beady eyes glaring at you as you walk down the street, sending coded messages back to Pyongyang by telegraph, letting them know your whereabouts.

They'd been tracking him since 1951 — he was sure of it. You don't kill twelve men named Kim from the top of a seawall at Inchon and think they're going to forgive and forget. Not the Koreans. They have Chinese patience, but an Italian-style vendetta streak. And they blend. Oh! It took Sheldon years to learn how to spot them, feel their presence, evade them, deceive them.

Not here, though. Here they stood out in a crowd. Each evil-hearted one of them. Each brainwashed manic nutter who was under the surveillance of the next brainwashed manic nutter, in case the first one started to suffer from freethinking.

"I have news for you bastards!" he wants to yell to them. "You started the war! And when you learn this, you will owe me a serious apology."

But Sheldon, even now, believes the deceived are not responsible for their actions.

Mabel never understood his aversion to Koreans. She said he was slipping, that his doctor also suspected it, and that it was time he listened to reason and accepted that he'd never been a romanticized sniper, but rather a pedestrian clerk in Pusan, and that the North Koreans were not following him. He'd never shot anybody. Never fired a gun in anger.

She was going on about this only a few months before she died.

"You're going senile, Donny."

"Am not."

"You're changing. I see it."

"You're sick, Mabel. How isn't that going to affect me? Besides, you've been saying this since 1976. And maybe I'm not changing. Maybe it's you. You're just growing immune to my charms."

"It's not an accusation. You're over eighty years old. Rhea told me that at eighty-five, over twenty percent of us get Alzheimer's. It's something we need to discuss."

"Is not!"

"You need to eat more fish."

"Do not!"

In retrospect, this was a rather childish response, but it was also a tried-and-tested rebuttal.

His memories were just becoming more vivid with age. Time was folding in a new way. Without a future, the mind turned back in on itself. That's not dementia. One might even say it's the only rational response to the inevitable.

Besides, what accounts for such memories?

He'd gotten lost in Korea in early September 1950. Through a series of events that only made sense at the time, he was picked up on the coast by the Australian ship HMAS *Bataan*, part of Task Force 91, whose job was to set up and maintain a blockade and provide cover for the American troops landing on the beach, of which Sheldon was supposed to be one, but wasn't because he was on the *Bataan*. Sheldon, who was called Donny then, was supposed to be with the Fifth Marine Regimental Combat Team that was hitting Red Beach, but he got lost during the reassignment, because armies lose things.

He was too young to fight when World War II came around. All he could think when Korea popped up five years later was that he wasn't going to miss *this* war, too, and he enlisted immediately, only to end up—at the moment of truth—surrounded by a bunch of outback hillbillies who wouldn't let him borrow their rowboat so he could get to shore and shoot people, like he was supposed to.

"Sorry, mate. Could need that. Only got four. Little ship, big guns, bullets flying around. You understand, right?"

So he decided to borrow without permission—he refused to use the word "steal"—a rowboat from his Australian hosts. It wasn't completely unreasonable, he realized, their wanting to keep the emergency gear during a massive amphibious assault mission, but people have different needs sometimes, and choices have to be made.

Donny Horowitz was twenty-two years old then. He had a clear mind, a steady hand, and a chip on his Jewish shoulder the size and shape of Germany. For the Army, it was only a matter of assigning him to the proper role and then tasking him with the right job. The role was scout-sniper. The task was Inchon.

Inchon was a tactically challenging mission. The North Koreans had weakened themselves against the Pusan Perimeter for almost a month and a half, and General MacArthur decided now was the time to flank them by taking Korea's western port city of Inchon. But the site had poor beaches and shallow approaches, and it restricted invasion options to the rhythm of the moon's tidal pull.

The naval bombardment had been going on for two days, weakening Inchon's defenses. There wasn't a man there who wasn't thinking of D-Day. Nor a man there not thinking about what happened at Omaha Beach when American bombers missed their targets and the DD tanks sank to the bottom of the sea during their approach, giving the Americans no armor on the ground to provide cover and firepower. No bomb craters to use as foxholes.

Donny would be damned if he wasn't going to be at the front of that invasion.

That morning, amid the smoke and the artillery fire, with birds flying wildly amid the noise, the Third and Fifth Marine regiments were advancing toward Green Beach in LSTs, with Pershing tanks in their bellies. Donny eased the borrowed rowboat down the side of the *Bataan*, slid down after it with his rifle, and rowed face-forward into the artillery fire directed at the naval craft.

On Red Beach, the North Koreans were defending a high seawall that the South Korean Marines were scaling on ladders. A row of sharpshooters on the top of the wall were trying to pick off Americans, South Koreans, and everyone else fighting under the UN flag. Missiles arced overhead. The North Koreans were firing green tracer bullets supplied by their Chinese allies, which crossed with the Allied red ones.

They started firing at Donny directly. The bullets came in slowly at first and then sped past him, splaying into the water or puncturing the rowboat.

Sheldon often wondered what the Koreans, a superstitious lot, were thinking when they saw a lone soldier standing face-forward in the water, illuminated by the reds, greens, oranges, and yellows of combat reflecting off the water and clouds of the morning sky. A diminutive, blue-eyed demon impervious to their defenses.

One barrage hit Donny's boat hard. Four bullets punctured the prow, and then the deck. Water started coming in, and ran around his boots. The Marines had already touched the beach and were advancing toward the wall. The green tracers were tracking low into his regiment.

Having come this far, and being a bad swimmer — from four hundred yards offshore, and with two feet in his watery grave — Sheldon decided to use his ammunition, *goddamn it*, rather than drown with it.

He had such soft hands for a boy. Five feet seven inches tall, he'd never done physical labor or heavy lifting. He added up the figures in his father's cobbler shop, and dreamed of hitting one deep into left field over the Green Monster for the Red Sox. The first time his fingers touched the bottoms of Mabel's breasts—under the wire of her bra during a Bogart movie with Bacall—she said his fingers were so soft it was like the touch of a girl. This confession had made him more sexually ravenous than any picture show he'd ever seen.

When he'd enlisted, they'd chosen him as a sniper. They could see he was even-tempered. Quiet. Smart. Wiry, but rugged. He had a lot of anger, but a capacity to direct it through reason.

We think of guns as brutal things used by heavy men. But the art of the rifle demands the most subtle feel—the touch of a lover or a watchmaker. There is an understanding between the finger and trigger. The breath is kept under disciplined control. Every muscle is used to provide only stillness. The direction of the wind on the cheek finds expression in the rise of the barrel, lifted lightly as from the heat of a warm blueberry pie on a winter afternoon.

And now, with his feet in the water, Donny focused on the distant objects above the wall, flickering in the fog. The artillery fire did not unnerve him. The water in his boots was just a sensation with no meaning. The bird that flew into his upper thigh, in the confusion of noise and smoke, was only a feeling. He was withdrawn, and to this day he remembers the event with music. What he heard, and hears even now in his memories, is Bach's unaccompanied Cello Suite no. 1 in G Major.

At this moment of deepest calm, of the most complete peace, he lost the anger of his youth. The venom against the Nazis was bled from his veins by the music, the fog, the water.

Now, in this moment of grace, Donny killed.

Through the business end of an unusually straight-shooting .30-caliber M-1 Garand, Donny emptied three clips of armor-piercing 168-grain ammunition in under thirty seconds. He killed twelve men, clearing them off the high wall from a distance of four hundred yards, allowing the first U.S. Marines to assault the peak without loss of life while he bled from a surface bullet wound to his left leg.

His action was the smallest of gestures, like dropping a pebble into a still pool of water and disturbing the image of the night sky.

He didn't tell Mabel any of this until much later, of course. So late, in fact, that she never came to believe it. They had a son to think about, and heroism was a private matter for Sheldon. He said he'd been a logistics officer, far south on much safer ground. The wound? The wound was caused by carelessly walking into a tool-shed, where he was punctured by a rake. He made it a joke.

*Compared to me, it was the sharpest tool in the shed.*

Sheldon was, as he recalls, awarded the Navy Commendation Medal and the Purple Heart for his part in the invasion. The question is, however, where had he put them? He ran an antique and watch-repair shop. They could be anywhere, in any crevice. They were the only tangible proof that he still had his marbles. And now the shop is gone, its contents sold off. Everything once so carefully assembled is scattered now. Back in the world, they will be assembled into new collections by new collectors, and then scattered again as the collectors return to the mist.

*This life.* What a question! No one really wants to know the answer to this.

*In this life, my body has become a withered twig, where once I stood tall. I distantly remember the lush earth and beech forests of New England—outside my bedroom window as a child—growing in kingdoms. My parents near me.*

*In this life, I hobble like an old man, when once I could fly over doubts and contradictions.*

*In this life, my memories are the smoke I choke on, burning my eyes.*

*In this life, I remember hungers that will never return. When I was once a lover with the bluest eyes she had ever seen—deeper than Paul Newman's, darker than Frank Sinatra's.*

*This life! This life is coming to an end without any explanation or apology, and where every sense of my soul or ray of light through a cloud promises to be my end.*

*This life was an abrupt and tragic dream that seized me during the wee hours of a Saturday morning as the sunrise reflected off the mirror above her vanity table, leaving me speechless just as the world faded to white.*

And even if they did want to know, who is there left to tell?

# CHAPTER 2

ITIS SOME UNGODLY hour, and Sheldon stands naked in the bathroom of their apartment in Tøyen. Rhea and Lars are out. They left in the middle of the night without a word, and have been gone for hours.

The light is off, and it is dark. He has one hand pressed against the cold tiles of the wall above the toilet, and with his other hand he is taking aim, such as it is. He's waiting for his prostate to get out of the way so he can take a well-deserved leak and get back to bed where he belongs, so that if by chance his heart stops this very second, he won't be found—holding his pecker, dead on the floor—by a bunch of twenty-year-old medics who will gawk at his circumcision and bad luck.

It is not only his age that is slowing things down. A man and a woman are fighting upstairs in some Balkan language, with all its acid and spleen. It might be Albanian. Or not. He doesn't know. It sounds vile, anti-Semitic, communist, peasant, rude, fascistic, and corrupt all at the same time. Every phoneme and slur and intonation sounds bitter. The fight is loud, and its constituent qualities cause his innards to constrict in some kind of primordial self-defense.

Sheldon slaps the wall a few times, but his strike is flaccid.

He recalls graffiti in the men's latrine during basic training: "Old snipers never die, they just stay loaded."

Sheldon shuffles back to bed, pulls the duvet up to his shoulders, and listens as the woman's hollers evolve into sobs. He eventually falls into a shallow, voiceless sleep.

When he wakes, it is — as expected — Sunday. Light is flooding the room. By the door is a large man who is clearly not Korean.

"Yuh? Sheldon? Hiyuh! It's Lars. Good morning."

Sheldon rubs his face and looks at his watch. It is just past seven.

"Hello, Lars."

"Did you sleep OK?"

"Where the hell were you two?"

"We'll explain over breakfast."

"Your neighbor is a Balkan fascist."

"Oh yeah?"

Sheldon scowls.

"We're about to put on the eggs. Come join us?"

"You heard it, too, right? It wasn't a hallucination?"

"Come have breakfast."

The apartment is on a small road off Sars's Gate near Tøyenparken. The building is brick, and the floors have wide, unvarnished planks. To Sheldon, there is a touch of the New York loft about it, because Lars's father had torn down the walls between the kitchen and living room, and the living room and dining room, to create a wide-open space with white floors and ceilings. There are two bedrooms off the now conjoined spaces, and a small bedroom down a short flight of stairs that now houses Sheldon.

Unable to avoid the day any longer, Sheldon gets up, puts on a bathrobe and slippers, and shuffles into the living room, which glows with early-morning sunlight as from an interrogator's bulb. He is neither unfamiliar with, nor unprepared for, this problem. It is caused by the Norwegian summer light. The solution is a pair of gold-rimmed aviator sunglasses, which he takes from his pocket and slips on.

Now able to see, he goes to the breakfast table, which is arrayed with goat cheese, a range of dried-pork products, orange juice, chopped liver, salmon, butter, and a freshly baked dark bread just purchased from the nearby 7-Eleven.

Rhea is in a pair of faded Levi's and a light blue, satiny blouse from H&M, and her hair is pulled back. She is barefoot and wears no makeup, cradling a hot cup of café au lait and leaning against the kitchen sink.

"Morning, Papa," says Rhea.

Rhea is familiar with Sheldon's morning look. She is also prepared for his traditional greeting.

"Coffee!"

Rhea is ready for this, and hands it over.

She sees that, beneath Sheldon's maroon flannel bathrobe, his legs are hairless and pale, but they still have some form and muscle. He is clearly shrinking, but is lean and has good posture. It makes him look taller than he is. He shuffles and complains and bosses, but he holds his shoulders back, and his hands don't shake when he carries his *Penthouse* coffee mug—a mail-order item from the back of the magazine during the 1970s, from the look of the girl.

Rhea has begged him to retire the mug . . . but no.

In any venue beyond this apartment, Sheldon would have been arrested in this outfit. The real question, however, is why Lars has agreed to house this forlorn creature whom Rhea loves so much.

But, of course, that is probably the answer right there. She adores Lars—especially for his gentle warmth, his dry humor, his calm temperament—and she knows he feels the same about her. He has a transformative masculinity that hides itself from public view but comes alive privately in the way a cuddly brown bear transforms into a predator.

Rhea attributes this to his upbringing, not just his character. It is as though the Norwegian nation has learned how to rein in unbridled masculine power and bring it into social balance, burying its rough edges from public view, but permitting expansive and embracing moments of both intimacy and force. He is such a sweet man, but he is also a hunter. Lars and his father have been shooting reindeer since Lars was a boy. Rhea has a year's worth of meat in the freezer. She has tried, but she can't imagine him pulling the trigger, slicing the hide, disemboweling the kill. And yet he does.

Lars is more than the mere product of his world, though. He has depths of kindness that Rhea feels she lacks in herself. She does not have his capacity for forgiveness. Her emotions and mind and self are more tightly wound, more intertwined in an eternal dialogue for meaning and purpose and expression. She has a compulsion to articulate and expound, to render the world explicable, if only to herself.

Letting it be, moving through, submitting to silence—these are not her ways.

They are for Lars. He comes to terms with humanity as it presents itself. He expresses himself not in a torrent of words and ideas and disruptions, revelations and setbacks, but through an ever-expanding capacity to face what comes next. To see it clearly. To say what needs to be said and then stop. What is for her an act of will is for Lars a process of life.

They'd wanted children. Only recently, though. Rhea needed time to find her place, to see whether she could graft her American soul onto the Norwegian matrix. And so, when the birth-control pills ran out, she simply stopped going to the pharmacy to renew her prescription. She remembers the day. It was a Saturday in December, not long before Christmas but after Hanukkah. It must have been one of the darkest days of the year, but their apartment glowed warmly with a Christmas tree and a menorah. In a game, they listed the sensuous accompaniments of holidays gone past.

*Clove. Cinnamon. Pine. Marzipan.*

"No, no marzipan."

"It's huge here," said Lars. "Covered in chocolate."

"So whose turn is it?"

"Yours."

*Bells. Candles. Pie. Apples. Ski wax . . .*

"Really! Ski wax? Here, too. That's exciting."

"I'm just screwing with you, Lars."

"Oh."

Three words in a row. Sometimes four. That's how much they had in common. A solid platform for a child.

Rhea sips her café au lait and looks at Lars reading *Aftenposten*'s front page. There is a picture of Kosovo's independence from Serbia. Something about Brad Pitt. Something about low-carb diets.

No, she hadn't told Lars that she was trying to get pregnant. It was somehow unnecessary. As though he already knew. Or that, being married, he didn't have to know. What might have unfolded as opera in her New York culture passed here with a hug and his fingers moving through her hair, then gripping it all in his fist.

Lars is reading the newspaper like a normal person, whereas Sheldon is holding a piece of the paper up to the light as though looking for watermarks. It is, as always, unclear to Rhea what anything he is doing might mean—whether he is seeking attention like a child, whether his age is merely expressing itself, or whether he's involved in some activity that, if probed, would sound misguided and demented and logical all at once. When the three are combined in this way—his personality, his condition, his reason—it is impossible to distinguish one from another.

This is Sheldon's third week in the country. They wanted him to find his place here, to settle into his new life. They all knew there was no going back now. Sheldon was too old, and the apartment in Gramercy was sold, so there was nowhere for him to go.

"I'm not taking the bait," she says.

"Huh?"

Lars and Sheldon each raise their newspapers a bit higher—one to hide, the other to provoke.

"I said, you nutter, that I'm not taking the bait. I have no interest whatsoever in why you're looking for the Da Vinci code in the newsprint."

"Norwegian sounds like English spoken backward. I want to see if it reads the same way. I can check by holding it up to the light and reading the article on the other side. But the words on this side of the newspaper are blocking the words on the other side of the newspaper, so I can't tell."

Lars speaks: "It's going to be good weather again."

"I think we should go out. Papa, how about a walk?"

"Oh, sure, they'd love that, wouldn't they."

"The Koreans?"

"You said that with a tone. I heard a tone."

Rhea puts her empty cup in the sink, runs her fingers under the cold water, and wipes them on her jeans.

"There's something we need to tell you."

"Tell me here."

"I'd rather go out."

"Not me. I like it here. Near the food. All the pork. It needs me."

"We could slip out the back."

At this, both newspapers drop.

"There's a back door?" Sheldon asks.

"Bicycle entrance. Not many people know about it. It's a *secret*."

"That's good to know."

"Little things like that can save your life."

"You're mocking me. I know you're mocking me, but I don't care. I know what's what. I still got all my marbles, my family jewels, and a bit of savings from my book. And I'm over eighty. That's something."

"So are we going out, or what?"

"What's with your neighbors?" asks Sheldon, changing the subject.

"How do you mean?"

"Sounds like the fascist beats his wife."

"We've called the police before."

"So you *have* heard it!"

"Yes."

"You got a gun? Lars, you got a gun?"

"Not here."

"But you've got a gun, right? I mean, you don't run through the forest naked, blond hair flapping in the breeze, and tackle the reindeer with your bare manly chest, right? Kill 'em with your teeth? Blood-stained peach fuzz on your chin? Big grin? There's a gun involved, right?"

"Up at the summer house. Moses and Aaron. They're in a lock box by the sauna. One of them is broken."

"You have Jewish rifles?"

Lars smiles. "Ah, no. A Winchester and a Remington. They're named after the two cannons in Drøbak that sank the German ship during the war. In the fjord."

"Norway has Nazi-killing Jewish cannons?"

"I never thought of it quite that way."

Sheldon raises his brows and opens his palms as though to ask what other way one could possibly think about two cannons named Moses and Aaron in Norway that sank a Nazi ship.

Lars relents. "Yes, Norway has Nazi-killing Jewish cannons."

"But the guns aren't here. Moses and Aaron are wandering."

"At the summer house. Right."

"That's OK. I'm sure we can win a knife fight. What does the Balkan mafia know about knife fighting compared to the three of us?"

"You know, the cabin is out by the Swedish border. The Norwegian resistance used to operate there. We called them the Boys in the Woods. My father says my grandfather used to hide them in the sauna out back. They used to wear paper clips on their lapels. Many people did. It was an act of rebellion against the occupation."

Sheldon nods. "So Operation Paper Clip was effective, was it?

That must have been what broke their backs. Who could tolerate such impertinence?"

Rhea says, "Papa, I think you need to take a shower, put on some matching clothes—some underwear even—and in return we can slip out the back door."

Sheldon changes the subject.

"You know why I wear this watch?"

"To tell time?" answers Rhea, submitting to the diversion.

"No. That's why I wear *a* watch. The question is why do I wear *this* watch. I used to wear one with the heart of your father in it. I'll explain someday. But I decided, on account of your news, and my coming to the land of blue and ice, to splurge and get a new one. And you know which one I bought? Not an Omega. Not a Rolex. I'll tell you what I bought. A *J. S. Watch and Company*.

"Never heard of them? Neither had I. Heard about them by chance. They're in Iceland. Between the Old World and the New. Four guys at the base of a volcano in the middle of the Atlantic who want to try making a buck by crafting exquisite and refined timepieces because they love them. Because they understand that a timepiece is an affirmative and creative act of engineering and beauty in response to a pitiless structure of functionality and form. Like life itself in response to death. Plus, mine's a looker! See this?"

"Outside. We're going outside."

"I don't have any keys to the house. I'm not autonomous."

"We'll make you a set. So what?"

"When your father was little, he deliberately stopped dressing in matching clothes. It was an act of rebellion against his oppressive father. So we bought him nothing but Levi's—the jeans named after a tribe of Israel that can magically match any top. Tie-dye, plaid, stripes, camouflage. You can throw anything at Levi's. With this I outmaneuvered your father. In return, we ended up with a child with no fashion sense."

"I think breakfast is over."

"He's in the book, you know."

"I know, Papa."

"And your grandmother."

"I know."

"And a lot of angry Europeans."

"Yup."

"And a dog."

"Right-o."

The book. "The book" was Sheldon's only verifiable claim to fame. In 1955, still a bit lost after the war and not much looking to be found, he somehow cottoned on to the idea of becoming a photographer. As it happened, he turned into a popular one. Long before thematic coffee-table books became the rage, Sheldon decided to travel and take portraits. Unfortunately, despite his talent with the camera, he lacked certain social graces—which was problematic, since taking portraits required willing subjects.

To Sheldon's credit, however, he turned even this to his advantage, by changing the subject of his portraits to *unwilling* subjects. In this, he demonstrated a certain *penchant*. And so, "Photos of Unwilling Subjects" became the name of the project.

By 1956, Sheldon had collected exactly six hundred and thirteen photographs, from twelve cities across five countries, of people apoplectically angry at him. More than two hundred made it into the book. The rest remained in storage boxes that he guarded, hid, and never let anyone see. It wasn't until Saul brought it up in conversation one time that anyone so much as suspected more photos existed. Nevertheless, Sheldon kept them hidden.

The book featured women screaming, men shaking their fists, children hysterical, and even dogs in midflight with their teeth bared. With his own graceless sarcasm, the book—which found a respected publisher and no small audience—was entitled *What?*

In a brief interview with *Harper's Magazine*, he'd been asked what he did to make everyone so angry.

"Whatever I could think of," he'd replied. "I pulled hair, teased kids, hassled dogs, knocked over ice cream cones, heckled the elderly, left restaurants without paying, snatched cabs out of turn, cracked wise, walked off with other people's luggage, insulted wives, complained to waiters, cut in line, knocked off hats, and I didn't hold the elevator for anyone. It was the best year of my life."

Saul was on page one. Sheldon had taken the toddler's candy away, and then took photos of him with a flash that enraged him entirely. Mabel became livid, thereby earning herself a place on page two.

There is a copy of the book in Rhea's living room. She has shown it to Lars. Their favorite photo is modeled on Robert Doisneau's *Kiss by the Hotel de la Ville*, which had just been printed in *Life* magazine. Sheldon had intuited the photo's iconic power of being a moment snatched from time during a period of change. In Sheldon's version, two lovers have been interrupted during a kiss. They are gripping the iron railing of a bridge, and the woman is hurling a bottle of wine at the camera (technically, at Sheldon). It was a bright day, so Sheldon had used a small aperture setting to capture a long depth of field, which managed to keep most of the scene in focus. The black-and-white photo—of superb composition—captured not only the angry face of the woman—her hand still extended from the throw, her face contorted, her body bent slightly over the railing as though hurling her very self at the camera—but also the vintage of the flying bottle (1948 Château Beychevelle, St. Julien, Bordeaux). It was a genuinely brilliant photograph. And in 1994, when Doisneau admitted that his own photo had been staged (because the girl in it wanted some cash forty years on, and sued him, thereby forcing the photographer's admission that she'd been hired, thus breaking the spell of the original photo), Sheldon went bananas and proclaimed himself the master.

"The original was a fake, and the fake was an original!" In 1995 his own photo was reissued, bringing him another week of notoriety and an opportunity to be incorrigible at family gatherings. This, for Sheldon, was a joy beyond description.

"Get dressed. We'll take a walk," Rhea says.

"You two go. I'll catch up."

Lars looks up at Rhea, who glances back knowingly.

"Papa, we want to tell you something about last night. Come with us."

Sheldon looks at Lars, who is innocently placing a piece of herring on dark bread.

"You don't want me wandering around alone. You want me supervised. Which is why you want to strap that mobile phone on me. But I won't have it."

"We like your company."

"Your grandmother was better at manipulating me than you two. I'm not giving in until you raise your game."

"Right, well, I'm going out. So who's with me?"

Lars raises his hand.

"Lars! Great! Anyone else?" She looks around the room. "No one else?"

"I have things to do," says Sheldon.

"Like what?"

"Private things."

"I don't believe you."

"So what?"

"It's a nice day, and I want you out of the house."

"Did you know that I went through eight cameras making that book? Six were brutally smashed by the subjects—Mario's was the first to go, one I dropped in the Hudson, and one was eaten by a dog. What I loved was how the dog blamed the camera and not me. The photo of the inside of his mouth is on page thirty-seven. And, of course, having pressed the shutter himself, the dog got the photo credit."

"What's your point?"

"It's cute how you think I have a point."

She scowls. Sheldon smiles. Lars announces he is going to get dressed. Breakfast is over.

Rhea is alone with Sheldon.

"What's with you? I said there was something I wanted to tell you."

"Go out with your husband. Go to the cabin. Make love on a fur blanket. Eat moose jerky. Drink *akevitt* that's crossed the equator a few times. Two hundred years ago, we Jews weren't allowed in this country. Now you've found a nice boy, and he loves you, and you're going to have pretty babies. I'll be here when you get back."

"Sometimes I think there's an actual person in there with you, and then other times . . . I think it's just you."

"Go get dressed and go. I'll rinse my mug."

Rhea, arms crossed, looks at Sheldon as if deciding something. And then, in a low voice touched with anger, she says, "I had a miscarriage."

There is a deep silence from her grandfather, and his face settles. The muscles release, and for a moment she sees him in all his force. The years flow into him. A frightening weariness comes to his mouth and brow. She immediately regrets saying this. She should have stuck to her agreement with Lars. To break the news slowly. To prepare the ground.

Sheldon stands quietly and wraps the robe around himself. And then, as though the tears were there all along, he walks back to his room and openly weeps alone.

Hours later, at two in the afternoon, he is alone in the apartment. His earlier insistence that Rhea and Lars go out had become quite different in tone when it was repeated later. He'd made it clear to them that he needed solitude, and so they went.

Dressed in jeans, a white button-down shirt, and a pair of workman's boots, he has recovered his composure and is comfortably stretched on the sofa with a book by Danielle Steel when the shouting starts again.

He has heard domestic squabbles before—the rounds of yelling, the escalation, the occasional banging, even the beatings and sobs. But this is something else. The cadence of the argument is wrong. There is no turn-taking between angry participants. The man had started screaming and then kept it up. The woman, this time, hasn't made a sound.

*She must be in there*, Sheldon thinks.

It doesn't have the pauses of a phone conversation. The diatribe is too linear, too intimate. The hollering voice is too present.

It doesn't matter in the slightest that Sheldon can't understand a word, because the message is clear. He has had enough experience with humanity, with its range of rage, to know what is happening. There is cruelty and viciousness in that voice. It is more than a squabble. It is a battle.

Then there is a loud bang.

Sheldon puts the book down and sits upright on the sofa. He is attentive, his brows furrowed.

No, not a gunshot. It wasn't sharp enough. He knows gunshots from his life and from his dreams. It was probably a door slamming. And then he hears approaching footsteps that are quick and even. The woman, perhaps. A heavy woman, or one wearing boots, or one carrying something heavy. She is coming down the stairs. First the one flight, then a brief pause on the landing, then the other.

It takes her the same amount of time to maneuver down the staircase as it does Sheldon to get to the front door and spy her through the peephole.

And there she is. The source, or focus, or even the cause of it all. Through the fisheye lens, Sheldon sees a young woman, around thirty years old, standing in front of his door. She is so close that he can see her only from the waist up, but it is enough to place her. She wears a dark T-shirt under a cheap brown leather jacket. She wears gaudy costume jewelry, and her hair is styled with thick mousse or gel that prevents it from responding to the normal force of gravity.

Everything about her says *Balkans*. Sheldon can only guess her life, and yet everything about it seems scripted, aside from her incongruous presence in Oslo. But that is easily explained by asylum practices. Maybe she was Serb or Kosovar or Albanian. Or maybe Romanian. Who knows?

His first feeling is one of pity. Not for the person she is, but for the circumstances she faces.

The feeling lasts until a memory transforms it.

*They did this with us, too*, he thinks, looking through the peephole. And then the pity vanishes and is replaced by the indignation that lives just beneath the surface of his daily routines and quick retorts.

The Europeans. Almost all of them, at one time or another. They looked out their peepholes—their little fishy eyes staring out through bulging lenses, watching someone else's flight—as their neighbors clutched their children to their chests while armed thugs chased them through buildings as though humanity itself was being exterminated. Behind the glass, some were afraid, some felt pity, others felt murderous and delighted.

All were safe because of what they were not. They were not, for example, Jews.

The woman spins around. Looking for something.

What? What is she looking for?

The fight has taken place only one floor above him. The monster upstairs could be down in seconds. Why is she delaying? Why is she hesitant? What is taking so long?

Sheldon hears rummaging upstairs. The monster is pushing and heaving and searching for something. He is moving walls and mountains. He is peeling the very darkness from the light to find it. At any moment he will stop and turn on her and demand it.

Sheldon mutters under his breath. "Run, you fool. Get out, go to the police, and don't look back. He's going to kill you."

A *bang* echoes from upstairs. Same as before. It is the door hitting the wall behind it.

Aloud, Sheldon says, "Run, you dummy. Why are you just standing there?"

On a hunch, Sheldon turns and looks out the front window. And there is the answer. A white Mercedes is parked outside. Inside, men in cheap leather jackets are smoking cigarettes, barring her escape.

And that seals it.

Quietly, slowly, but without hesitation, Sheldon opens the door.

What he sees is not what he expected.

The woman is clutching an ugly pink box just big enough to

hold an adult pair of shoes. And she is not alone. Pressed against her belly is a small boy, maybe seven or eight years old. He is clearly terrified. He is dressed in little blue Wellington boots with yellow Paddington Bears hand-painted on the sides. Carefully tucked inside are beige corduroy trousers. On top, he is wrapped in a green jacket of waxed cotton.

The footsteps from above pound the floors. A voice hollers a name. Laura? Clara? Vera, maybe? Two syllables, anyway. Barked out. Coughed up.

Sheldon ushers them in with his finger pressed against his lips.

Vera looks up the stairs, then out the door. She does not look at Sheldon. She does not wonder about his intentions or give him a chance to reconsider by looking into his eyes for clarity. She pushes the silent boy in front of her and into the flat.

Sheldon closes the door very quietly. The woman with her wide Slavic face looks at him in conspiratorial terror. They all squat down with their backs against the door, waiting for the monster to pass.

Again Sheldon raises his finger to his lips. "Shhh," he says.

No need to look out the peephole now. He is no longer one of the people he abhorred. Sitting next to his neighbors, he wants to stand in the middle of a soccer field with a bullhorn, surrounded by Europe's oldest generation, and yell, "Was that so fucking hard?"

But outside he is silent. Disciplined. Calm. An old soldier.

*When you sneak up on a man to kill him with a knife*, his drill sergeant explained sixty years ago, *don't stare at him. People know when you're staring at the back of their head. I don't know how, I don't know why. Just don't look at their head. Look at the feet, make your approach, get the knife in. Head forward, not back. Never let him know you're there. If you want him dead, make him dead. Don't negotiate it with him. He's likely to disagree.*

Sheldon never had trouble with this end of things. Never pondered the imponderables, questioned his mission, doubted his function. Before he got lost and ended up on the HMAS *Bataan*, he was shaken awake one night by Mario de Luca. Mario was from San

Francisco. His parents had emigrated from Tuscany with the intention of buying wine land north of San Francisco, but somehow his father never got out of the city, and Mario was drafted. Where Donny had intense blue eyes and sandy-blond hair, Mario was dark like a Sicilian fisherman. And he talked as if he'd been injected with some kind of truth serum.

"Donny? Donny, you up?"

Donny didn't answer.

"Donny. Donny, you up?"

This went on for minutes.

"Donny. Donny, you up?"

"It will not help my cause by answering you," Donny said.

"Donny, I don't get this invasion. I don't get this war. I don't know what we're supposed to do. What are we doing here?"

Donny had on flannel pajamas that were not government issue. He replied, "You get out of the boat. You shoot Koreans. You get back in the boat. What confuses you?"

"The middle part," Mario explained. "But now that I think about it, the first part, too."

"What about the third part?"

"No, that part is like crystal."

"So what about the first two?"

"My motivation? What's my motivation?"

"They'll be shooting at you."

"Then what's their motivation?"

"You'll be shooting at them."

"What if I don't shoot at them?"

"They'll still be shooting at you because other people will be shooting at them, and they won't differentiate. And you'll want them to stop, so you'll shoot back."

"What if I ask them not to?"

"They're too far away, and they speak Korean."

"So I need to get closer and have a translator?"

"Right. But you can't."

"Because they're shooting at me."

"That's the problem."

"But that's absurd!"

"Yes, it is."

"It can't be true!"

"Most things are both true and absurd."

"That's also absurd."

"And yet . . . ?"

"It may also be true. Jesus, Donny. I'm going to be up all night."

Then Donny whispered, "If you don't go to bed, there will be no tomorrow. And it'll be all your fault."

The monster's feet stop outside the door. What were stomping, pounding footfalls of a pursuer are now gentle shuffles. Whoever is chasing them is now spinning around, looking for them as though they might be hiding in a shadow or under a ray of light. Outside, a car door slams. Then another slams. There is fast talking in Serbian, or Albanian, or whatever it is. The conversation is easy to imagine.

"Where did they go?"

"I thought they were with you."

"They must have come out the front door."

"I didn't see anything."

And then, because they are amateurs, because they are fools, they turn on each other and away from the task at hand.

"That's because you were smoking and talking about that slut again."

"It was your job to bring them out. I'm just waiting."

And so on.

One sound is all it would take to give them away. One squeal of glee from the hiding child who thinks it is all a game, or a whine because of his immobility. Or simply a cry of fear—something as human as a cry of fear.

Sheldon looks at him. The boy's back is against the door like his own, and his knees are up. He has wrapped his arms around them and is looking down at the floor in a gesture of defeat and isolation. Sheldon understands at once that he is assuming a familiar position. He will be silent. In his world of terror, this is a learned skill.

And then the talking, the bickering, ends. The doors to the Mercedes open and close again, and the powerful engine starts. In a few moments, the car pulls off.

Sheldon sighs. He rubs his hands over his face to stimulate blood flow, and then forcefully massages his scalp. He has always imagined his brain to be like the liquid-iron core of the earth—gray and heavy, in constant motion, producing its own gravity, and carefully balanced on his neck's vertebrae like the earth is balanced on the backs of turtles in the cosmos.

Events like this tend to cause the iron flow to slow or even reverse, which can result in ice ages. A little massage usually takes care of the gray matter, though.

This time he is cold all over.

He stares at his companions, who are still sitting in his entryway. The woman looks more pasty, more podgy, than she was when viewed through the fisheye lens. The thin leather jacket is thinner. The trampy shirt is trampier. It all bespeaks a lower-class Balkan immigrant. He never saw the man outside the door. He can only imagine him being fat and sweaty, wearing a Chinese-made Adidas tracksuit with white stripes down the arms and legs. His equally foul-breathed colleagues are probably in dark open shirts under poorly fitting, fake designer jackets the texture of vinyl.

It is all so hopelessly predictable. Everything except the Paddington Bears on the boy's bright blue Wellingtons. These have been painted by someone with love and imagination. Sheldon is, at this moment, inexplicably prepared to credit them to the pasty hooker on his floor.

The car has moved off, so Sheldon says to the boy, "Those are nice boots."

The boy looks up from the crook of his arm. He does not understand. Sheldon can't be sure if it's the comment itself that he doesn't understand, or the timing of the comment, or the language. There is no good reason, after all, to think the boy speaks English, except that everyone these days speaks English.

I mean, really. Why speak anything else? Stubbornness. That's why.

It also occurs to him that perhaps it is the soothing and encouraging male voice that is so rare and so unfamiliar. He lives in a world of violent men, as so many boys do. With this thought, Sheldon can't help but try again.

"Nice bears," he says, pointing at the bears and giving the thumbs-up.

The boy looks down at the boots and turns one leg inward to get a look at them for himself. He does not know what Sheldon is saying, but he does know what he's talking about. He looks back at Sheldon without a smile and turns his face back into the crook of his arm.

The woman stands up and begins to speak quickly. Her tone is grateful and seemingly apologetic, which seems to follow, given the circumstances. The words themselves are gibberish, but luckily Sheldon speaks English, which is universally understood.

"You're welcome. Yes. Yes—yes. Look, I'm old, so take my advice. Leave your husband. He's a Nazi."

Her babbling continues. Even looking at her is exasperating. She has the accent of a Russian prostitute. The same nasal confidence. The same fluid slur of words. Not a single moment taken to collect her thoughts or search for a phrase. Only the educated stop to look for words—having enough to occasionally misplace them.

Sheldon labors to his feet and brushes off his trousers. He holds up his hands. "I don't understand. I don't understand. I'm not even sure I care. Just go to the police and get your boy a milkshake."

She does not slow down.

"Milkshake," says Sheldon. "Police."

Sheldon decides her name is Vera. Sheldon watches Vera gesture toward the boy and nod. She points and nods. She nods and points.

She puts her hands together in a praying gesture. She crosses herself, which causes Sheldon to lift his eyebrows for the first time.

"In that case, why not stay? Have a cup of tea and wait this out for an hour. Waiting is wise. He might come back. You don't want to go back to the apartment. Believe me."

He thinks for a minute. There is a word they used in the Ukrainian part of Brooklyn. Yes. *Chai.* It is Russian for tea. He makes sipping sounds and says it again. To be absolutely certain he is communicating, he sticks out his pinkie finger and makes yummy slurping sounds.

"Tea. Nazi. Milkshake. Police. Are we clear?"

Vera does not respond to Sheldon's pantomime. Exasperated, Sheldon throws up his hands. It is like persuading a plant to move.

As Vera keeps talking and the boy sits, Sheldon hears a rumbling—the familiar if distant sound of a German diesel engine pinging and ponging its way slowly around a nearby bend.

"They're coming back. We have to leave. Now. They might not be as stupid as they absolutely seem to be. Come on. Come-come-come-come-come." He gestures, and when the car stops and the door opens, he decides the time for niceties has ended.

With extraordinary effort, Sheldon bends down and lifts the boy up, cradling him under the bottom like a toddler. He is not strong enough to use his free arm to grab Vera's sleeve and pull her. He needs all his strength for the boy. He has nothing to move her but his power to persuade. And he knows his power is limited.

"*Puzhaltzda,*" he says. *Please.*

It is the only real Russian he knows.

He moves with the boy to the three stairs that descend into his own apartment.

There is a bang at the door.

"*Puzhaltzda,*" he says.

She talks more. She is explaining something crucial. He cannot make any sense of it and then makes the kind of decision a soldier makes with simple, irreproachable logic.

"I cannot understand you and I am not going to. A violent man is at the front door. I am therefore leaving through the back door. I am taking the boy. If you come with us, you will be better off. If not, I am removing you from the equation. So here we go."

Sheldon steps down into his bedroom, goes past the bathroom and the closet on his right. Beyond the bookshelf there is a hanging Persian rug that covers the bicycle entrance, which Sheldon has known about for three weeks—not just this morning—but didn't want to admit finding on the day he moved into the apartment.

Say what you want, but there is a value to knowing the entrances and exits to places and problems.

With his elbow, he pushes the rug aside and sees the door behind.

"Right, that's it. We're going. Now."

The banging has changed from a firm knock to a frontal assault on the door. The monster is kicking it with his boot. Hammering at the spot where the thin deadbolt holds the fifty-year-old dry-wood door to the opposing wall.

It is only a matter of time.

The problem is that the door in front of Sheldon is also locked, and he can't manage to get it undone while holding the boy.

"Come here, you fruitcake," he orders Vera. "Open this. Open it, goddamn it!"

But she does not open it. She has crouched down under his bed.

Is she hiding there? That would be madness. Why hide when escape is possible?

There is no option. Sheldon has to put down the boy to struggle with the lock. And when he does, the boy rushes to his mother.

Just then the front door is kicked in.

It slams into the wall. Though he can't see the front door from his angle, he hears the wood splinter and something metallic clank on the ground.

What Sheldon does next is focus.

"Panic is the enemy," said Staff Sergeant O'Callahan in 1950. "Panic is not the same as being scared. Everyone gets scared. It is a survival mechanism. It tells you that something is wrong and requires your attention. Panic is when scared takes over your brain, rendering you utterly fucking useless. If you panic in the water, you will drown. If you panic on the battlefield, you will get shot. If you panic as a sniper, you will reveal your position, miss your mark, and fail your mission. Your father will hate you, your mother will ignore you, and women across this planet will be able to smell the stench of failure oozing from your very pores. So, Private Horowitz! What is the lesson here?"

"Hold on a second. It's on the tip of my tongue."

Sheldon focuses on the lock. There is a chain lock that he slides off. There is a deadbolt that he twists. There is a door latch that he presses downward as he also lowers his weight onto it in the hope that the hinges will not squeak.

The steps down into Sheldon's flat are not immediately visible from the kitchen. There are two other bedrooms off the living room for the monster to search before reaching the stairs.

It is just a matter of seconds now.

Sheldon grabs the boy by the shoulders as the mother emerges from under the bed. There is a moment when all three are standing silently. Looking at each other. Pausing before the final assault.

A stillness settles.

Vera is framed by the doorway leading upstairs. The Norwegian summer light floods around her, and in that blessed instant she looks like a saint from a Renaissance painting. Eternal and beloved.

And then the heavy footfalls come.

Vera hears them. She opens her eyes wide, then—slowly, quietly—pushes her boy toward Sheldon, mouths something to him Sheldon doesn't understand, and turns. Before the legs of the monster can descend the three steps, Vera, determined, rushes up the stairs and launches her whole body at him.

The boy takes a tentative step forward, but Sheldon grabs him. With his free hand, he tries the back door one more time. It still won't open. They are trapped.

Releasing the rug and letting it fall back into position, Sheldon opens the closet door and leads the boy in. He raises his finger to his lips to signal silence. His eyes are so stern and the boy is so terrified that not a sound passes between them.

There is screaming, heavy-body heaving and crashing, and cruelty upstairs.

He should go. He should grab the poker from beside the fireplace, swing it with all the force of mighty justice, and lodge the spike in the monster's brain stem, standing tall as the invader's lifeless body collapses full force to the floor.

But he doesn't.

With his fingers under the door's edge, he pulls it closed as far as it will go.

As he hears the sound of choking, the smell of urine fills the closet. He pulls the boy to his chest, presses his lips against his head, and places his hands around the boy's ears.

"I'm so sorry. I'm so sorry. This is the best I can do. I'm so sorry."

# CHAPTER 3

SIGRID ØDEGÅRD HAS been a police officer with the Oslo *Politidistrikt* for just over eighteen years. She joined after completing her advanced studies in criminology at the University of Oslo. Her father persuaded her to go there, rather than study farther north, because in his view "there will be more eligible men in the big city."

As so often happens in police work and in life, her father's theory proved both true and irrelevant.

"The question, Papa, is the ratio of available men to those who are interested in me. Not just the number of available men." Sigrid had made this point to her widowed father in 1989, before going to Oslo.

Her father was a farmer from the countryside. Though not a formally educated man, he did understand numbers, as they came in handy for organizing life on the farm. He was also a reader of history. He did not call himself a student, since he had no tutor, but he found reading pleasurable, took an interest in the worlds that have passed before this one, and had a good memory. All this served him, Sigrid, and the animals rather well. He also had a fine mind for reason, and he and Sigrid found comfort there when emotions were too tender.

"If your argument holds," he had responded over a quiet dinner of salmon, boiled potatoes, and beer, "then it is not a matter of ratios at all, but a statistic of likelihoods. What is the likelihood of there being a man sufficiently observant as to note your desirability and availability? And again, I stand by the claim that such a young man is more likely to be found in the big city."

"It's not such a big city," Sigrid said.

Her father slid each section of pink meat off the subsequent section of pink meat to see how well prepared it was. They slid easily, and he said nothing.

"It is the biggest one available," he offered.

"Yes, well," she muttered, reaching for the butter.

Sigrid's older brother had moved to America on being offered a position selling agricultural machinery. It was a good offer, and their father had insisted he take it. Though he stayed in touch, Sigrid's brother almost never came home. This was family now. This and the animals.

"I'll grant you the point about the city, but there are still two problems," she said.

"Oh?" Her father raised the pitch of his voice just enough to suggest a question.

"The first is that I'm not pretty. I'm plain. The second is that it is near impossible to know whether a Norwegian man is interested."

She had learned this by way of empirical observation and comparison.

To wit, she had once met a British man named Miles. Miles was so forthcoming with his advances that the alcohol merely affected his aim rather than his behavior.

She had also met a German boy who was sweet and affectionate and clever, and whose only flaw was being German—which was unfair, and she knew it, and she felt bad about it, but Sigrid still didn't want to spend every other Christmas in Hanover. To the boy's credit, though, neither did he.

Norwegian men, in contrast to the others, were problematic—even for Norwegian women, who presumably had the greatest motive to crack the code of their behavior, if only for reasons of proximity.

She explained. "They are polite. Occasionally witty. They dress like teenagers no matter what their age, and will never say anything romantic unless it's during a drunken confessional."

"So get them drunk."

"I don't think that's the first step in a lasting relationship, Papa."

"Things can't last unless they begin. Worry about duration after commencement."

Sigrid pouted, and her father's shoulders dropped.

"Daughter, it's not hard at all. You look for the man staring with the greatest intensity at his own shoes while in your presence. The kind of man who is too tongue-tied to try talking to you. This is the one you're looking for. And take it from me, you'll have his love and you'll win more arguments. In the long run, this is the key to longevity, which is apparently your goal."

Sigrid smiled. "You know, Papa, they tend to be more loquacious in Oslo."

"Yes, well," he said, "the world is a tricky place."

Her father finished his second beer and sat back with a heavy briar pipe that he lit with an experienced hand and a long match.

"So," he asked, "what will you do after university?"

She smiled broadly. "I'm going to fight crime."

Sigrid Ødegård's father nodded approvingly. "That's the spirit."

Sigrid's interests had led her to specialize in organized crime. Traditionally, this meant drugs, weapons, human trafficking, and a smattering of economic and corporate crime—though Oslo's police department was woefully understaffed to deal with white-collar offenses. Back when she started, organized criminals were more opportunistic and disorganized than today; they were generally not linked with global criminal networks and terrorists. Only in recent years, as Europe's borders grew soft, and wars raged on in the Balkans and the Middle East and Afghanistan, did organized crime come to resemble the sorts of American TV shows she often watched alone in the early evenings after returning from work.

Sigrid, just over forty, had recently been promoted to the rank of *Politiførstebetjent*, or Police Chief Inspector, in her district, after dutifully working her way up from constable, to sergeant, to inspector, and now this. Not politically minded, she had little interest in this post, but it did provide an opportunity to survey the wider range of crime in the city and to observe the movement of the times from a greater height and wider angle. She confidently believed this job was her final destination, and she was grateful that she had reached her potential without undue strain or frustration.

*From now on*, Sigrid thought, *I will work, witness, and assist when possible.*

Being a professional witness, she was aided by a corps of able, respectful men in her unit who understood that she took pleasure in odd events. They each made a concerted effort to bring the most noteworthy matters to her attention, and no one was more eager to do so than Petter Hansen. Petter, thirty-six and still not needing to shave daily, was able to spot oddities with the discerning eye of an antique collector.

His job had become easier over the past few years because Oslo was no longer the silent, uneventful city it once was. There were now rapes, thefts, armed holdups, violent domestic disputes, and a growing tide of young people who did not respect the police. Recent immigration from Africa and Eastern Europe — and Muslim countries farther east — created a new social tension in the city that still lacked the political maturity to address it. The liberals expounded limitless tolerance, the conservatives were racist or xenophobic, and everyone debated from philosophical positions but never from ones grounded in evidence, and so no sober consideration was being given to the very real question now haunting all of Western civilization—namely, How tolerant should we be of intolerance?

Sigrid sets her sandwich—now half molested—onto the brown paper bag that had sheltered it for the night and looks up as Petter walks to her desk with a smile, which can only mean he's uncovered another buried treasure.

"Hi," she says.

"Hi," he says.

"Have something?"

"Yes," he says.

"Good for you."

Petter says, "Something awful."

"OK."

"But different."

"Start with the awful."

"There's been a murder. A woman in her thirties in Tøyen. She was strangled, then stabbed. We've already secured the scene. We're starting the process now."

"When did this happen?"

"I got the call twenty minutes ago. We've been there for five. A person in the building heard a fight and called us."

"I see. And what's different?"

"This," says Petter, handing Sigrid a note. It is written in English. A sort of English, at any rate. She reads it carefully. And she reads it again.

"Do you know what this means?"

"No," Petter says. "But it has spelling mistakes."

"Yes."

"We've called the owner of the apartment. The woman who was killed didn't live there. She lived upstairs with her son. The son is missing. The owner is Lars Bjørnsson."

"Do we know him?"

"He makes video games. He's really good."

"You're thirty-six, Petter."

"They're very sophisticated video games."

"I see."

"He's here in room four. They came right away. Lars's wife says her grandfather is missing from the apartment."

"He lives there?"

"Ah, yup. American. Retired."

"I see. Are they suspects?"

"Well, you know. We have to figure out where they were at the time, but I don't think so. You'll see." Petter pops his lips and says, "So let's go, then."

Sigrid looks down at her baby-blue shirt and black tie to see whether any of the sandwich's contents are stuck to them. Satisfied, she stands up and follows Petter down the hallway, past the overhead Geographic Information System that maps the whereabouts of all police officers and vehicles in the city, and past the coffee machine that has been broken for so long that someone (probably Stina) has placed flowers in the pot. The coffee pot is now regularly watered.

Police room four has a round wooden table and five office chairs. There is no two-way mirror, and the chairs do not screech across the floor during an interrogation. Instead, there is a box of tissues and a few bottles of Farris water. There is a window on the far wall that is locked, but there are no bars or grates covering the glass. Opposite the window on the far wall is a public-awareness poster from the Norwegian Reindeer Police Service, with a uniformed woman on a snowmobile speaking with two Sámi herders. Sigrid secretly imagines that the officer is asking directions.

At the table sit a man and a woman. The man is Norwegian, and the woman is not. He is tall and fair, with a boyish expression. She has black hair and unusually deep blue eyes. Both look grave.

They look up as Sigrid enters the room and Petter follows.

The two police officers sit at the table. In English, Petter says, "This is Chief Inspector Ødegård."

Rhea speaks in English. "They say there's a dead woman in my apartment."

"Ya, ya," says Sigrid. "We're curious about that, too."

"Does this sort of thing happen often around here?"

"No. Not so much."

"You don't seem very surprised by it," says Rhea.

"Ah, well, not much point in that now, is there? So, Petter told you about it. Did you know her?"

Lars and Rhea both nod.

Sigrid notes how the woman does all the talking.

"She lived upstairs from us with her son. She didn't talk much. I think she's from Eastern Europe somewhere. She used to fight with a man a lot."

"What man?"

"I don't know. But he was there a lot recently. They spoke the same language. He was very violent."

Sigrid takes notes, and Petter does as well. The conversation is also being recorded.

"What was she doing in your apartment?"

"I have no idea."

"The door was kicked in," says Petter.

"See, that's interesting," says Sigrid. "A small woman like that. Probably didn't do it herself, right?"

Petter shakes his head. "A man's large boot print is all over the door."

"So she was in your apartment when it was locked. Did she have a key?"

"No," says Rhea.

"Do you usually lock the door when you leave?"

"Yes, but my grandfather was there. Sheldon Horowitz."

"Ya," Sigrid says. "Do you want to tell me about that?"

And so Rhea speaks and does tell her something she has never heard before. She speaks about her grandfather who is missing. She talks about New York City in the 1930s when Sheldon was a boy.

She mentions E. B. White's memoir of the city. About the coming war and Sheldon watching the older boys go off to fight the Nazis, and how he stayed behind because he was still a boy. How many of them never came back. She speaks of Mabel and their courtship. How he enlisted in the Marines and worked as a clerk in Pusan, though he's started to say something different these days.

How Sheldon and Mabel had a son, Saul, and how Saul spent countless hours in Sheldon's antique and watch-repair shop, learning how to take everything built between 1810 and 1940 apart with a screwdriver, and then run like hell.

She talks about how Saul died in Vietnam. How all of Sheldon's friends have died of old age, how Mabel died, how the pressures of this world were weighing her grandfather down, and how this move to the northern frontier of Western civilization was her own failed effort to share his final years before the end came. She explains his fears. Now the unimaginable has happened in her home, and her grandfather is missing.

Rhea has spoken carefully and with love. She has spoken with some terror of what she is experiencing. She has spoken in waves of insight and humanity.

She has spoken for a long time. When she is finished, she has a question for Sigrid.

"So, do you understand?"

Sigrid has indeed been listening closely. So she answers with precision.

"An eighty-two-year-old demented American sniper is allegedly being pursued by Korean assassins across Norway after fleeing a murder scene. Either before or after."

Rhea furrows her eyebrows. "I don't think I'd phrase it quite like that," she says.

"What did I miss?" Sigrid asks, looking at her notes.

"Well . . . he's Jewish."

Sigrid nods and makes an additional note. Then she looks up.

"Well," says Rhea, "that part's important. It sort of frames everything else. It's not just a fact. It's not like he's wearing a blue coat and not a brown one. It matters."

"How so?"

"Well," says Rhea again, trying to find words to express the essence of the thing. "It means, well . . . he's Jewish. He's not your normal whacko. His name is Sheldon Horowitz. Can't you hear it? It's like his whole history is built right into his name. He's a missing old man in a foreign country. He has dementia. He must have seen something. Something happened."

Nothing Rhea has said makes any sense to Sigrid, who has grown puzzled by what is a new and clearly sensitive topic. She knows little about Jews. There are only a thousand Jews in all of Norway. His name just sounds foreign.

All the same, Sigrid appreciates that Rhea is trying to impart something she considers so obvious as to not need explanation. So in trying to explain it for the first time, she is frustrated and halting. Though Sigrid still needs to discuss it with Petter, she can sense already why this woman and her husband are not suspects.

Rhea, sitting across from the policewoman, sees on her face the very foreignness of the Jewish experience to Norway, and she now feels a tremendous guilt in bringing her grandfather here.

It wasn't as though Sheldon hadn't attacked the issue head-on one morning during a breakfast rant while gesturing with his coffee mug . . . in Rhea's mind forever conjoining Norwegian Jewish history to images of airbrushed *Penthouse* nudes.

Not that this wouldn't have delighted Sheldon, had he known.

"A thousand Jews!" Sheldon had said. "I read it in the Lonely Planet guidebook! Five million people, and one thousand Jews. The Norwegians do not know what a Jew is. They only think they know what a Jew is *not*."

What Sheldon said next upset her because he said it in front of Lars, who is married to a Jewish woman and who has a strong affection for Sheldon. When Lars looked at her afterward, she just stared at the floor.

"Jews, the Norwegians have been taught, are not greedy, duplicitous, weak, pale, sneaky, plotting, impotent, salacious, or mendacious. They do not have crooked noses, bony fingers, or evil appetites. They are not scheming, evolutionarily inferior to the Nordic blond, not working on secret plots to overthrow the world," said Sheldon. "They have been taught this so they can grow up to be nice liberals with their ears flushed of bad old Nazi propaganda. The thing is, this sort of description doesn't exactly make you want to rush out and date one, does it?

"So, despite being here—or somewhere, anyway—for three thousand years, all they think of when they hear the word 'Jew' is the Holocaust and the Israeli-Palestinian fiasco. The problem is, nowhere in that twisted and limited story is there a place for Sheldon Horowitz or a brooding little siren like you. Nowhere is there three thousand years of history, philosophy, theater, art, craftsmanship, scholarship, writing, pontificating, fornicating, or well-timed and perfected humor, goddamn it!

"Don't worry," he added for Lars's benefit. "That's what everyone else in Europe has been told, too."

And this is what he said next, for his own benefit, mug lowered to the table: *Look to the cemeteries on France's northern coast. Look, Europe. Look and see the tombs of Jews who landed on your beach. Over here. Here in the oppressive silence of Europe that has squandered the music of Jewish ideas. Where we were your victims. You look carefully, because we came from America, where we were five hundred thousand Sons of David fighting under Old Glory against the apocalypse of Western civilization.*

*Breathe deep this lesson, Europe: as you killed us, we liberated you.*

But not Sheldon. Sheldon did not go to that war. He was too young.

"What I mean to say," says Rhea to Sigrid, "is that he's a remarkable old man who is coming undone at the end of a long and hard life, and he's missing."

Sigrid nods. Lars and Petter remain silent. Sigrid looks again at her notes, and says, "I'd like to revisit the discussion of his dementia."

"Yes, OK."

Sigrid notices a change on Lars's face, but cannot make sense of it.

Rhea explains. "My grandmother died not long ago. Sheldon has been lost ever since. They were unusually close. Before she died, she told me he was suffering from dementia. She recommended I watch it and stay informed."

"This was in New York."

"Yes. I looked up the symptoms from the National Institutes of Health in America."

At this, and for the first time, Lars audibly snickers.

"What?" says Rhea.

"You must admit that your grandfather had an answer to each of those symptoms."

The conversation Lars is referring to took place three weeks ago, outside Vestbanen, near Aker Brygge in Oslo Harbor. The entire area was being developed. The Tourist Information Office had been moved out of the old train station and replaced by the museum for the Nobel Peace Prize. They sat at Pascal's, with its excellent cakes and absurdly priced ice cream served in pathetic plastic cups. A massive ocean liner was at anchor by Akershus Fortress, and a stream of large humans with cameras and appetites was approaching.

On seeing the hungry tourists, Sheldon pulled his twelve-dollar cup of ice cream a little closer.

"Papa, all I'm saying is that there are five symptoms, and we should consider them." Reading from a piece of paper, she said, in as cooperative and supportive a voice as she could muster, "First, asking the same questions repeatedly. Second, becoming lost in familiar places. Third, being unable to follow directions. Fourth, getting disoriented about time, people, and places. And fifth, neglecting personal safety, hygiene, and nutrition."

It was Saturday morning, and the edge of spring was giving way to the long, lush days of Norway's eternal summer.

Sheldon listened and nodded. Then he ran two fingers up the

sides of his beer glass and collected the condensation. He closed his eyes and ran the cool water over his eyelids.

"Ever do this? Feels great."

"Papa."

"What?"

"Why do you keep buying beer if you never drink it?"

"I like the color," he said, his eyes tightly closed.

"Do you have any thoughts about what I just said?"

"Yup."

"Do you remember the question?"

That provoked him. Sheldon turned to Lars, who was attentive. "Watch this."

"Number one. Getting people to repeat their own questions forces them to figure out what they're asking. If you're not willing to ask a question three times, then you don't really want to know the answer. Number two, you have brought me to Norway. Nothing's familiar. I can't become lost in familiar places. I just become lost. Number three, I don't speak Norwegian, so I can't follow any directions. If I understood . . . *that* would be demented. Number four, I don't know of any half-intelligent, self-aware person who, if they give it a moment's thought, doesn't find time, people, or places all highly disorienting. In fact, what is there to disorient us *other* than time, people, or places? And for the three-part finale, I say this. I have no idea what it means to be neglectful of personal safety. As measured against what? Under what conditions? As judged by whom? I've sailed into a storm of tracer bullets, face first, on the Yellow Sea at dawn. Was I neglectful? I married a woman and stayed with her until the end of her life. You call that safe? As for hygiene, I brush my teeth and shower daily. The only one who thinks I'm dirty is someone who thinks I don't belong, and so is probably an anti-Semite, and you can tell him Sheldon Horowitz says so. And nutrition? I'm eighty-two and I'm *alive*.

"How did I do, Lars?"

"Better than I could have done, Sheldon."

Rhea remembers the story. But she says to Lars, in front of Sigrid, "He was lucid. He has powerful reasoning skills. He was show-ing off."

Lars shrugs. "It worked on me."

"OK, maybe it isn't dementia per se. But he's odd. Really odd. And he's increasingly talking to the dead."

Even as she speaks, she accepts the doubts. Whatever is going on in his overtaxed mind is complicated. It comes and goes. She does know that Sheldon isn't well. That Mabel's death has fundamentally altered his place in this world. That he is unmoored. Beyond that, she can't say.

Sigrid listens and then says to Lars, in English, "You don't think it's dementia."

Lars taps his fingers on the table. He doesn't want to disagree with Rhea. Not in public. Not about her own family. But he feels an obligation. Before saying it, though, he wonders whether he can set the scene so Rhea will arrive at the same truth herself. The moment can be hers.

"Rhea told him something this morning. Something that af-fected him."

Sigrid turns to Rhea and waits.

"I had a miscarriage last night. They sent me home from the hospital. I was still in my first trimester. I told Papa this morning."

It is Petter who responds to this. "I'm sorry," he says.

Rhea nods. She does not want to be the center of attention.

Lars says, "We weren't unprepared for this. But I think Sheldon was."

Rhea says nothing. So he goes on.

"I don't think it's dementia. Sheldon has outlived everyone he knows, including his own son and wife. I think he came to Norway because of the baby. For a chance to see life continue beyond him. But then the baby died."

"What do you think it is?" Sigrid asks Lars.

"I think it's a kind of guilt. I think he is consumed by guilt for surviving. His son, Saul, Rhea's father, for starters. Maybe also his older friends in World War II. His cousin Abe. The Holocaust.

People in Korea. His wife. This baby. I don't think he can take any more guilt. Even with the Koreans. I know there's some debate about whether he actually saw combat, but I think he did, because he sees them hiding in trees. I don't think they're just any Koreans. I think he sees the people he killed, and feels bad about it. Even though it was a war."

Rhea does not agree. "My grandfather does not feel guilty for surviving the Holocaust. Trust me. If anything, he feels guilty for not lying about his age and going to fight the Nazis."

"He was fourteen when America entered the war. He was a boy."

"Have you met him?"

Sigrid writes this down in her notebook, along with other observations about Rhea and Lars and the timing of the disappearance.

There is only one last order of business.

"What do you make of this?" Sigrid asks, handing the murder-scene note to Rhea.

The note rests lightly in Rhea's hands as she reads and rereads it.

"It's from my grandfather."

"And what do you think it says?"

"Well," she says, "it isn't so much what it says as what it means."

"Ya. OK."

"This is why Lars and I disagree on Sheldon's diagnosis."

Sigrid takes back the note and reads it aloud as best she can, not knowing what accent it is meant to mimic:

> I reckon I got to light out for the Territory, because they's going to adopt me and sivilize me, and I can't stand it. I been there before.
>
> —River Rats of the 59th Parallel

"So," Sigrid says, "that's what it says. What does it mean?"

"Yeah," says Rhea. "I don't know."

# CHAPTER 4

SHELDON NEVER SAW the attack on his son in Vietnam. But he imagined it over and over again. It appeared faithfully in his dreams night after night. Mabel would shake him awake. "You're dreaming," she'd say.

"No. It's not like a dream."

"A nightmare, then. It's a nightmare."

"No, not even that. It's like I'm there. In the boat with him. Patrolling the Mekong. Up a tributary at night. I can taste the coffee. My feet itch."

Mabel was forty-five. She slept naked, except for her wedding ring and a thin, white-gold necklace adorned with a tiny diamond pendant. She'd made the pendant from the engagement ring that Sheldon gave her in 1951, and never took it off.

Mabel did not have trouble waking up at odd hours of the night. Her husband's bouts of fear did not disturb her. Twenty-three years earlier, Saul used to keep her up, as he was a colicky baby. Since then, she'd never needed much sleep. After Saul died, it no longer mattered.

Sheldon's dream started one summer night in New York, in 1975. Saul was already buried. Mabel lay on top of the white sheet. She was curvy and petite, and liked to stretch her body by pointing her toes and arching her back and extending her fingers as far as she could until everything tingled. She'd hold the position until she cramped and then released . . .

Donny was also lying naked on the white sheet. It was scorching that summer. They had no air conditioning. An antique ceiling fan, which looked as though it had been imported from colonial Kenya, was spinning slowly. It forced the hot air down.

Mabel switched on the bedside light.

They had not had the conversation yet. Donny had not asked the question that upset him. He had been, at least until tonight, prepared to go on like this. To wake in the morning, go to the watch-repair shop, put on an eyepiece, and replace a hairspring, oil a wheel train, change a broken balance staff, or affix a new crown. Eat a sandwich. Come home. Make small talk. Read a paper. Smoke a pipe. Have a drink. Go to sleep. Day after day, quietly allowing time to pass while fixing the instruments that measured it.

But that summer night in 1975 was different. There was no way of knowing what made it different. Maybe it was the temperature—the way the heat in his imaginary Vietnam followed him to the Lower East Side of New York, and the sweat from the jungle soaked into the bed sheets.

Maybe there was no more room left inside him to contain his inner world any longer, and regardless of the possible consequences, it needed to be released.

When she took his hand in hers and sighed, Donny asked the question.

"Why are you still with me? Why haven't you left me?"

His voice, as he remembers it, was calm. Sincere. Drawn from a subterranean reservoir of humanity, still and quiet in our collective souls.

There was a long pause before Mabel answered. He looked at her painted toes as they flexed. She had beautiful arches.

"You know what I've been thinking about?" she said.

"What?"

"I've been thinking about those two spaceships that just found each other in all that emptiness."

"I don't know what you're talking about."

She turned her head and frowned. "You don't watch the news?"

"I've been keeping my head down."

"The *Apollo* and a Russian spaceship. The *Soyuz*. They linked up two days ago. Out there in the blackness. In all that silence, they connected. I wonder what it was like to hear that sound. To be floating. Weightless. And suddenly you hear the clang of metal against the hull of your spaceship. Your enemy extends his hand. You grip it with your glove. Above it all, finally. It gave me a feeling I used to have. I don't remember what you call it. It was like . . . sort of like a smell that you walk past one day, and this world rushes back in and time vanishes, and you're there again. What would you call that?"

"Hope."

"You should have watched the news."

"I can't tell if this is an answer or not."

"I'm still here, Sheldon. Does it matter why?"

"Yes."

"Why?"

"I need to know how fragile it is."

"It isn't science, Donny."

"I'm working on a tough watch back at the shop. It's an Omega Speedmaster. There's a broken screw that sits just below the surface of the hammer spring. I have to strip the whole thing down to the bones to get a grip on it, and I'm not sure I know how to put it all back together again once I do. All these in-house calibers are a little special. Anyway, it's the same watch your astronauts wear out in space."

"Is this a coincidence?"

"It's a popular watch. I had one myself, but Saul took it. I don't know where it went."

"That's too bad. I like coincidences."

"Do you blame me?"

"Do you blame yourself?"

"Yes. Entirely. I brought him up on war stories. I told him that a man fights for his country. I encouraged him to enlist. Jews can't get out of Russia. They file their papers to emigrate and they get blacklisted—they call them refuseniks. They live like nervous rats. We live like men. That's because we're Americans. And America is at war. So, Johnny, go get your gun, I said."

"You said so before."

"They're smoking dope and listening to records. We're all a bunch of change-the-world liberals now, I said."

"You said this before. We don't need to go over this again."

"I had to fill my kid with ideas."

"I know."

"I remember when Harry James hit that C note above high C at Carnegie Hall in 1938. It was Benny Goodman's orchestra. No one was sure if jazz deserved that level of respectability—if those musicians were serious enough to deserve Carnegie Hall. And then that one note. The city went wild. Can you imagine a single note being heard across this country anymore? They smash their guitars on stage now. My son could have played music. I sent him to war."

"It wasn't his nature," Mabel said.

Sheldon shook his head and said, "We used to worry that if we picked him up when he cried, he'd never learn self-reliance. What the hell were we thinking?"

"I'm staying with you, Sheldon. I think it's enough for now. OK?"

"Yeah. OK."

And that was it, the last time they brought it up. If there was more to be said, she took it to the grave.


They manage to escape shortly before the police arrive.

Sheldon gently cracks open the closet door and listens in silence for several minutes. Listens for the crush of glass on the steps, the sound of doors opening, closing. He knows there is no defense if they are discovered, but he can help prevent that from happening.

The struggle had been horrible and long. The boy had buried his face in Sheldon's chest. And when it was over, Sheldon had felt a wave of shame and regret as powerful and unavoidable as the years after Saul died. In his mind, any other sequence of events—not opening the door for her, not keeping them there so long, calling the police, anything—would have resulted in that poor woman living on to raise her gentle son. He may as well have murdered her himself.

He fully opens the closet door and looks around the room. Nothing has been disturbed. The monster has not come here.

Sheldon yanks down the rug that covers the back door and works the lock. He jiggles it, presses on the door, lifts it, and finally manages to push it open just enough to let them out. The door is noisy and hard to move. Something heavy had been pressed against it. He could not have opened it without being heard. This is small comfort.

Speaking into the dark closet, Sheldon whispers—so as not to startle the boy—"You stay here for one minute. I'll check to make sure the coast is clear and then we'll go. Because we can't walk through the living room."

Sheldon slips through the doorway into a small alley behind the building. A garbage bin had been pressing against the door. Rust had formed on the hinges, from neglect. And together these could have killed them.

He walks a few meters to his left and emerges on a side street where the sun is shining and couples stroll by. It is calm and safe. The events in the apartment do not radiate from it, disrupting the world around. *We are all truly unconnected.*

Before Sheldon returns to collect the boy from the apartment, a white Mercedes slowly drives by. It is the same Mercedes he saw from the window. In the driver's seat, looking straight ahead, is a man in a black leather jacket with gold chains. Beside him is another man.

This other man and Sheldon look at each other as the car goes by. There is no recognition on the man's face. He has never seen Sheldon before. He has no reason to suspect that the old man is anything more than a random bystander near a murder scene.

But there is a connection. Some message has passed between them. Sheldon feels it immediately.

As the car drives past, Sheldon mutters quietly so that the words have been spoken, even if there is no one there to hear them: "You can't have him. As God is my witness, you can't have him."

Inside, he writes the note. The words come to him as if they were prophetic. Rhea will understand, won't she? She'll get the reference. She'll know where he's going. She'll know what it all means.

He leaves it on his dresser, by the photos and under his Marine Corps jacket patch. Though the idea comes to him, he chooses not to write down the time.

On leaving the apartment through the back door, Sheldon and the boy do not need to wander far to find a safe and public place where they are unlikely to be found. Like so many other Norwegians, they drift into the Botanical Garden and hide themselves in the beauty of the day. Only they are not like other Norwegians.

Sitting on a park bench after buying the boy an ice cream cone, Sheldon checks his watch so he can know precisely the moment he ran out of ideas.

*2:42 p.m. As good a time as any.*

A police car drives by behind them with its lights on and siren going. Soon after, another follows. He knows immediately that they must have found her. And soon they'll find the note.

"What we need to do, kid, is hole up in a cave like Huckleberry Finn for a while. Do you know that story? Huck Finn? He went upriver after confronting his evil father. Faked his own death. Met up with a runaway slave named Jim. Sort of like you and me, if an old Jew and a little Albanian dressed like Paddington Bear are reasonable stand-ins for the original cast. Point is, though, we've got to hole up somewhere. Our own version of Jackson's Island. We've also got to go upriver. Go north to freedom. And I've got an idea about how to do that. The trouble is, I'm out of my element here. I don't know what use I am to you. I can't give you up. I can't hand you over to the police and hope that the Norwegians don't just hand you over to the monster from upstairs. How should I know who he is? What I do know is that it isn't your fault, and that's enough for me right now. So I'm on your side. Got it?"

The boy chews what remains of the cone in silence, looking down at his Wellingtons.

"You're going to need a name. What's your name?"

The Paddingtons dangle.

"I'm Donny." He points at himself. "Donny. You can try Mr. Horowitz, but I think that's a doomed proposition. Donny. I'm Donny."

He waits.

"Eye contact would be helpful here."

He waits again. Another police car drives by with the sirens blasting.

They are sitting on a bench not far from the Zoological Museum. Plush grass surrounds trees in full flush. Lilies line the base of bushes, and children—many about the boy's age—glide along on odd sneakers that seem to have wheels in their heels.

A dark cloud passes over, cooling the air and bringing with it a thousand shadows.

Sheldon continues speaking for both of them. Silence is not a practiced skill of his.

"My son's name was Saul. He was named for the first king of Israel. This was three thousand years ago. Saul had a hard life. And it was a hard time. The Philistines had taken the Ark of the Covenant, his people were miserable, and he had to pull it all together. Which he did. But he couldn't hold it. He was a flawed man in many ways. But not in others. One of the things I like best about Saul is how he spared the life of Agag. This was the king of the Amalekites. Saul's army defeated them, and according to Samuel—whom I do not like—Saul was supposed to put Agag to death because it was the will of God. But Saul spared him.

"I see these men, men like Saul, men like Abraham. They hear God's vengeful voice raining down to destroy Sodom and Gomorrah, to take the life of the defeated king. But these men stand between God and what he'd destroy, and refuse to let it happen. And so I wonder: Where are they getting these ideas about right and wrong, about good and evil, if not from God himself? It's as though, at one time, the river of the universe flowed through the veins of these men and connected us to eternal truths—truths deeper than even God could remember in his anger. Truths that Jewish men stood on like firm ground and looked into heaven and insisted remain. What are these truths? Where are these men?

"I picture Abraham standing on a hilltop, a rocky, reddish hilltop, above Gomorrah as the clouds gather for their attack, and he extends a hand to the sky and says, 'Will you destroy this city if there are still a hundred good people?' And at that moment, wretched though he is, standing before the forces of the Eternal, Abraham is the height of everything man can be. That one person. Standing there alone with dirty feet, a filthy robe in the hot oncoming wind. Confused. Alone. Sad. Betrayed by God. He becomes the voice beyond the voice. The gathering. Is God acting justly, he wonders. In that instant, humanity transforms itself into a conscious race.

"God may have breathed life into us. But it was only when we used it to correct God that we became men. Became, however briefly, what we can be. Took our place in the universe. Became the children of the night.

"And then Saul—my Saul—decided to go to Vietnam because his father had gone to Korea, and his father went to Korea because he didn't go to Germany. And Saul died there. It was me. I encouraged him. I think I took the life of my boy in the name of a moral cause. But in the end I was nothing like Abraham. Nothing like Saul. And God didn't stay my hand."

For the first time that Sheldon can recall, the boy is looking at him. So he smiles. He smiles the kind of smile that only the old can deliver. The smile that appreciates the importance of the moment more than the reality of it.

The boy does not smile back. So Sheldon smiles for both of them.

"And then there was the other Saul—Rabbi Saul of Tarsus. A Roman. Liked to fall off horses. According to you Gentile types, he persecuted the early Christians until he had a revelation, a vision, on the road to Damascus. And so Saul became Paul. And Paul became a saint for the Church. And a good man he was.

"You didn't know I knew all this stuff, did you? I do. No one ever asks me. Lucky for me, though, I've got a rich inner life. Now I've got you.

"What if I call you Paul? A boy transformed? The one who fell and got up again? The Christian reborn from the fallen Jew? Would you mind that? It'll be my own private joke. All the best ones are.

"All right. Let's go hide at the movies."

It is hard for Sheldon to remember the last time he'd held a boy's sticky hand in his own. The chubby fingers and light but purposeful grip. The trust and responsibility. The moderation of gait and the slight stoop of his own shoulder. Was the last time really with Saul? That would make it over fifty years ago. The feeling is too familiar, too *immediate*, to assimilate that answer, even if it is true. The prospect of half a century existing between this feeling and the last time he had it fills him with remorse.

There was Rhea, of course. A love he never expected. But this was a boy's hand.

Rhea and Lars stand outside the police station in silence. They are free to go but are instructed to remain reachable at all times. Lars watches the cars pass. Rhea bites a piece of her lip, takes it into her fingers, and flicks it off her fingertip into the light breeze. They stand there for a couple of minutes. Eventually, Lars speaks up.

"So now what?"

"I don't know," she says.

"I suppose we could take the bike around town and look for him," he says.

"I can't believe he doesn't have a mobile phone."

"He refused. Said we'd use it to track him."

"And we accepted that."

"Only because he never left the house."

"He's left now," says Rhea.

A few more cars go by and a thick cloud passes overhead, bringing a quick chill. It is a reminder of the distance they have all come. How far they are from home.

"Yes, he did," Lars says. "He sure did."

# CHAPTER 5

I T IRRITATES SHELDON to no end that movie theaters in Oslo assign seating to its patrons.

"You think we can't sort it out for ourselves? We need supervision? Direction?"

He says this to the innocent girl behind the ticket counter.

Her pimply face puckers. "Is it different where you're from?"

"Yes. First come, first served. Survival of the fittest. Law of the jungle. Where competition breeds creativity, and out of conflict comes genius. In the Land of the Free, we sit where we like. We sit where we *can*."

Sheldon snatches his ticket and mumbles. He mumbles at the price of hot dogs at the concession stand. He mumbles about the temperature of the popcorn, the distance between the restroom and the theater, the steepness of the theater's banked seats, and the average height of the average Norwegian, which is well above average.

It is when he stops mumbling—for only the briefest moment as he catches his breath—that the murder rushes back in and finds purchase. It occupies the space.

He's familiar with this problem on a larger scale. This is just an instance of it. History itself constantly threatens to take him over and leave him defenseless under its weight. It's not dementia. It's *mortality*.

The silence is the enemy. It breaches the wall of distraction, if you let it.

*Jews know this. It's why we keep talking at all costs. With what we've been through, if we stop for a second, we're done for.*

Turning to Paul, he says, "I don't know anything about this movie other than it's over two hours long, at which point we'll get you the world's most expensive pizza at Pepe's, and then we're going to relax in style tonight at the Hotel Continental. It's near the National Theater. The Grand Hotel, I'm sure, is all booked. It's the last place they'd think to find us, because it's not the kind of place I tend to haunt. But personally, I think we deserve a little calm tonight."

And then the trailers end and the movie begins. It involves a spaceship on its way to the sun in order to save the world. The movie begins with wonder but degrades into horror and death.

Sheldon closes his eyes.

Jimmy Carter did not remain president long enough to see the hostages come home from Iran in 1980. On the day of Ronald Reagan's inauguration, the planes departed from Tehran with the Americans who had been held in captivity for four hundred and forty-four days. The cameras filmed Reagan taking the oath of office in a light rain—his wife wore red under a gray sky.

But the drama was on the airplane where these people cried, and talked, and worried that it was all a lie and that they were merely being flown in circles in a further act of cruelty. What Sheldon understood, watching it all on TV, was that the grand sweep of American history was not in Reagan's poised pronouncement, but in the lonely and pensive look on Jimmy Carter's face as he stood, no longer president, on the tarmac. And beneath the grand sweep of history were the lives of people like him and Mabel and Bill Harmon, his colleague from the pawnshop down the block from his own place in New York.

Mabel read the newspaper in those days. She formed her opinions at the end of each article, and then allowed them to evaporate like so much water off a dead pond. She did not allow Sheldon to discuss politics in the house, and he had no desire to do so anyway. Saul had been dead for six years by 1980—which, as time works, was no time at all.

The city had become still for them, purposeless. It was a succession of yellow streaks of cabs going by. Black sheets of rain. A palette of greens from a farmers' market. A red steak for dinner. Sleep again. The only movement came from the watches in Sheldon's shop.

The watch-repair and antique store was in Gramercy, off Park Avenue South. It was inconspicuous, but locals knew it was there. Passersby could easily miss the thickly barred iron door that opened into the small workshop in the front and the larger showroom in the back.

By the 1980s, Sheldon's business was suffering from an invention called the digital watch. They had few moving parts, kept remarkably accurate time, inexplicably excited people's imaginations, and were cheap. Worse yet, they were disposable. And so the Swiss watch industry was in turmoil, and those who depended on it for their livelihoods were, too. No longer did men and women of every economic stratum come to Sheldon's shop for a minor repair, or to clean and oil the movement, or to put in a new gasket. Instead, only the old-timers were coming in. The quality of Swiss watches improved steadily, as people replaced the cheap ones and fixed the good ones. Sheldon had fewer clients, the work was more complicated, and the pay did not improve. The decade grew silent and unremarkable.

Bill Harmon's pawnshop was three doors down on the right. Bill was also in his fifties, was American of Irish decent, and had a shock of pure white hair over his ruddy face. He and Sheldon sent customers back and forth between them as if they were Ping-Pong balls.

"Not for me. Try Bill's shop. He buys power tools."

"No, no. You go to Donny's with the fancy gold watch. I don't know the first thing about these."

"This is a Nikon. What am I going to do with a Nikon? Go to Bill."

"Go to Donny."

"Go to Bill."

"So Donny, take a look at this one," said Bill one day. He handed Sheldon a thin gold watch with its original leather band, a Patek Philip. "Guy says he bought it in Havana before they went Red. Wanted to sell it to me. I sent him to you, but . . ."

"I got in late."

"You got in late. So I bought it."

Sheldon was wearing a leather apron and a white shirt, and had slid his reading glasses to the top of his head. He was looking a bit scruffy, and his blue eyes caught a glint of the afternoon. Not that Bill noticed. Bill had no sense of the dramatic, the fleeting, the ethereal. Nothing magical existed for Bill. Which was a pity because, as Sheldon saw it, Bill had one of the most magical shops in New York—aside from his own—and no one knew this better than his son had.

To Saul's boyish delight, Bill's shop was the exact size and shape as Sheldon's. Something about their sameness gave Saul a proprietary feeling whenever he was in the pawnshop. Bill, divorced and childless, welcomed being adopted by the boy.

To enter his father's shop, Saul had to walk down a few steps and through the single gated door. On the left was the repair area. Sheldon had a big wooden workbench there, and along the wall behind him were hundreds of little shelves, each one smaller than a library catalogue drawer, with nothing but numbers on them. The light was good here, and Saul watched as people passed through, all of them nice to his father.

In Bill's, there was a large display case so people could look in and see all the strange things he had for sale. At one time he had a Viking shield with fur on the front side. Another time he had

Rock 'Em Sock 'Em robots, an antique pistol from the Wild West, a broken typewriter, a letter opener from France, a vase with fish for handles, and a mirror surrounded by gold leaves.

Bill did not wear a leather apron as Sheldon did, nor a watchmaker's loupe, so there was still something special back at Saul's father's shop. Sheldon's apron was faded and folded, and had been worn by knights when they fought dragons. Saul knew this because Sheldon had told him. In fact, Sheldon had no special interest in looking like an Old World *horlogeur*, but he couldn't deny that leather aprons came in handy when he dropped tiny watch parts. With the apron on, he could hear a part hit the leather, which let him know that, yes, he had dropped something. Also handy was how the tiny pieces could be easily collected from the folds. So while it actually was a cobbler's apron, not a watchmaker's, it had both utilitarian and magical dragon-fighting qualities. Together, they made it easy to don and hard to remove.

When Bill walked in that morning, Sheldon had a thermos of coffee on the workbench and was carefully fitting a used balance spring into a new Ollech & Wajs diver's watch.

"Congratulations," said Sheldon. "Now you have a watch."

"What are you doing?" asked Bill.

"Something that's been on my mind for a while."

"What?"

"You wouldn't understand."

"It's complicated, right? Technical? I wouldn't understand." Bill shook his head and whistled. "You Jews. You're so clever. There's nothing you're not good at."

Sheldon didn't take the bait. "Staying out of trouble doesn't seem to be our thing."

"So tell me what you're doing, Einstein."

Sheldon took off the eye loupe and placed it to the right of the workspace. He pointed to the watch casing on the left.

"That was Saul's. They recovered it from his body. It came home with his personal effects."

"So you're fixing it."

"No. I don't want to fix it. I'm doing something else. Have you ever heard of elinvar?"

"No."

"It's a metal alloy that's resistant to changes in temperature. The word is from the French *elasticité invariable*, which they shortened to elinvar. It's used to make the balance spring on a mechanical watches like these two."

"Valuable?"

"No. It's just iron, nickel, and chromium, but it makes a lot of stuff useful. The balance spring is a very delicate piece. It coils around and around. When you wind a watch, you're coiling the balance spring. As it uncoils, the tension causes the watch parts to move and the whole thing to tick. The balance spring is the heart of the watch.

"Thing is, there are only a few foundries that produce the stuff. So most balance springs can be traced back to the same foundries. It's like . . . the hearts all come from the same place. Like every watch has a soul, and is connected to every other one because they all came from the same home.

"I bought the watch from a magazine. Nothing you'd have ever heard of. Fancy people don't own them. Working-class people do. Soldiers. And they get what they pay for. I like them. So I bought a new one recently, and I'm taking the balance spring from Saul's old watch and placing the old heart in the new one. This way, when I go about my day and check the time, when I make some decision or other, we're connected. It makes me feel a little closer to him."

"That's something, Donny."

"It's what I'm doing, anyway."

"So how's that any different from taking a battery from one watch and sticking it in another?"

Sheldon rubbed his face. "And you wonder why you never get laid."

"I don't know what you mean."

"You really don't, do you?"

"How much for the new one?"

"About thirty-five bucks or so. They used to be around seventeen."

"So look, guess how much I paid for the gold watch."

"How much?"

"Oh, come on, Donny. Ask it like you mean it."

Sheldon opened his hands a bit and asked in the same bored tone of voice, "How much?"

"That's more like it. Eight hundred."

"Eight hundred what? Dollars? Jesus, Bill. For a watch? You'll never be able to sell that!"

"I'm not gonna sell it. It's an investment. I'm gonna buy a dozen of these things, stick 'em in a vault, and in twenty years when we sell these shops those watches will be worth thousands! We'll retire. Get a place on Long Island. Fill it with Playboy bunnies and drink champagne."

Sheldon's desk chair creaked as he rocked on it. "What are we going to do with Playboy bunnies when we're in our seventies? Admire the way they carry drinks?"

"You mark my words, Donny. By that time, with the way science is rushing on today, they'll make a pill or give us a shot or something that'll build a rocket in every old man's trousers. We just landed on the moon ten years ago. That's a young man's dream. By the time those same scientists are our age, they'll set their sights closer to home. They won't want to go where no man has gone before. They'll want to go where *every* man has gone before. And you know why? Because it's *nice* there."

"What about our wives?"

"Our wives . . . ," said Bill, taking the question seriously. "I won't be married, and . . . by then . . . Mabel will be glad you've found a hobby."

Sheldon leaned forward and opened a drawer under the workbench. "You're a visionary, Bill. I'll grant you that. A horny, spendthrift visionary."

Sheldon took out a small box and handed it to Bill.

"What's this?" Bill asked.

"I want you to store these at your place. Just stick them some-place. Don't sell them."

"What are they?"

"Some medals they gave me, coming home from Korea."

Bill accepted the box without opening it.

"Why do I have to take them?"

"I don't want my wife to find them. Or Rhea. She's getting big-ger and running around asking questions."

"You're the one who taught her to speak."

"If I'd known the consequences . . ."

Bill looked around the antique shop. "You can't hide them here? You could hide Jimmy Hoffa here."

"Do something useful."

"When do you want 'em back?"

"Let's see if I do."

"Is it really about the girls?"

"In part. But mostly I don't want to be reminded that I let Saul see them. And since I'm doing this thing with the watches, I can't handle them being so near me. Look, you don't have to understand it. You just need to do it because I'm asking. Isn't that enough?"

"It's enough."

"Good."

Bill took the box but hovered there as Sheldon worked. After a few minutes, Sheldon looked at him.

"What's with you today?"

"I'm dead."

"What did you do now?"

"I'm dead. Actually dead. Don't you remember? It happened in November, during the elections. Drunk driver. You took it hard. I guess you're still taking it hard. I'm your first death since Saul. That's why you're doing the watch thing."

"I'm doing it because of my boy."

"Yes. But my death is why you're doing it now."

"So this isn't just a memory, then."

"Sure it is."

"Not this part. I mean, I can't be remembering a conversation with a ghost. I have to be making this up."

"Well, no. I guess it's not a memory per se. It's more like a vision or something. Neither of us is here. You're at the movies with the little foreign kid you picked up in Iceland."

"Norway."

"Whatever."

"You don't sound quite like Bill."

"Who do you think I might be?"

"I don't like that question."

A little bell over the door announced that a customer had entered the shop.

"I think we should wrap this up."

"What happened this morning?" asked Bill.

"Which 'this morning' are we talking about?"

"The one with the little Balkan kid. Why did you hide in the closet? Why didn't you save the woman?"

"I'm eighty-two years old. What could I have done?"

"I'm just saying."

"I made a choice. Whatever strength I had, I chose to use for the boy. Life is choice. I know how to make a choice."

"Now what?"

"Every direction is upriver. Ask me when I get there."

A young usher wearing the nametag "Jonas" is leaning over Sheldon with a kind expression. He says something in Norwegian.

"What?"

In English, Jonas says, "I think you fell asleep. The movie is over, sir."

"Where's the boy?"

The lights are on and the credits have stopped.

With some back pain, Sheldon walks up the aisle and out to the lobby, where he finds Paul holding another ice cream cone — presumably a gift from the concessionaires.

"I've been looking for you," says Sheldon.

Paul does not smile when he sees Sheldon. He has not softened at all since they've met.

Sheldon holds out his hand.

Paul does not respond.

So Sheldon calmly places his hand on the boy's shoulder.

"Let's get out. Get you changed. You can't keep wearing those pants. I should have changed you out of them earlier. I wasn't clear yet. I am now."

Petter taps Sigrid gently on the shoulder to draw her attention away from the computer screen. "There is urine in the closet."

It is almost eight o'clock at night, and the sun is still high. The temperature is over eighty degrees in the office. The building was built without central air conditioning. It was unnecessary back then, but now global warming is killing them.

Unlike some of the men in the office—buzzing with energy—Sigrid has not unfastened the top button of her uniform. She is entitled to, and the office does not stand on formality, but for reasons she cannot entirely explain to herself, she prefers not to.

"Definitively new urine. It was still wet a few hours ago."

"You sure it wasn't one of the cops?" she asks sarcastically.

"We're testing it for DNA against the dead woman's. It isn't hers, because her trousers were not wet. I wonder if it belongs to the missing boy."

"Hiding in the closet, hearing his mother being murdered? It's a terrible thought."

Petter says nothing.

"How long to run the test?"

"Normally? Six months."

"How about this particular time?"

"By morning. Inga is going to stay late at the lab. She just broke up with her boyfriend. I think she likes being busy, and I broke six laws asking her to put this one in front."

"Doesn't she have a dog?"

"A cat."

"Victor?"

"Caesar."

"Well. Good for us, then."

"Are you going to the crime scene?" Petter asks.

"Aren't you doing a good job?"

Petter puckers his lips.

"Yeah, eventually," Sigrid says. "I'm getting the woman's name from the landlord, as well as her son's and the man who probably did this. I figure I'd catch the bad guy first, then worry about the rest later."

"We're going to Pepe's after for a pizza."

"After what?" says Sigrid.

"It's a nice night. Have a drink."

"I'm not in the mood."

"I've never seen a woman murdered before," says Petter.

Sigrid does not look away from the computer screen. She sternly says, "You still haven't."

Sheldon checks in at the reception desk. "Name, please?" asks the woman.

In an accent that neither Sheldon nor the Swedish woman behind the desk can quite place, he says, "C. K. Dexter Haven."

"C. K. Dexter Haven," she repeats.

"Esquire," he adds. Looking down, Sheldon says, "And grandson. Paul. Paul Haven."

"May I have your passports, please?"

Sheldon turns to Paul and says, "She wants our passports. The ones with our names on them."

He turns back to the receptionist. "Actually, my dear girl, there is bad news and good news there. The bad news is that we were robbed of our bags — passports included — no more than an hour ago when coming in on that fancy train you have from the airport. The experience was so traumatic that my boy actually wet himself. But I say this to you in confidence — I wouldn't want to embarrass him, even at his age. But the good news is that my office faxed them over to you before we left, so luckily you have copies. And please, could you make me two more? I'll need them for the police report tomorrow morning and for the embassy, so they can issue us new ones for the sad journey home."

There is a moment when nothing is said.

As the slender, inviting, stylish woman opens her mouth to speak, C. K. Dexter Haven raises his hand and says, "But no need to do it now. Thank you for the offer. Our day has been so long, so tiring, that—given my age, I'm eighty-two—I think it's best if we address the matter in the morning. What I would like to do is give you cash for the room now so we can settle accounts. And then I'd like one of your bellboys to go out to a local shop and buy my grandson some clothes. Socks, sneakers, trousers, underpants, a shirt, and a nice jacket for walking in the woods. Charge it to the room and bring it up as soon as possible."

The woman is trying to speak. She makes the sorts of gestures one proffers when trying to contribute to a conversation. Some hand movements. An occasional open mouth. Eyes narrowing and widening, with the practiced head-tilt being used for emphasis. But such subtleties are, against Sheldon, like whispering to an elephant. Sweet and pointless.

"Mr. Haven, I'm sorry that—"

"Of course. So am I. And with the medication missing that I use to offset the side effects of my cancer, I'm so grateful to have been robbed in a country filled with such kind people. This is what they say in America. The Norwegians are the kindest people. If I make it home alive, I'll confirm that message. And if I die before returning to my native land, the boy will do it for me."

It was a nice room.

Sheldon found a TV station playing cartoons in Norwegian. Paul sat quietly on the bed with a bottle of Coke watching Tom chase Jerry. Sheldon sat next to him, doing the same.

"I had an idea for a television commercial once," Sheldon says. "Picture this. First shot, a field of wheat and wildflowers, all in golden shades. The sound of insects buzzing away. You can feel the heat. Next shot, gentle ripples on a pond. A dreamlike patina on the water. Then, splash! A dog jumps in. The camera tracks him as he single-mindedly swims from left to right. Then, coming into view on the right side, an empty Coke bottle floating in the pond. The dog—a golden retriever—takes the bottle in his jaws, huffs and puffs as he turns back. He bounds out, shakes himself off, runs with the bottle onto a dock, where there is a boy lying on his back, lazing away under the clouds. The boy, without looking, picks up the bottle and tosses it back into the pond. Then, as the dog jumps back in, the words appear on the screen: 'Coca-Cola. Summertime.'

"It eats you up! There's nothing you can do! It reaches into your gut and plucks your piano string! But what do you do with an idea like that? Nothing. You send it in, they steal it. Meanwhile, I don't have my own soft-drink company."

Paul says nothing. He has not uttered a word since they met. Has not so much as smiled.

But a child does not know how to manage silence. About the need to keep comedy and tragedy as close to each other as humanly possible—as close as pathos and words will allow—to try to shut out the voices of the dead. He is only a little boy. He is enveloped in the silence of terror, where words fail and every utterance slips from reality like raindrops from a leaf. He is not old enough to distract himself with games, is not yet adept at finding solace from dialogue and drama. He is defenseless. His mother is dead. And this is why Sheldon will never leave him.

"God made the world, said it was good," says Sheldon aloud. "Fine. But when did he reappraise?" he asks as Tom chases Jerry on the television.

"OK, I know what you're thinking. You're thinking, well, he reappraised before the Flood. Before Noah made the arky-arky made of hickory barky-barky. But that was a while ago. And it's not like he went back to the drawing board. He just smudged it all out, except for the ark. I think we're due for some reconsideration. Not necessarily the same juvenile response, like a kid crumpling up a bad drawing and pretending it never happened, leaving Noah with a question. The question was 'Why me?' Unable to answer it, he hit the bottle. Personally, I'd like to see some growth in God. Some maturation. Some responsibility. Some admission of guilt. Some public testimony about his negligence. The trouble is, God is alone. No one to push back. Set him straight. No Mrs. God. I'm not the first one to think this, I suspect.

"Now, you might say, being as you are Saint Paul and therefore a theologian and a philosopher, and possibly the most interesting person in history, that it is impossible for God to make amends, because how does he know when he's done wrong? After all, does being all-knowing include self-knowledge? As He is the source of everything, can He possibly deny His own actions and condemn them? Against what? What's the yardstick other than Himself?

"So, I have an answer, and thanks for asking. The answer lies in the biblical story of masturbation. I wouldn't mention this, not at your age, but seeing as you don't speak English and you've been through worse today, it'll cause little damage.

"Onan. We remember him as the one who spilled his seed. The original jerk-off. But what happened there? Onan had a brother, and his brother and his wife couldn't conceive. For whatever reason, God decides that the family needs a child, so, as was the custom in those days when people seemed to be replaceable, God tells Onan to go into his brother's tent and *shtup* his sister-in-law. But Onan finds this wrong. He goes into the tent and, thinking God can't see inside tents—and don't get me started on that one—proceeds to masturbate instead. Spills his seed, as it were. He comes out, tells God the deed is done, and walks off. God, being God, gets angry with Onan. The lesson we all derive from our Judeo-Christian clerics is that masturbation is abhorred by God, and we're to keep our hands off our willies. But my question is this: Where did Onan get the idea that instructions from God could possibly be immoral? That there was a morality, a code, that came from a place deeper in the human soul—from our uniqueness and our mortality—that already knew right from wrong with such clarity that it could deny the most powerful authority and navigate its own course?

"And so the real question becomes: Why couldn't I instill some of that in my own son so he could have had the courage to stand up to me, deny me my own failings, and refuse to go to a futile war that killed him? So he could have outlived me. Why couldn't I have given more of that . . . whatever that is . . . to my son?"

Sheldon looks at Paul, who is staring at the screen.

"Now come here, and let's get your Wellingtons off."

# CHAPTER 6

WHEN RHEA AND LARS left the police station, they rode around for hours looking for Sheldon. Their search was random at first. They rode through neighborhoods close to the city center, and up and down the most popular roads. Karl Johan's Gate. Kristian IV's Gate. Wergelands-veien, by the new Literature House. Up Hegdehaugsveien onto Bogstadveien, and all around Majorstuen. Back to Frogner Park, down into Frogner, down to Vika, down to the port.

Then they chose particular locations. There was a synagogue, but no sign of Sheldon. There was an all-day topless bar, but no sign of Sheldon. There were bookstores, but no sign of Sheldon.

Lars suggested they stay overnight in town. Someplace nice. Someplace expensive. Perhaps the Grand Hotel?

But the Grand had no rooms, so they stayed at the nearby Continental.

Lars slept deeply. He was exhausted.

Rhea lay awake, staring into the ceiling, her life playing backward and forward.

The breakfast at the Hotel Continental this morning is good, but Rhea is not hungry. She dips her finger into the hot tea and places it on the edge of the water glass. Holding the base with her other hand, she circles the ring until a low tone rises like the mournful cry of a lost baby whale.

"If I did that, I'd be in trouble," says Lars.

"I'm sorry."

"How did you sleep?" he asks.

"I'd rather be at home."

"No you wouldn't."

"How are we going to go back there, knowing a woman was murdered in our apartment? How long can we live at a hotel?"

"There are people with worse problems than ours."

"That's true. And it would be rude if they were here right now, but they aren't, so let's talk about us."

Lars smiles, and for the first time since checking in, Rhea smiles, too.

"You sound like your grandfather sometimes. Mostly when he isn't around."

"He raised me."

"You're worried about him?"

"I'm too shocked to be worried."

"We don't have to stay in the hotel. We'll go to the summer house. I can get time off from work."

"I don't have anything with me but a toothbrush."

"We have some things there. We can get what we need before we leave."

"Are we allowed to leave?"

"I'll call Sigrid Ødegård and let her know where we're going. Unless they want to pay the hotel bills."

"It's in the paper this morning, you know. I saw a photo of our building on the front page."

Lars is drinking black coffee and eating toast with an egg. He is wearing a white, short-sleeved dress shirt, untucked, over fashionable jeans and leather shoes.

"How can you eat?" she asks.

"It's breakfast."

"All this doesn't invade you somehow? Disrupt everything? Hollow you?"

Lars puts down the coffee cup and taps the table a few times. "I try not to think about it. I just try and think of what to do."

"Like a video game."

"That's not fair, or nice."

"You make it sound like a choice. Doesn't it get into you? Terrify you? I'm terrified. My grandfather has all these hostile images in him. All this pent-up rage. I remember him, when I was little, looking at me with such love and tenderness and then, in a flash, becoming angry. Not at me. He never really got angry with me. Exasperated. He got exasperated all the time. He would throw up his hands and ask me what I was thinking. 'What makes you think that's a good idea?' he'd say.

"It was the world itself he railed against. When I was older, he said that looking into my face showed him the infinite depth of humanity and all that is lost every time a person is taken from us. And it brings into focus the kinds of people who can look into children's faces and harm them, and what the rest of us need to do about that.

"And then he'd talk about the Holocaust. The Nazis shooting children in the head in front of their parents, to prove to themselves that they were above petty human kindness and were the supermen that Hitler said they were. Tying families together with piano wire along the Danube and shooting only one, so the others would drown. Gassing them. Throwing them into pits and covering them, still alive, with lime . . ."

"Stop it," whispers Lars.

"You want *me* to stop it?" she says, slapping the table.

Sheldon wakes, and does not shave or bathe. Instead, he opens the door and sees a copy of the *Aftenposten* newspaper just outside. He can't understand it, but he is looking for something specific, and he finds it.

The word for murder in Norwegian is *mord.* There is a picture of his building, a headline, and police tape across the entrance. There is a huddle of people standing around it. She is really dead. It is as if the reality of the experience is made doubly real by the world's confirmation. Perhaps it's just a function of the dementia that Mabel insisted he has.

*You need proof.*

*Fine. Proof. I'll find proof. May I go now?*

"I didn't even call the ambulance," he says to no one. "What kind of animal am I? How did I forget to do this? Could she have survived if I'd fought? If I'd have so much as called out?"

And then here is the boy. Who is peeing in the bathroom. Trying to aim over the rim and not make a mess. Who flushes and turns on the tap. Who washes his little hands under the water as his mother taught him to do, and turns off the faucet as tightly as he can and dries his hands on a fresh towel before coming out of the bathroom while trying to buckle his belt.

Sheldon learns that her name was Senka, not Vera. There is, as far as he can tell, no mention of a boy. If this is true, someone is being very careful about how this story is being told.

Sheldon showers, shaves, and dresses them both in the new clothes that the porter brought up. He looks under the bed, in the bathroom, the drawers, and the folds of the bed and chairs to be doubly sure that nothing in the room can identify them. He hasn't skipped out on a bill since 1955, and there is a skill to it. He doesn't want to get it wrong when the consequences are so unusually high.

When he finishes preparations to leave, he sits on the edge of the bed and thinks. He thinks slowly and he concentrates.

If the police know about the dead woman, they know about the boy. And seeing as Sheldon didn't come home last night, Rhea is probably losing her mind right about now.

It occurs to Sheldon that Rhea may have walked in on the dead woman. That Rhea might have thought he'd been murdered as well. A day after the miscarriage.

*This life? You want my views on this life?*

He holds the paper and looks at the building. They will hunt for the killer and possibly for the boy, too. They will be looking for him for one reason or another. And if the killer is after the boy, the police will be checking every plane, train, and bus to lock down the city.

"It's like in the Navy," he says aloud. "You control the choke points, like Gibraltar or the Bosporus or Panama or Suez. Control that, and then you wait for the enemy to come to you. On your terms. It's what they'll do. It's what I would do. The Norwegians might lack a certain assertiveness, but they're no fools. They'll wait for us all to fall into the trap."

Sheldon looks over at Paul, who is watching a cartoon in Norwegian.

"I know what you're thinking—I should turn you in, drop you off. But what if they don't suspect the monster? What if they hand you over to him? What if they think I'm a crazy old man and that my testimony isn't worth spit? And I never saw his face anyway. I'll bet Rhea already told them I'm cuckoo. So then what?

"Look, I'm not turning you in until they catch him. OK? So how do we get out of here?"

Sheldon imagines the city as he knows it. He imagines it as a crystal in the midst of a wild, emerald-green forest with flowing rivulets of blue. He pictures planes and trains and taxis and cars. He imagines the police and the monster sitting on either side of the crystal city, peering into it. Looking for the old man and the little boy.

"The river," he says at last, referring to the Oslo Fjord.

Sheldon puts down the paper and rubs his face.

"I don't want to go on the river."

At breakfast, Lars takes the napkin from his lap and places it on the table beside his plate. He sits back in his chair. Rhea rests her chin on her open hands and slumps forward. They say nothing for a long while.

"What would we have done today?" Rhea finally says.

"You mean, if all this wasn't happening?"

"Tell me a story."

When she was little and lived in Manhattan with her grandparents, she dreamed of New England the way Sheldon had described it. The hills of the Berkshires would crest and dive like waves covered in wet autumn leaves. A giant doll's house floated on that sea of leaves. Inside, blueberry pancakes slid back and forth across the breakfast table. When the pancakes arrived at Sheldon's side, he'd take a bite, then slide them back down to Rhea's end, where she'd take a bite. Mabel sat in the middle, trying to pour freshly pressed cider into a cup without spilling it.

The teddy bear behind her on the hutch rocked and rolled, too, its blue bow tie flapping like a butterfly.

At breakfast, in the doll's house, they would tell stories.

The summer house was her doll's house now; Hedmark, her Berkshires. And so life unfolds itself, and our dreams come true in ways we never imagined.

Lars is her imagination. He tells her stories in their doll's house. They lie on the grass in summer and under the duvet in winter, and fly together in worlds both wonderful and sad.

This morning—the morning of the second day—he wants to be somewhere else.

So Lars talks. He tells of a nice day at the bookshop with the terrace at Aker Brygge, and the midsummer sales on Bogstadveien, and ice cream on some corner of Grünerløkka, and cinnamon buns at the Åpent Bakeri across from the new Literature House near the Royal Palace. Rhea follows the circuitous route in her mind and imagines herself pushing a pram.

Inside the pram is her baby, who is between three and four months old. She looks in. It is a boy, and he is sleeping. He sways as the pram sails the city streets. He doesn't wake when the wheels cross the frequent drainage runs in the sidewalk. It is part of the rhythm of the city, and the boy was born here. Born here, so far from her home. He both is, and will never be, of this place.

As she listens to Lars, she populates the city with familiar and unfamiliar faces. She matches the clothing styles to the neighborhoods. She recalls Sheldon mapping the city against New York.

"Frogner is Central Park," he'd said. "Grünerløkka is Brooklyn. Tøyen is the Bronx. Gamlebyen is Queens. And that peninsula—what do you call it?"

"Bygdøy."

"That's Long Island."

"What about Staten Island?"

"What about it?"

The boy's name is Daniel. They pass a toy store and she looks in the window. Suddenly she imagines Sheldon standing inside, holding a bloody knife.

"I think we should settle the bill and go to the summer house," Rhea says abruptly.

Outside the window, in a white Mercedes across the street from the hotel, Enver's fingers roll back and forth across the black vinyl of the steering wheel to a rhythm that no one else hears. His trigger finger is permanently stained yellow by old Yugoslavian cigarettes. A CD is playing the music of a dark and raspy singer strumming a gypsy guitar.

The car's engine is off. The hood crackles under the sun.

The woman he is watching inside the building is slumped onto her hands, and the man is stretched over his chair. They have been there for over an hour as the hot morning sun shines into Enver's weathered face. The sun doesn't just set late here; it rises early.

He puts on a pair of gold aviator sunglasses and inhales deeply.

Soon his exile from his native land will end. After the war—when Kosovo was still Serbian—he fled. He was wanted and hunted. But now things are different. Kosovo has declared independence. It has been recognized by states all around the world. And there, Enver is not a wanted war criminal. There, in that new state, with new laws, new rules, and a new memory, he will return a quiet hero. Yes, the new state has all the trappings of a modern government. It will be good, of course. It will act in accord with all international laws and treaties. It will be grateful for the support of the kindly nations that have recognized its right to exist. But it will be crafty and wise, too. It will first remember its own. It will protect Enver and his comrades. It will welcome him into its warm embrace. It will learn to justify his past actions in the way that all states celebrate their soldiers.

Before all that, however, there is something that needs to be done here, in this Nordic land. Before all that, he needs to find the boy.

Kosovar independence should have been a time of rejoicing—of dancing and drinking and fucking—a decade of fighting in the KLA against the Serbian scum finally vindicated. His comrades in arms have been living in every godforsaken land, furtively, like rats hiding from the light. When you fight for a land that has no government of its own, there is nothing to protect you. But now Kosovo is free. And the government knows who helped make it free. And it will be good to its returning sons.

Enver was there in March '98 when Adem Jashari's house was raided a second time by the police. He personally put a knife in the soft space between the ribs of a burly cop wearing a flak vest, and stared him down as the life drained out of him, watching the last emotion register on his victim's face.

Hate. It is always hate. Never remorse. Never regret that this life is ending, or for the beauty that is passing.

Perhaps if he saw sadness—the sadness of final knowledge in all that is still undone, unlived, unloved—he could look onto something new in the light of this asylum summer. But it never comes. You cut a man open and all that flows out is the hate that is inside. It drips from the knife, and sanctions the kill.

He wipes his brow with a white handkerchief. *They never said it would be so hot here.*

During the war, the Serbs tried to drive him, his family, his clan, his fellow Kosovar Albanians, from the land, in what the West called ethnic cleansing. But when NATO starting dropping the bombs, and the KFOR soldiers moved in, the tide turned. Enver and his men quickly formed a militia. Their revenge was not random. Enver and his men targeted the family members of the men who terrorized their families and his people. After the war ended, there was still justice to deliver.

The day that brought him to Oslo began in Gracko. The Serbian boys and men were working the fields. It was scorchingly hot. Enver was lying beside a sickly gray brook with a rifle resting on his fist, looking down the long barrel's iron sights. The flies on his hair and face made him twitch. They made it hard to keep the farmer covered by the iron pin.

He and his men, twelve in all, were in the forest at the edge of the field. Enver had picked the target. It was his mission. The killing would begin as soon as he pulled the trigger.

And he did. But the farmer didn't fall. Instead, the man turned to his left, looking for the source of the small explosion. Perhaps a car had backfired? A stone had hit another stone? An ax had struck a buried brick? Anything but this. The war was over, wasn't it?

Then the farmer fell, shot by someone else's rifle—killed in his confusion and tranquility. Perhaps his last thought was of the peace he lived in and the safety of his family. Enver hoped so. Because in the afterlife he would be ashamed of his final moments. And perhaps this would be the first shame he ever felt. And through that feeling he might come to understand what he and his people had done to others in this life.

Enver was a poor shot. His targets dropped, one by one, at the hands of other men in the team, and his own rage mounted. He couldn't seem to put a bullet on target. His compatriots would complain that he didn't do his fair share, that he didn't earn his fair share of the honor. They would secretly scoff at his manhood—at his failure to avenge his people against the marauders.

Because of flies. The distraction of the damn flies.

With no bullets left, he dropped the rifle and ran into the field to find someone to kill with his bare hands and teeth.

The field was dry. His feet pounded the cracked earth as his heart pumped in his chest. A boy, maybe fourteen, clutching a rake, stood frozen like a panicked deer as Enver charged at him. The boy peed into the left leg of his trousers like a child. But before Enver was on him, before he could slit his throat, a bullet clipped the boy in the neck, splaying blood over the golden field.

The boy thrashed on the ground, crying for his mother, as Enver picked up his rake and ran toward the farmhouse.

What right did they have, these Serbs? They did this to him in Vushtrri. They created this moment. Wrath does not invent itself; it is the product of the ways of others. We all must brace for the impact of what we put into this life. These farmers—these killers—were fools not to do so. And now, God the merciful, in his infinite wisdom, is taking them.

Vushtrri. Enver's own family had been toiling over their own land. It was an unremarkable day, just like this one. Daily life was in the details: a bit of thirst, a blister, a bad joke half heard, a stubborn root. The Serbs came in uniform, walking slowly. They were in no rush. They were on government business. To terrorize them. To drive them out like rodents from the Garden of Eden.

Enver's family was surrounded.

His sister was raped. Her ears were cut off. One eye was gouged out. She was left to live like this. Enver was a boy, hiding alone in a closet as he listened to the screams of his sister outside, too scared to try to stop it. He heard it all. When he entered the kitchen to see what had happened, he heard someone laughing. To this day, he is sure it was the devil.

And now, years on, here they were, the killers. The torturers. The families of these people had been sipping water from flasks, and their women were serving them cold beer in the noonday heat, to soothe them. These murderers. These parasites. Acting as though they, too, knew human emotion. But they were empty. Soulless. Without remorse or faith.

Past the wounded boy, Enver broke into a run and entered the front room of the farmhouse. Water still ran from the tap. Outside, he heard the *pop-pop-pop* of low-caliber rifles and a few muffled yells. But inside it was so quiet.

*They are hiding.*

Even an empty house speaks more than this. You can hear an empty house breathe. This one was holding its breath.

He put down the rake and took a thick knife from the sink. He tried to control the beating of his heart.

"Come out. Face your fate," he called out.

He walked into the living room. The television was on, playing a Western film dubbed in Serbian. A black American cop with a gun was running down a city street after a robber. The city was New York. The robber was clutching a bright red handbag and sprinting between a line of cars.

"Come out!" Enver yelled. Perhaps his voice was scary enough, because he heard a muffled cry in the closet.

*If there is a gun, and should the bullet kill me now, so be it. At least I died honoring my dead.*

Prepared for his last breath, he opened the closet door and looked into the darkness.

Outside, the killing was steady and without mercy. The iron circle closed in around the farm, as the others had done to his own village. Snipers covered three directions, ensuring that no one escaped the shrinking perimeter.

It took time for his eyes to adjust to the dull gray and flecks of gold in the closet. But when they did, it was as though God himself had placed them there for him.

There was a woman in her early twenties, barefoot, wearing a flowered skirt. And beside her, nestled into her sister's neck, was a soft little one. Maybe twelve years old.

It was clearly a gift. A chance to have his revenge and assert his moral superiority, both in the same simple gesture. There was such purity to the offering, its cosmic balance almost made him cry.

He addressed the older one.

"Get out. Get on your hands and knees and prepare yourself for me. Otherwise, I will slit her throat and have you anyway."

He remembers the feel of her hips in his hands, the movement of the flowered skirt across her back, the whimpers of fear, pain, and pleasure confusing her. And when the moment came, he raised his face to the heavens and, unsure if his act was profane, shouted that God is truly great.

It was over. And yet these moments do not merely end. They do not pass unremarked and drift lightly into the hinterlands of memory, to be eclipsed—like so much else—by the present and its seductions of imagined futures. Sometimes, they live. And they grow. And the past matures until it takes over the world and gives birth to a new reality that commands us and subjugates us, making us face who we are and all we have done. And so, when Enver learned that this girl, Senka, had become pregnant and had fled to the Nordic countries to hide her shame, he was unprepared for the feelings that came over him, and the bright light that shone down on it all—directly from above—casting no shadows in which to hide from this new world of his own making.

Now Enver was a father.

He opens his eyes in the car, realizing he has nodded off like an old man. He looks again, in vain, for a cigarette to place in the crook of his fingers and the corner of his lips, where it belongs. He wipes his face with a tissue that leaves bits of white on his temples and snags on his glasses.

The couple in the hotel sign some paper and stand to leave. Enver shakes his head in bemusement. The mailbox of the apartment where he and Senka had words yesterday showed that these two people lived together. If they have been together long enough to share a mailbox—married, perhaps—how could they have so much to talk about? Does this man have no friends to confide in that he will chat for hours with this girl?

Such a strange place, this Norway. Such strange people.

The CD in the car ends, and he turns on the radio. He checks his mobile phone for messages, but there are none. The radio begins to play American rock-and-roll from the 1950s, and he leaves it on. He fiddles with the rear-view mirror and wonders when he'll have time to eat today. He'd forgotten to eat breakfast, and now that he is tailing these two to find the old man—the one Kadri saw in the alley—he can't see when he'll get something to eat.

There might be a chance for an ice cream. That would be delicious. Maybe strawberry. Or mint. They have good mint here. And a cone. Or a cup.

No, a cone.

He sees a 7-Eleven. They don't have especially good ice cream, though. But they do have the Lollipop, which is icy and fruity. Assuming a short line, he could be in and out in, say, four minutes.

Which is too much time. Such is his fate, they are coming out of the hotel now, carrying two unusual pieces of hard-cased luggage. They are wearing leather jackets and carrying helmets. They walk around the corner, still in sight, and mount a large off-road motorcycle that immediately makes Enver worry. It is very hard to tail people on motorcycles. Even when they don't know they are being followed, they can weave through traffic, cut past cars to the front of lines at red lights, and take sudden turns onto roads that disappear into forests.

The Norwegian places a call on his mobile phone, speaks for only a moment, and puts it back in his jacket.

The white Mercedes will be conspicuous. No one drives a white Mercedes here. His friends bought it for him. Stupid. You leave it to a bunch of foreigners and they inevitably bring their own ideas with them to new places where they don't belong.

The proper vehicle would have been an Audi A6 wagon, in silver. That would have been the least suspicious car in Oslo. Schools of them swim through the city. Instead, he is in a gangster's white Mercedes, with no air conditioning and one CD, following a BMW motorcycle now pulling away onto the road, heading east.

He starts the CD again. Despite himself, Enver smiles.

At least the hunt has begun.

# CHAPTER 7

THE BMW GS 1200 runs high on the road, and the boxer engine thumps gently. Rhea looks over Lars's right shoulder as the bike glides undramatically at 65 kilometers an hour past the new Opera House, shimmering white and angular against the blue fjord, as Oslo's city center disappears behind her.

She unzips the vents on her leather jacket to let in more warm air.

*River Rats of the 59th Parallel.*

It wasn't madness. It could mean only one thing—that Sheldon was headed north and east along the Glomma River, into the hinterland, where the cold-water summer house hid two rifles he'd learned about just yesterday.

Lars had made the case plainly back at the Continental.

"If we're wrong, we can be back here in four or five hours to keep looking for him, though I'm not sure what good that would do, and we should probably stay there, given that we can't go home. If we're right, and we get there before him, I can lock up the rifles more securely, and we can wait for him. Then, depending on what we think, we take him to the hospital, or maybe to the police."

Rhea had been wringing her riding gloves like dishtowels.

"The guns aren't locked up?"

"Well, yeah, sure, but he can get to them."

"How do you figure?"

"He was a watchmaker." Lars shrugged. "I'm sure he can pick a lock. Don't you think?"

"That's not very reassuring."

"No." Then Lars asked, "Was he really a sniper in Korea?"

Rhea shook her head. "I don't think so. My grandmother told me he started saying that after my father was killed. She thought it was a kind of fantasy."

"He wanted revenge?"

"No. He always blamed himself. There was no one to take revenge on."

After that, they had mounted the bike and left.

It took more than two hours to get to Kongsvinger and the little town past it, out in the forest by the Swedish border, way beyond the edge of Sheldon's known universe.

"It all started when you came to live with us," Rhea's grandmother had said. "First he lost one marble, then another. After a while he'd lost all his marbles. But he kept playing." Mabel never said that Sheldon got worse because of Rhea. But she did say it started around the same time.

She was only two years old in July 1976, at the height of America's bicentennial. Wide-eyed and frightened, with nothing but a one-eared blue bunny, she was handed over to her grandparents. They were near strangers.

Her mother? Gone. One day she didn't come back. Saul had been dead for more than a year. She drank, she yelled, and then she disappeared when the flags started coming out. It was simply more than she could take.

Sheldon and Mabel had both tried supporting her during the

pregnancy. Her own parents were disgusted with her, and she clearly needed help. Unfortunately—for her, for the child, for them all—she was beyond reach. The Horowitzes didn't know her well enough to know why. There was an anger inside her that, they were sure, preceded Saul and her predicament. Why he was attracted to her they could never say. Beyond the obvious curves and sexual invitations, Mabel had speculated that Saul had wanted to disappear, and the only way to do that without being alone was to find a woman incapable of seeing him.

In the end, none of this mattered. Only the child did.

Rhea asked her grandfather where her mother had gone. She was a little older then. Five. They were in the shop, and she was holding a brass sextant that she'd found in a purple box. Sheldon had been working intensely on something small and complicated.

When she asked, he was momentarily diverted.

He'd put down whatever he was holding and said, "Your mother. Your mother, your mother. Your mother . . . grew wings one day and flew off to become the princess of the dragon people."

Having answered, he put on his eyeglasses and started working again.

Rhea pulled on his leather apron.

"What?"

"Can we go find her?"

"No."

"Why not?"

"Aren't you happy with us?"

Rhea did not know how to respond to this. She wasn't sure if it was related to her question or not.

Sheldon sadly accepted that Rhea wasn't going to let this go.

"You got wings?" he asked.

Rhea frowned and tried to look behind herself, but couldn't.

"Turn around."

Rhea turned. Sheldon lifted the back of her dress, exposing her red panties and pale back, and then dropped it.

"No wings. You can't go. Sorry. Maybe some other day."

"Will I grow wings someday?"

"Look, I don't know. I don't know why people suddenly fly off. But they do. One day some grow wings, and then they're gone." Seeing her expression, he added, "Don't worry. I won't grow wings. I'm a flightless bird."

She remembered from when she was five. But 1976, when she'd arrived, was too far back. She was too young. She couldn't remember the flags everywhere. The streamers. The bands playing in the streets. The speeches by politicians. The newly minted coins and toy drums. It was two years after the near impeachment of a president, one year after the failure of a twenty-five-year war, in the midst of civil rights turmoil, an emboldened Soviet Union, a declining economy, an oil crisis, a baffled intelligentsia, and a movie about a giant shark that ate people. America celebrated its existence as this little girl was transported to a new life, set on a new course, and would forever live in the shadows of the dead and disappeared.

Under fireworks and a combat-jet escort, Rhea was dropped off by Social Services with her grandparents—thumb in mouth, bunny in tow—in a parking lot by a Sears department store, way past her bedtime. She'd been alone for two days by the time the neighbors realized that her crying was not being soothed by anyone, and they placed a call.

Mabel put her in the back seat of a borrowed Chevy wagon and pulled the thick black seat belt across her with a click. Rhea watched the explosions in the sky, watched the clouds turn green, then red, then orange.

But she didn't remember any of this. Mabel told her. Just as she told her how Sheldon started slipping and became a sniper.

"I remember the conversation. We got you home, put you into some of Saul's old baby clothes because that's all we had, and your grandfather said, 'Well. We killed the first one, but God's giving us a second chance to get it right. I wonder if we get a prize if this one makes it to adulthood.' It was a horrible thing to say. Even to think. Only a madman could have uttered a sentence like that. He started making up stories about the war shortly after that. Dementia was the only explanation I could imagine."

Rhea sits on the back of the motorcycle and wonders. She wonders when personality lapses into eccentricity. When genius merges into madness. When sanity gives way to—what? Insanity is merely the absence of sanity. It is not a thing in itself. It is everything but sane. And that's all we know about it. We don't even have a real word for it.

She knows what Sheldon would say, and can't help but smile. "Sanity? You want to know what sanity is? Sanity is the thick soup of distraction we immerse ourselves in to keep from remembering that we're gonna bite it. Every opinion and taste and order you place for brown mustard instead of yellow mustard is just a way to keep from thinking about it. And they call our ability to distract ourselves sanity. So when you get to the end, and you forget whether you prefer brown or yellow mustard, they say you're going nuts. But that isn't it. What's really going on is this. In those little senior moments of clarity, when your head is flipping back and forth between brown and yellow like a tennis match on fast forward, and you suddenly pause, you find yourself undistracted. And it happens. You look straight across the net at all the other people trying to choose between brown and yellow mustard and . . . there he is! At the seat in center court! Death! He's been there all along! Mustard on the left and right, distractions everywhere, and Death straight ahead. It hits you like a swinging vat of onion soup."

The ride grows wilder. The trees thicken as they leave the still, blue water of the fjord far behind and forgotten in the scented winds of pine and maple and birch. Lars steers the bike onto a secondary road to avoid the big rigs and anxious drivers of the city. They climb over the rolling hills and lean into the turns of the valleys. The 1200 cc adventure bike pulls up and then passes with the power of a team of Clydesdales.

It is a horrible thing happening to them. It is. Lars allows the circumstances to confront him as he shifts up into fourth. Sheldon is missing, and a woman has been murdered in their apartment. But Lars believes the murderer will be found, that Sheldon will be found, and that there is no real danger. Sigrid Ødegård had explained it. Domestic disputes often take tragic and violent turns. And, as awful as it was, Rhea would need to understand that it wasn't a random act of violence. It doesn't have to evoke ideas of the war, or genocide, or all the historical weight she carries with her so intimately he sometimes wonders if, in another life, maybe she was there. She seems so able to describe these worlds.

There is something about the way the Jews bear witness to history that Lars has always found unsettling. They speak as witnesses. Since Egypt. Since the morning of Western civilization, when its light shone west from Jerusalem and Athens, and blanketed Rome and all that it would leave behind. They have watched the Western tribes and empires rise and fall—from the Babylonians to the Gauls, from the Moors to the Hapsburgs to the Ottomans—and have alone remained. They have seen it all. And the rest of us wait for the verdict that is still, even now, to come.

The road narrows again, and Lars drops into second gear, bringing the rpm up to four thousand and holding it steady—light hands, weight tipped backward—over the sand by the edge of the road.

It is awful, yes, the miscarriage. But no one did anything wrong. Rhea was in great shape. She ate well, didn't touch a drop of wine, and steered clear of tuna fish and blue cheeses. It simply wasn't meant to be. She's taken it better than he expected. But then again, there have been some distractions. Maybe he doesn't know her mind as well as he thinks.

But is it wrong to be enjoying the moment? To feel her warm, leather-clad thighs wrapped around him? They haven't ridden since learning about the baby. It took all his powers of persuasion to get permission to keep riding at all. No, not at night. Never after a beer. I'll try to stay out of the rain. I won't yell at truck drivers and encourage them to crush me under the wheels of their rigs.

*I will not even get irritated at Swedes.*

It feels good to have her here, despite it all. In the middle of un-expected chaos. Isn't that what a good marriage should be all about? Isn't this what life is while we have it?

There is nothing but forest now. At the turn of the last century, this road was a dirt path that led through a dense dale and opened over a wilderness inhabited by the northernmost wanderers of the species. It was only paved after World War II. Norway extends end-lessly northward from here. But out here, away from the city, the entirety of Scandinavia begins to form on the wind. The Finns came down through here, and some of them settled. The popula-tion bleeds over from Sweden. The Nordic tribes march past one another like nomads, and the vastness of humanity's farthest-flung outposts lies open and wild.

Lars slows even more now, and turns off the smaller road onto a dense dirt path that in winter he traverses on skis—the car left on the side of the road, with a battery charger, an electric blanket, and a jerry can of gas in the trunk, the doors unlocked in case a poor soul, including him, needs shelter. He has had nightmares of fingers so frozen that he cannot get into the car and turn on the blanket.

The bike crunches over the gravel and rolls up the winding path, which soon lets out into a wide mews that gradually climbs to the horizon, where the squat red house sits clean and fresh against the blue sky.

As Lars rolls on a bit more power to cross the grass, he and Rhea have the same sense. He hears her through the carbon fibers of his helmet.

"He isn't here," she says.

There is no way for either one to know this, but it feels true. They come to a stop on the left side of the house, near a patch of tall grass and a cistern, and Lars turns off the motorcycle.

The engine's fan whines and then halts.

His helmet off, Lars goes to the front door and tries the han-dle. It is locked. He presses his face against the glass and looks into the rustic and orderly kitchen. Nothing is out of place. The coffee grinder is where he left it. The propane tank is still unconnected to the hob. The cutting board hasn't been used. The four chairs around the small wooden table are pushed in and at rest. The hand-crank transistor radio sits mute on top of the cupboard.

On his way back to the bike, he sees that the water in the cistern is low. It hasn't rained in some time. The grass in the mews has faded to a mustard yellow in the hot sun. Lars walks around to the back of the house, past the axes, hoes, and rakes, and presses his hands against the window and looks in. Still nothing: books and magazines, puzzles and games, oil lamps and blankets, an armful of dry wood for the fire. The blue-and-white plates and cups on the hutch along the north wall, and the pillows on the window bench, are all unmoved.

Little has changed in the cabin over the last century, aside from the backup generator and some communications equipment. It is how he and his father like it. While Rhea's New York sensibility first found it quaint to the point of hokey, she has since learned about the sounds one can hear without interruption. And this has rescued the cabin from being a sentimental relic. For her the place has become a refuge in an ever-encroaching universe.

They could stay here tonight. It's past four o'clock already, and the sun is high in the sky. It's possible that Sheldon is on his way. It might even make sense. There's a train and a bus that come out to Glåmlia from Oslo; being resourceful, he'd probably hitch a ride to where the road ends and the path begins. He doesn't know the address, but he knows it's the red house on the hill at the end of the mews. There's only one. And everyone knows who owns it. Getting here wouldn't be a problem.

Unless she's right. Unless he does get disoriented and ends up in Trondheim or elsewhere. Or the police catch him. Or unless something has happened to him already.

Lars comes back around the house and sees Rhea standing several meters away from the motorcycle, staring back across the mews into the forest. She's still zipped into her gear and is holding her helmet under one arm. Her black hair hangs low, and she is as motionless as a statue.

As Lars comes up behind her, Rhea silently moves her hand away from her thigh, her open palm toward him, signaling him to halt.

Then she raises the same hand and points to the woods as she turns back to him. Her voice is low.

"I think there's someone there."

# CHAPTER 8

F IRST WE WATCH," says Sheldon quietly. "We learn their ways. How they move. What they wear. We mimic their behavior so we can blend in and become one of them. So we can merge into their culture and go native. Then, and only then," he tells Paul as he raises the binoculars to his eyes, "do we make our move."

From the edge of the Akershus Fortress along the fjord, Sheldon and Paul squat on the grass by a cobblestone street and look down at several extraordinarily fat people emerging from a Carnival cruise ship. They flow from the gangplank like thick blubber from a wounded white whale, washing into the road below the fortress and then oozing into the city, by the city hall and Aker Brygge.

"There, there, look over there. Near that big sailing ship, the *Christian Radich*. Look at them. Those little boats. Maybe a twelve-footer with an outboard. Looks like it hasn't moved in years."

Sheldon puts down the binoculars and flips through his Lonely

Planet, which has become awfully handy for finding his way around the city and figuring out what he's looking at.

If he'd had one of these for North Korea, his scouting missions would have been far easier.

"We're going to blend in with the lard-asses, we're going to borrow one of those boats, and then we're going south. I'd go north, but we'd need a car."

Sheldon sits up and looks at how Paul is dressed. He still looks like Paddington Bear without the red hat.

"We need some camouflage. Come on. They're not going to disembark forever. We've got about fifteen minutes to use them as cover while we take the boat."

With Paul in hand, Sheldon takes the path away from the city, past obsolete cannons, and down to the edge of the fortress, where a small path descends to a squat stone tower and then on to the harbor.

At the waterfront they turn right and stroll casually toward the cruise ship, where the colorful blobs have coagulated into small groups flowing northward toward Sheldon's intended mark.

"Watch this," he says to Paul.

As they pass an especially large and distracted pod of vacationers, Sheldon bumps into one of them and, with unusual grace, lifts a thin orange Gore-Tex jacket from an open backpack. Rather than hide it, he immediately slips it on, despite the fair weather.

"You hide in plain sight. It's where they never look," he says to Paul. "Now, over there, onto that pier."

Walking among the sandal-clad minions now, Sheldon and Paul flow like leaves on a river current. He talks to Paul as they shuffle up the road.

"Why do people always compare the size of a growing fetus to food? 'It's the size of a pea. Size of a lima bean. Size of a cherry. Size of a banana.' There's something creepy about that. Don't you think that's creepy?"

Paul looks at his feet as they walk. It has been less than twenty-four hours since he hid in the closet. Sheldon is not unaware of this. He simply does not know what to do about it.

"They never say, 'It's the size of a small-change purse' or 'It's the length of a parking ticket.' They're thinking of eating you before you even show up. There, there, look. Over there. That's the one. All we have to do now is look purposeful."

Sheldon and Paul walk past the three-masted steel ship and hug the waterfront, breaking off from the colorful flow of city-goers. Like convicts, they slip behind the port authority office and go down a small flight of stairs to a short dock. To the right is an unoccupied police boat bobbing on the calm water just in front of the boat that Sheldon has decided is now his.

Long ago painted in the bright red, white, and blue of the Norwegian flag, the little boat now looks haggard and wan. It's an oversized rowboat with a small outboard motor at the stern that has to be steered from the tiller.

Sheldon regards the small craft. He shakes his head at Paul.

"Jews aren't supposed to eat shellfish. I think it was His way of letting us know we aren't a seafaring people. All right, let's do what needs to be done."

Sheldon takes hold of a mooring line and pulls the boat so it is close enough to step into. He puts one leg cautiously inside and then reaches out to Paul.

"Come on. It's OK."

Paul does not step forward.

"Really, look, I've been in a rowboat before. And that one didn't have an engine. I can do this. No problem. None at all. I'm sure. More or less."

The impulses and inner worlds of children have never been clear to Sheldon. When Saul was under two years old, he would spring out of his stroller and run like a little drunkard to the toddler swing.

*Go da, go da*, he would say.

"Go there? You want to go there? Sure. Why not."

So Sheldon would lift Saul onto the swing, upon which Saul would immediately break into tears and a squirming fit.

"This wasn't my idea. It was your idea. I'm nothing but a human forklift! I pick you up and put you down. You said in, I put you in. So down now? OK."

And out Saul would come, which would enrage him further. This sort of behavior Sheldon blamed solely on female influence.

How come Paul wouldn't get in one moment, then did the next? *Who knows. That's why.*

Once in the johnboat, Sheldon works quickly. He hasn't hotwired an outboard engine since his training for Korea. At the time, it was part of a host of fun and unexpected lessons they taught his group as part of the scouting portion of their training. The logic came down from his drill sergeant, as so much wisdom often did.

*We can't push you out of a plane with a rifle, have you march twenty miles across enemy terrain, evading commie forces and local wildlife, only for you to show up and realize you forgot the key. So we're going to learn to live without keys. Lesson one starts with a hammer . . .*

Lesson ten (or so) involved more sophisticated techniques, like how to find the relevant bits in a motor's power head and get around the main wire harness to jump the starter directly from the battery. It wasn't brain surgery, so long as the motor was simple. And this one was.

Sheldon checks the fuel level by following a tube from the intake pump to a plastic tank under the rear seat. On the outside of the tank are indicator marks showing that it contains about ten liters of fuel. It is a small four-stroke engine—which gives it a better range than the older two-stroke—so he guesses they can get about four or five hours out of it, which is plenty. No telling where they might end up, of course, but that doesn't matter for now.

As Sheldon checks whether the spark plugs are corroded, a police officer walks down the stairs onto the pier and heads in their direction.

Sheldon is removing the engine's plastic housing as the officer walks by without looking at them.

"I know what you're thinking," he says to Paul as he works. "Don't we look suspicious? The truth is, we don't. When was the last time you heard of an octogenarian wearing a bright orange jacket steal-ing a boat moored next to the police? Never, that's when. It's incon-ceivable! This is how you get away with things on this planet. Do the unimaginable in plain view. People assume it *has* to be some-thing else."

When the engine starts with a sputter and cough, Sheldon un-ties the mooring lines from the cleats and throws the lines to the pier.

"Tougher to do this in New York. Some smart-ass would have come over to tell me how to fix the engine, or asked what I thought of the Yankees losing to the Red Sox. You know what I think? I think it's great—that's what I think. The Yankees deserve to lose. Let's just hope no one asks us anything in Norwegian."

Sheldon pushes the tiller hard to port and gently twists the throttle, easing them away from the dock and out into Oslo Fjord. He runs their small raft along the edge of the *Christian Radich* and its gleaming white hull, and out to the deep, blue sound, leaving Oslo and the little he knows of this strange country far behind him.

# PART II

# River Rats

# CHAPTER 9

UNTIL TODAY, SHELDON has been on the water only in his imagination. It started with visions he described to Mabel in 1975. Their source was vivid, though mercifully simple: a letter from Herman Williams, one of Saul's buddies from the boat, who was with him when he was wounded. The letter explained the circumstances of Saul's death.

In this way, the visions were derived from facts, but they were larger than the facts themselves. They were terrifying and alive, and became truly enveloping and relentless when Rhea came to live with them in 1976.

In his vision, Sheldon was patrolling the Mekong Delta with Saul, Herman Williams, Ritchie Jameson, Trevor Evans, and the captain—a man they called the Monk.

The visions all began with a sort of open-hearted optimism.

Sheldon was on assignment for Reuters. His well-known photography book was just the sort of in-your-face realism Reuters needed then. His own war record gave him the credibility among the younger men that he needed to document their contribution to the war effort. He was only in his forties and, while not stupendously fit, was slender and alert. The call came late one night while he was watching Johnny Carson. Carson was interviewing Dick Cavett, and their comic timing and quick repartee had him and Mabel in stitches.

"This is Reuters calling. We need you there. You up for it?"

"My bags have been packed since the Tet Offensive."

"Good man. Leave in the morning?"

"Morning? Why wait? How about now?"

In an hour he was transported to Saigon, where an elephant took him to Saul's base in three minutes while Nepalese Sherpas carried the luggage. The colonel in charge shot Sheldon a thumbs-up, and Donny winked back. It was good to be on the line again, out among the men. How young they were now! Not like in his day. Was he ever this young? Of course not. Korea was fought by men, and not just any men. Men with better taste in music.

All the guys gave a "hoo-ah!" when the old Marine walked into the barracks. Despite his low rank, they all saluted him, and he returned it. Respecting the old guard. They knew he was one of them and not some chump from *Stars and Stripes*, here to snap a few shots to put over whatever propaganda the brass had just thought up. And he wasn't some hippie dreaming of planting a wet one on Jane Fonda's misguided ass. Nope. This was a real man, here to take photos of life on the *river*. Where the insects were big enough to carry away Vietnamese children, the air was thicker than the tension, and the only rule was that you couldn't eat the dead.

Donny tossed his duffle bag on an upper bunk and swung himself up. He'd need a good night's sleep, because tomorrow he would board the boat with his son. And he didn't want to make Saul look bad in front of the guys.

Before drifting off, he whispered, "Hey, Herman? You up?"

"Yeah, Donny. What's up?"

"Why do they call the captain the Monk?"

"Oh, yeah. That. He doesn't want to be here."

"Who does?"

"No, I mean, he *really* doesn't want to be here."

The Oslo Fjord runs gently under the hull of the johnboat, and the 20-horsepower motor pushes them steadily southwest. Sheldon is seated on the white plastic bench near the stern, with his hand on the tiller. He wears the stolen Gore-Tex shell and has put on the aviator sunglasses he found in the pocket. Paul sits on the third bench, closest to the prow. Sheldon wonders if the boy has ever been in a boat before.

The Lonely Planet has a map of the fjord, and Sheldon uses it to navigate. Rather than follow the wider channel to the north, where the Danish ferries and cruise ships run—and could run over him—he passes through the sound between Hovedøya and Bleikøya islands, and then between Lindøya and Gressholmen, hoping that Norwegians don't have an overly nervous Coast Guard that asks too many questions.

Their boat is not the only one making the summer run south. There are ketches, kayaks, and catamarans; skiffs, scows, and cat-boats. People wave to Sheldon and Paul. From the calm of splendid anonymity, Sheldon waves back.

Most of the smaller leisure craft seem to be headed out past Ne-soddtangen, at the tip of a massive peninsula, and then south. Slow and steady, staying as close to land as possible, Sheldon follows them like driftwood. He and the boat and the boy putter on together, away from the horrors of yesterday and into a blue-and-green world that knows nothing of who they are or where they came from.

Against the gentle wind and glimmering waves, Sheldon and Paul make their escape. As the tension of the city recedes, along with the harbor, the Opera House, and the city hall, silence returns, bringing with it the unheeded cries of the previous morning and all the mornings before it.

From inside the closet, Sheldon had heard Senka gasping for air. He had heard her being choked, her arms losing purpose, grace, and fight, flailing and clawing for any purchase on life. He had heard the hate that possessed the hands of the killer. He imagined her eyes growing wide as the terror overcame her, robbing her of any chance to save herself.

Looking at Paul sitting on the prow of the boat, leaning over to touch the water passing under their shallow draft, he wonders what the boy imagined as the tortured sounds of his mother's life settled into stillness. He hopes that the boy's imagination is not as refined as his own, which inevitably returns to the journey upriver in Vietnam.

*It's the dementia, Donny,* said Mabel.

She didn't understand. She had other anchors to steady her. But he wanted to correct her all the same.

"How demented is it to have the past rush up to meet us just before the end? Isn't that the final act of the rational mind as it struggles to comprehend its step into the darkness? The last push for coherence before the great unraveling? Is that so mad?"

"We should be in and out in about three or four hours," Herman said to the team. "An F-4 went down about seven clicks from here, and HQ thinks the pilot bailed. So we're to go recover his skinny ass before he has to do any actual soldiering."

The Monk was speechless, as usual, while the other men loaded the supplies on the boat. It was raining, and everyone was a little hung over from a three-day bender in honor of Saul's rejoining the Navy for a second tour and getting back to the boat.

Saul didn't talk to his father very much. Just normal stuff. "Pass me that rope" or "Can I have a cigarette?" Sheldon didn't mind that. He watched what the boys were doing as closely as he could. He didn't want to get in the way. But in this vision—in this memory of a place he has never been—he was terrified of losing even a single moment. He felt that Jewish compulsion to document. To remember. To hold on to every last ray of the day and ensure that others would know that it had been seen. What once existed and no longer does.

The Monk was a careful pilot. Sheldon photographed his hands on the wheel and took the Monk's portrait when the sun was over his shoulder, and all you could see of his face and body were the dark edges and his stance against the river.

There was a darkness to his demeanor. A hidden pain. A plan of some kind. Sheldon, through the lens, saw it all.

He photographed Herman's slender and delicate black fingers, which could have been trained to repair watches, had they all been born on a different planet.

He watched Trevor clean his rifle with the painstaking attention one would give to a hunting weapon inherited from a grandfather.

He photographed Ritchie and his smile, and wondered why people so often resemble their own names.

It was good to be on the boat. Since Sheldon had started traveling with them regularly in 1975, he seldom worried about Saul, despite knowing the end of the story. He didn't watch his son with the plaintive gaze of a father or a war buddy. He just went along for the ride. Taking it in. Being there. Basking in the warmth of camaraderie and life.

He enjoyed watching his son as a man. This is what he wanted, Sheldon reminded himself. Right? For his son to be a man? To become an American soldier.

The F-4 Phantom had been shot down with a Soviet-supplied surface-to-air missile. The pilot, as everyone knew, was utterly blameless. But airmen had it easy, and everyone knew that, too. They sat in their air-conditioned tents, filing their precious nails, sipping tonic, playing gin, and jerking off to new and unsoiled magazines. Then, when the dinner bell rang, they would don their spiffy gear that made all the girls swoon, get in the cockpits of their shiny planes — that some lackey had cleaned and polished for them — and for fifteen minutes they'd drop napalm on huts, people, cattle, crops, and whatever else. Then, once their thumbs got tired, they'd go back to base, wipe a single drop of sweat from their foreheads as the press took their photos, and then resume their so rudely interrupted card hands as Red Cross girls named Heather or Nicky massaged their exhausted shoulders while the pilots flooded their ears with stories of derring-do.

Given the pilots' cushy life, the boat boys weren't going to give them the benefit of any doubts. It didn't matter a lick to them, for instance, whether or not that SAM was the finest heat-seeking missile the communists could design, and it was fired at a low-flying plane that had only 1.7 seconds to respond before losing the left half of its fuselage. They didn't care whether that pilot was outgunned or not. He was going to catch nothing but shit on his ride home, and knowing that gave each and every man on the tiny boat something really great to look forward to.

The real trick to a search-and-rescue mission was getting to the downed plane before the Vietcong did. The VC were murderous bastards, but it *was* their country, and they had a demonstrable knack for knowing where things were. So when a plane went down, they just headed on over. The Riverines, on the other hand, had to find their way.

That was the Monk's job as skipper. As they all puttered up the river, there wasn't much to do other than train the M-60 into the woods and think of jokes and the girls they'd surely never have sex with. Not in person, anyway.

The rain came down steadily as the boat grunted through an estuary about twenty meters wide. Local boatmen passed by under the rifle barrels of the men, but none stopped, and no one looked up as they passed.

Trevor sat behind the Monk in a manner that Sheldon found tense, as though he was prepared to spring from the bench and . . . something. It was hard to predict what would happen. Jump overboard, maybe? Tackle the Monk?

Sheldon sat far back in the boat, snapping pictures. Taking in the jungle. Trying to understand the terrain, the men, this war. It was so different from Korea. In Korea, the communists attacked the South with Soviet backing, and the United Nations passed a resolution while the Soviet ambassador was in the bathroom, and so the whole to-do was pretty straightforward. This war was less straightforward. And, of course, the big trick in Korea was that the southern ones wanted us there. Over here, not so much.

After three hours on patrol, the boat came to a rest by a small pier. The Monk didn't move. He just tossed a radio to Saul and looked at Herman. Ritchie, who outranked them both, said, "Witzy and Williams. Go."

That's what they called Saul: Witzy. Because "Horowitz" was too long, and "Saul" was too old-fashioned.

Why those two? Witzy and Williams? *Because who can avoid saying it, that's why.*

"I'm going, too," said Sheldon. No one replied. It was as though, for the first time on the trip, Sheldon wasn't really there.

Saul handed a letter he'd been writing to Ritchie. "Mail it for me if I bite it."

All Ritchie said was "OK."

Saul stepped up to the pier with his M-16 in one hand and the radio in the other. He said to Ritchie, "My girl's pregnant. Does that just take the cake or what?"

"You should go home," Ritchie said.

"I probably should," Saul said, and then he started hoofing it along the pier with Williams.

They walked through a very small village that seemed deserted. Four thatched huts were clustered together on a patch of brown, muddy ground. A bicycle wheel rusted in the rain. A basket of rotten vegetables sat overturned on a table. Sheldon photographed them and walked on.

Saul took point, followed by Williams and then Sheldon. Saul was a good soldier. He paid attention, didn't allow little things to distract him, and didn't talk while they walked. But he was also in his early twenties, and so didn't walk slowly enough, didn't pay close enough attention, and didn't talk softly enough when he did open his mouth.

As the jungle opened into a small rice paddy, Saul took a bearing with his compass and pointed off to his left. He turned and looked behind him, right past Sheldon, and got a sense of the terrain they would see on their way back. This was a valuable lesson that Sheldon had been taught in Korea. Once again, his drill sergeant's voice came back to him: *The reason nothing looks familiar when you're heading back is because it isn't. You've never seen it before, have you? If you don't turn around, how will you know what to look for? Huh? You! Shithead! What's the answer?*

On that day, it was another shithead. But it could have been Sheldon, and often was. By the time his own day came at Inchon, he would be glad for the lessons he'd learned.

They smelled the plane before they found it. The F-4 had been halfway through its bombing mission, and so went down with a lot of fuel, which burned with a different odor than napalm, rice paddies, cattle, and people. According to Herman, it was only a 2 on the gag-o-meter, whereas the rotting corpses of children in the hot sun was a 9.

A 10 was saved for the smell of letters received from bureaucrats.

Saul couldn't tell from the odor which direction they needed to travel. But soon they started to find pieces of the plane on the ground. Just scraps at first, bolts and bits of twisted metal, but enough to know they were getting closer.

Sheldon looked at his watch. They'd been in the jungle for only fifteen minutes.

Saul directed them toward a small rise. This was a good idea, because it gave them a more commanding view of the grid. Before they reached the top, Williams whistled through his teeth and said, "Over there. Check it out."

Saul and Sheldon turned to their left, and there, about a half click away across easy ground, lay large chunks of the plane.

"Anyone see the shithead pilot?" Williams asked.

Saul pointed off to the left. "That could be the parachute."

"Right, then. Let's go see if there are any pink bits in the cockpit first," said Williams.

As they walked down the hill toward the jet, Sheldon made out an incongruous figure leaning against a tree by the side of the footpath. Saul walked right past him, as though he weren't there. As Williams approached, Sheldon shouted, "Herman, on your right."

"Oh, that's just Bill. Forget about him. Fucker shows up all the time. Never helps, though."

When Sheldon caught up, he saw that it was indeed Bill Harmon, his friend from New York. Bill was wearing shabby trousers, penny loafers, a blue button-down shirt, and a Harris Tweed jacket. Bill did not show up during these trips between 1975 and 1980. It was only after he died that he popped up and chimed in. Only Sheldon wasn't sure that Bill was really Bill. He looked like Bill. He had the same stupid things to say that Bill did, but he didn't feel like Bill. His presence was both more vast and more juvenile. Bill, in life, had never left Sheldon feeling perturbed. This guy did.

"What are you doing here, Bill?"

"Antiquing."

"What?"

"The French colonials were here for ages. Indochina has some amazing hidden treasures that I can get top dollar for back at the shop."

"Are you drunk?"

"It's two o'clock in the afternoon and we're in Vietnam. Of course I'm drunk. Want some?"

"I got to go. We have to find the pilot."

"Pilot's dead," said Bill. "They put a bullet in him before his parachute hit the ground. Very unsporting. There's really no need for you to go on."

"So I'll tell the guys and we can go back."

"They won't believe you."

"Why? Are you the ghost of Christmas past?" And without waiting for a reply, Donny shouted, "Hey, Williams. Hold up. The pilot's dead. We should go back to the boat."

"How do you know?"

"Bill said so. He knows."

"Can't put your faith in Bill, Donny."

"But sometimes he's right."

"Sure, but who knows when? Besides, it's not my call."

"Well, then tell Saul."

"Fine."

And so Herman told Saul, and Saul just shrugged and kept on going. After a few minutes, though, he became pensive and stopped. For the first time on the trip, he turned and addressed his father directly.

"What are you doing, Dad?"

"I want us to go home. I want you to grow up."

"You should have thought of that before suggesting I come here."

"You're right, and I'm sorry. But I never said you should go back. This second tour was all your idea."

"You don't remember our conversation very well, do you?"

"I might have said something about America being at war. But if I did, I didn't mean you had to go back. You did your duty. More than most people."

"It was your idea to join me here. I can't go back. I can't write a report saying that Bill Harmon appeared in the woods and had the inside scoop on the pilot's whereabouts."

"You loved Bill."

"Still do," Saul said. "But he's hardly a quotable source, is he?"

"This is madness!"

"Your madness. So what's it going to be? Are you heading back, or do you want to watch this play out?"

"I want to be with you."

"Well, come on then. And be quiet. There are VC around here."

And so they walked on, leaving Bill behind.

In what seemed like no time at all, they arrived at the plane. It hadn't crashed straight down or managed a controlled landing. It had its bits shot off in midair, and had fallen to the ground with the graceless tumble of a meteor.

The cockpit was somewhat intact, because that is how randomness works. Sheldon took a picture.

Saul, on an impulse, said, "Herman — go check the cockpit. I'm gonna see about that parachute."

Saul turned to his father and said, "Well? You coming or staying?"

"I want to be with you."

What Saul wanted was to take his shithead brother pilot home. That's what he'd been sent to do, that's what he had been trained to do, and that's what he wanted to do. Because an American shouldn't be left to rot in a green pile of Asian compost. He should be home with his family.

The parachute was hanging from a very tall tree at the end of the marshland that Saul and Sheldon had to cross in order to reach it. The pilot was black, which surprised both of them: you didn't see many black pilots in 1974. And the pilot, as Bill had said, was dead. The poor bastard hadn't even been given a chance to land. The Vietnamese didn't understand blacks; they had never seen anyone from Africa before. They thought blacks were white men who were dyed black as camouflage. There were documented cases of the VC using steel brushes on these men, trying to get their blackness off.

"Right, that's it. Let's go," said Sheldon.

"We've got to get him down," said Saul.

"No we don't."

"Yes we do."

"No. We damn well don't!"

"You carried Mario home," Saul said. "You told his parents. His father hugged you and cried."

"I was on a secure beach. You're in the jungle alone. This poor man here . . ."

"Come on. Help me cut him down."

"Saul, be reasonable. The VC know you're coming for the pilot. They know it, and there's a fifty-fifty chance they got here before you did."

"Then why didn't they shoot me?"

"Because an injured man needs to be carried, and that way they immobilize two or three men, not just one."

"Why not capture me?"

"How the hell should I know?"

And then Saul got enraged and everything came to a head. "There's a Negro hanging from a tree. A Negro who is an American soldier. How do I let him stay there? How do I walk away from that man? Explain to me how I can walk away from him and still be your son, and I'll do it. I swear I will."

And at this precious moment, Sheldon had nothing to say. Nothing at all.

So Saul swung his rifle across his chest like a bow and started climbing the tree.

When he was high enough, he grabbed a branch and used his service knife to slice away at the cords and silk of the parachute. The pilot's boots were about six feet off the ground. It wasn't a long fall. Somehow, though, it felt like a slow one. Nausea came over Sheldon when the man tumbled to the ground.

As Sheldon watched, the first waves of resignation passed through him. He'd been here on assignment so many times, watched this event so many times, that he knew both when and how terror comes. It would all happen soon. Saul would start off down the only path toward the plane as Herman came up the same path—having burned maps and papers to deprive the enemy of intelligence.

He knew what would come. Still, just in this moment, it had not happened yet. He was between the knowledge and the reality of what was to come—just where Cassandra found herself before it drove her mad. It was a precious moment. So precious that Sheldon delayed, allowing himself to sleep each night with this knowledge of what would happen.

During this moment—as Saul dropped from the tree, put his knife away, and took off the pilot's dog tags and put them in the upper-left pocket of his own shirt—Sheldon watched as his son became a man.

It was not a grand moment. There were no witnesses to it. There were no heroics. It was merely a small gesture of dignity and respect between one man and another. And in that, for Sheldon, the possibility of a better world was created. All humanity had accomplished thus far—as little as it may have been—was expressed in the unseen and forgotten gesture of Corporal Saul Horowitz recovering the mortal remains of Lieutenant Eli Johnson.

And so, before the end, there was a moment of grace.

In that moment, Sheldon raised the camera to his eye and took their picture.

The release of the shutter freed time to carry onward. Sheldon watched Saul step on the tripwire, setting off the explosion that killed his only child. He watched from a position in front of Saul and Eli Johnson, just off the footpath to their left.

When it happened, Herman came running up behind him and toward Saul.

The VC had packed the bombs with nails and ball bearings and—perversely—casings from American rifles they'd picked up in a previous battle.

All these items tore through Saul's legs, his groin, and his lower torso.

Before the pain registered on his face, he collapsed, because there were no longer bones, muscles, or ligaments to hold him up. Lieutenant Johnson's body came down on the side of the path, and would not be recovered by the team. Only his dog tags, in Saul's pocket, would make it back to the States, to his parents and the coffin they would be buried in.

Herman screamed and started to cry almost immediately. He grabbed Saul by his shirt and, with the strength of the terrified, hoisted him onto his back, much as Saul had carried Johnson, and as Donny had carried Mario, and as men throughout history have carried one another.

The shooting began as soon as Herman started running.

No one looked at Sheldon anymore. No one paid him any heed at all. Even Bill Harmon was gone.

Herman ran a full click through the jungle, into the tiny village, out to the boat. Ritchie was manning the M-60 and firing wildly into the undergrowth to provide covering fire, but he didn't know whether there was anyone even hiding there.

Trevor was still poised on the bench behind the Monk.

As soon as the three men were back on board, the boat began moving, and soon they were free of the land.

But it wasn't over.

The Monk turned the boat around so they could open it up heading downstream, to put more distance between themselves and whatever was in the bushes.

Herman checked Saul's airway, stuck a morphine syringe into his carotid artery, and pressed two large pads on the femoral arteries of his legs.

This field dressing would keep Saul alive for three days once the boat made it back to port, but he would never regain consciousness.

Sheldon sat on the bench next to Trevor. There was nothing he could do for Saul—the son who had once stood on his lap to study his nose with the intensity of a scientist, and had put his fingers in his father's joyful tears.

He watched passively as the boat rounded a bend toward a line of wooden rafts. He opened his eyes wide as machine-gun fire from those rafts started pelting the hull.

As the bullets came in, the Monk let go of the wheel.

Trevor, who was already coiled, sprang forward and grabbed it, steering them directly toward the first raft at ramming speed.

The Monk walked to the bow of the boat, stood upright at the prow, and raised his arms like a Brazilian cliff diver, or Jesus and the criminals on their crosses.

Ritchie eviscerated one of the rafts with the M-60. Splinters and the red spray of blood made a small cloud around it as the base broke apart.

Herman worked on Saul, Trevor piloted the boat, and the Monk stood there, untouched by man or movement as Saul bled.

This was Sheldon's last vivid image in the dream. It was the one that woke him that night to talk with Mabel and ask his question. The one he still wakes with in the mornings. Somehow, the events of that day are not clear to him beyond this point. He knows the boat made it to safety. Saul was evacuated to Saigon, where he died in the hospital. The letter was mailed as promised, and Rhea received her name. Trevor and Herman stayed on the boat until the end of their tour, and then went home.

The Monk never got shot. But one day, in another battle, it was said that he dived into the Mekong River and never came up.

# CHAPTER 10

THEY APPROACH THE small village of Flaskebekk over the port side, and Sheldon sails as close to the coast as he dares. He figures the Coast Guard won't be interested in a small craft skirting the shore, a good place to be in case something goes wrong. The weather is not going to change, and the current is not strong.

He has no idea, of course, what is under the surface, but one of the great benefits of the johnboat is its shallow draft. While not especially seaworthy, the boat is easy to pilot.

The rifles he needs are named Moses and Aaron. The cannons they are named after, according to the guidebook that Sheldon leafs through, are located in the Oscarsborg Fortress, on an island not far ahead, called Søndre Kaholmen. Evidently, on April 9, 1940, the Germans sent a fourteen-thousand-ton warship, called the *Blücher*, into the Oslo Fjord to attack the capital, capture the king, and steal the national gold reserves. Though the fortress was poorly manned, it did have three 28-centimeter Krupp guns named Moses, Aaron, and Joshua, as well as a commanding officer who didn't mind the odds.

As the German warship entered the sound near Drøbak, Colonel Birger Eriksen and the few men under his command engaged the *Blücher* at eighteen hundred meters with Moses and Aaron. They fired only two shots, but they were decisive. The first round penetrated the hull, setting off the German ordnance and oil drums, and the second made it impossible for the ship to return fire.

As the ship burned on, the secret torpedo batteries on the island fired, sinking her and all hands from a range of only five hundred meters.

It is argued that Oscarsborg gave the government enough time to escape and form a resistance in exile that put Norway officially in the Allied camp. Norway soon fell to the Nazi invaders, and a puppet regime took over. Seven hundred and seventy-two Norwegian men, women, and children, who were Jewish, were rounded up by the Norwegian police and the Germans, and deported. Most were sent to Auschwitz.

Thirty-four survived.

After the war, few of the Norwegian police who had collaborated received any punishment, and some were even kept on in their jobs until retirement. The Holocaust itself was not on Norwegian university curricula for decades after the war. It took more than fifty years for Norway to build a national memorial commemorating the events, and a few more before the Norwegian Centre for Holocaust and Genocide Studies was opened.

The entire event, it seemed to Sheldon, was spoken of as though by witnesses, not participants. And where Norwegian actions were suspect, they were too easily dismissed in the easy memory of victimhood.

"The question," Sheldon says aloud, looking south toward the Oscarsborg Fortress, "is whether we have enough gas to get there."

The day draws on and on, and the sun never seems to move.

Sheldon has never felt time pass so slowly. The whole trip from Oslo to just north of Drøbak is less than seventeen nautical miles, but time and distance on the water are a property of mind.

They sail for four hours before they run out of gas.

They drift for thirty more minutes as the rising tide carries them to shore in a small, rocky bay surrounded by evergreens.

Sheldon considers the line of sight of passing boats, and ties up the johnboat at an angle where it will attract the least attention.

If it were made of wood, he would have sunk it.

If he'd had the strength, he would have pulled it to shore and hid it.

If he'd been younger, he would have plunged a knife into the heart of the attacker and saved the boy's mother.

But things are as they are.

Once safely on shore, with everything removed from the boat, Sheldon is winded. "Aren't you going to say anything?" he asks Paul. "You can hit me if you want. I deserve it. I'm sure I do. I should have called the police the second I heard the fight upstairs. Never even occurred to me. I was too superior to the whole thing. I figured I knew what was what, and that this was all going to play out with your mother running down the stairs and out to where someone else would look after her. I didn't open the door for her. I opened it for me. Out of spite. To prove to everyone that this is what you're supposed to do. At my age I still think there's an audience for my actions. Can you believe it? I'm playing to an audience that died fifty years ago. I should have called the police, and if we'd been lucky, they would have showed up on time."

Sheldon is taller than the boy, of course, but he does not tower over him. Right now he is slightly stooped and weary from the voyage. His back curves. They become almost the same height, and Sheldon tries to look him in the eyes.

"Is it a coincidence," Sheldon asks, "that the older we get, the more we actually look like question marks? What I mean to say is this: I'm sorry. My best never seems to be very good. I've had a couple of moments. Not so many, though, when you consider how many chances I've had. I even missed Saul's birth.

"I don't want to turn you in yet, do you understand? What if that guy is your father? He was in your apartment at all hours of the night, from the sound of things recently. He was probably there a lot. A boy like you doesn't go mute all of a sudden. You had to learn this. You've probably been terrorized for ages. I could drop you off and then he could rush out and say, "My son, you found my son," and then I'd be handing you into the clutches of your mother's killer. What kind of a friend does that?"

Paul listens. Sheldon does not know why.

"You hungry? You must be famished." Sheldon extends his hand to the boy. "Come on, let's go borrow some food."

Paul does not take Sheldon's hand, but he does follow. They move slowly, because the long hours of sitting have hurt Sheldon's lower back. Sharp pain juts down his left leg with each step, and he readjusts the satchel over his shoulder.

"Let's call it a day. We're going over there."

Sheldon points to a lovely blue house close to the water. They are walking south, with the fjord to their right. On the coast is a private metal pier for a boat that is not there.

Sheldon leads the boy around to the front of the house and looks for signs of life. There are no cars in the driveway, and few on the street. The house feels empty.

Together, they head around to the back again, and Sheldon shows Paul how to cup his hands while pressing his face to the glass. Paul doesn't mimic him, but Sheldon feels it is a valuable lesson all the same.

Inside, no lights are on. The television is off. Everything is tidy and clean. Unmoved.

Sheldon walks a few more meters along the house to the back door, which lets out to the backyard and down to the pier. He presses his face against the window one more time, still sees nothing of interest, and comes to a decision.

"So this brings us back to lesson one," he says to Paul.

Putting the satchel down on the wood porch that leads to the kitchen, Sheldon takes out a hammer and, without comment, smashes the window pane next to the door handle.

He pauses, listens carefully, and then says, "No alarm. That's helpful. Now watch your step. There's glass there."

In an Eames-inspired living room of fine Scandinavian and mid-century American furniture, Sheldon finds a magazine cradle with maps and the local bus and train times, which he gathers up and takes into the kitchen for review as he sets a pot of water to boil for pasta.

Finding a good area map, he unfolds it delicately across the tabletop and, using the tip of a wooden spoon, he points to the Glomma, tracing the meandering blue line up a few centimeters to Kongsvinger.

"That's where we're headed. I've never been there, but I've seen a photo of the place on the refrigerator door in Oslo. So I'm pretty sure we can find it." Sheldon starts tracing an overland route. "I never knew this country had so many lakes. There's a lake everywhere."

When the water boils, Sheldon makes instant coffee for himself in a glass from IKEA. He opens the cabinet to the left of the sink, finds a box of fusilli, and dumps the whole thing into the pot—he has no idea how much a hungry child can eat. He finds a can of tomatoes, some salt and pepper and garlic powder, and with the nuanced expertise that only a grandfather can summon, he combines them into a concoction that only a child could eat.

He adds three heaping teaspoons of sugar to his coffee and goes back to the table, where Paul has grown transfixed by the maps.

"We're going there," Sheldon points, "but the issue is how to get there. I can barely make heads or tails of these timetables here, but what is clear is that almost all buses getting you from Drøbak to Kongsvinger seem to pass through Oslo. And I don't want to go to Oslo. I want to avoid Oslo. Oslo is where we came from. So now we're stuck again. We could hitchhike, but I hardly think that's inconspicuous, and the chance of a police car coming by and finding us is higher than I'd like. We still can't rent a car. I suppose we could borrow one, but let's consider that as a last resort. What I'm saying is, we have some thinking to do."

When Sheldon puts two bowls of pasta on the table. Paul devours his in one long, continuous, and strangely fluid movement.

The experience covers them both in tomato sauce. The boy does not smile. Instead, Sheldon senses a sort of convergence, as though the child's body and mind are in the same place for the first time since his mother's murder.

"All right. Now let's get you out of those clothes and into bed."

Once Paul is clean and his teeth are brushed—with whatever toothbrush is in the bathroom—they look for clothing in the junior bedroom, and find a long white T-shirt that Paul can use as a nightgown. The bed is made, and covered by a thick woolen blanket that reminds Sheldon of the Hudson's Bay blankets he used as a child in western Massachusetts—the kind that had tick marks on the side. His mother said they showed how many beaver skins they should be traded for, but he wasn't so sure. The method didn't seem to account for inflation.

It occurs to him that he's spent so much time remembering his son's childhood that he has almost entirely forgotten his own. At his age, it can be overwhelming and painful to harbor a thought accompanied by too much nostalgia. Not that he wanted to. Mabel, in her final years, had stopped listening to music. The songs of her teenage years brought her back to people and feelings of that time—people she could never see again, and sensations that were no longer coming. It was too much for her. There are people who can manage such things. There are those of us who can no longer walk, but can close our eyes and remember a summer hike through a field, or the feeling of cool grass beneath our feet, and smile. Who still have the courage to embrace the past, and give it life and a voice in the present. But Mabel was not one of those people. Maybe she lacked that very form of courage. Or maybe her humanity was so complete, so expansive, that she would be crushed by her capacity to imagine the love that was gone. Those of us with the courage to open ourselves to that much lost love and not fear it—who can give joy to a dying child until the very end without withdrawing to save ourselves—those are our saints. It is not the martyrs. It is never the martyrs.

With the boy prepared for bed, Sheldon presses his nose into the thick wool and takes in as much of the past as he can handle. Then his eyes begin to tear up, and he stops. He composes himself and goes to the bathroom to wash his face. In the mirror, he sees a man he does not entirely recognize. And for this he is grateful.

At the police station in Oslo, Sigrid loosens her tie just enough to let the blood flow again, but not enough to suggest the pressure is getting to her. Her team is working hard, it is late, and everyone is tired. She has issued more orders in the past twelve hours than in the past twelve weeks, and while not overwhelmed, she would certainly welcome a break.

For solidarity and convenience, she's taken a seat in the big central room with most of the other police, and left her office vacant. There's nothing in her office of special use, other than her work terminal, and she can get the same access to the servers from Lena's desk, now that Lena's been sent out to the asylum reception center to interview known associates of this former KLA guy whom Immigration—in its infinite, well-meaning wisdom—decided to allow into the country and to provide with a taxpayer-supported stipend—"to help him get on his feet."

Her conversation with her counterpart at Immigration—just to get the name of the director of the reception center, really—was terse, and ended on a sour note far off the intended topic.

"They come here with nothing," the man on the other end said with unyielding idealism. "How are they going to integrate without some support?"

"We've grouped them together in centers outside the city, where they're forming gangs," Sigrid said. "How's that helping them or strengthening Norway?"

"It's a transitional measure," the man said. "The Kosovars have been through a terrible war, and they're traumatized by the conduct of the Serbs. The best way to provide the needed psychosocial counseling is by working with them all together. You saw the war coverage. It was like the concentration camps."

Sigrid sighed. Everything these people avoided ended up on her desk sooner or later. She had a theory that many of her compatriots took the same cooperative, optimistic, goodhearted approach to every problem, domestic or international, because it helped them feel more Norwegian. It might even be how they *achieved* being Norwegian.

It wasn't the compulsion to be good that irked her. That, she admired. It was how they tried to solve every problem with the same approach, independent of the problem. Because that just won't do. The analysis and the solution simply have to align, and anything else is dreamlike and unrealistic. It's not for cops, anyway.

Her father—and, as best she could tell, her father's entire generation—did not exhibit this kind of self-assured confidence in their own goodness. Something new is clearly afoot, and she doesn't like it.

She also lacks that particular skill of keeping it all to herself.

"Did you know that a large proportion of Europe's heroin is trafficked through the Balkans?" she asked the man on the phone. "Much of it through Kosovo? You didn't help them integrate—you created a new, isolated node in that network."

"That's bigoted."

"That's a fact," Sigrid said. And, since she knew this interview was going nowhere, she added, "I'm sorry to have bothered you," and hung up.

The sun is finally below the horizon now, and she switches on her desk lamp. As she does, the bulb blows out with a *pop*.

Enver Bhardhosh Berisha, aka Miftar Vishaj. Against the dimming light, Sigrid picks up his file and leans far back in her chair. This man, this killer, is here. In Oslo. There is a file on him, but no charges against him. No warrant for his arrest. No request from the Serbs for extradition. He is here with the Norwegian government's blessing, using taxpayers' money to take the tram and buy cigarettes. It might not have incensed her so much had all the facts not been laid out so clearly in the file. Immigration knew he was KLA, knew he'd been in death squads, knew he was fleeing from the Serbian government. Somehow, that information had been used to make the case *for* his asylum. After all, didn't he have a legitimate claim that his life was under threat? Wasn't he able to prove, through new DNA testing, that he had a son in the country, and thereby was entitled to benefit from Norway's efforts to unite families?

Why haven't the Serbs tried to get him? She can only speculate. Maybe they have, and she doesn't know the story. Maybe they plan to kill him off the books, given that Serbia abolished the death sentence in 2002. Maybe they're happy to be rid of him, and want to call it a day. Maybe they know about his family, and worry that a prosecution against him will open up their own crimes to further international scrutiny.

So much falls through the cracks. This veil of equal justice under the law is always breached by those who practice realpolitik on the international stage. The further we get from the crimes and their victims, the more justice is sacrificed for the sake of expediency. So, for whatever reason, here he is—shopping at Glassmagasinet for saucers and at Anton Sport for winter socks, like the rest of us.

Families. Such a loose term. Sigrid picks up the woman's file. Background, birth date, education, date of immigration—all of this is stapled to her new file. Date of the murder, location, cause of death. It's still an open file, of course. Information is being added all the time.

There is a list of her personal effects. Everything is remarkably common. A Pulsar wristwatch. Some costume jewelry from Arts and Crafts in Oslo. Clothing. A little key for a lock box of some kind—maybe a diary or the mailbox key. A lovely white-gold ring with a single blue sapphire that must have been a gift or something of sentimental value. No earrings. No money.

Despite the buzz and energy of the main office, Sigrid hears only silence as she imagines Enver placing the cord around the woman's throat and squeezing the life out of her.

"Where's my file on the boy?" she shouts.

An officer yells something about its being on the way. Sigrid shakes her head. Things should be moving faster than this.

"Where's my information on Horowitz?"

"The records from the Marines are in the archives and haven't been digitized yet, because they're so old, so some private is spelunking for them with a flashlight."

"I need to know what we're actually dealing with from that end, OK?"

Whether he was a sniper or a clerk, Sheldon Horowitz had been a Marine. And this being a murder case involving a former American soldier, Sigrid had the idea of placing the request for information through the Foreign Ministry, given that Norway and the United States were NATO allies, to see how that worked out. To her surprise, the Americans were getting right on it.

Her theory was that the staff at the massive, fortified American embassy in Oslo on Henrik Ibsen's Gate were bored. Yes, Norway is in NATO, and there is a lot of fish and oil and gas here. But . . . really. What could they possibly be doing in there?

"Yes. Absolutely. We're tracking down that information," said one of her officers. "It just hasn't arrived yet."

"Nothing from the terminals?"

"No," said another. "Nothing from the bus lines, the trains, the taxis, the airport, or the central tourist office. Nothing from the patrol cars. Nothing from the bicycle police. Nothing from the lookout across from the apartment building. Nothing from the hospitals."

"What about the granddaughter?"

"They're at the summer house at Glåmlia," replies yet another officer. "They have a phone. They've been calling in like we told them to."

"Maybe the old man is headed there," Sigrid says.

Everyone is quiet.

*How?* they wonder silently.

But no one says anything. Then someone suggests, "They'll call us, won't they? They've been staying in touch like we asked." And some people agree. Others mumble.

"Call the local police and send someone out there tomorrow morning. Let them know there's a problem. What about car rentals?"

"Faxes were sent around. We've got nothing there."

Sigrid would be content to have nothing if there was nothing to have. She was always reasonable about aligning her expectations with reality. But surely, in a search for an old man, a younger man, and a boy in such a small city, there had to be something out there.

The conversation with the immigration official grated on her. This was no time to be thinking about it, but how could the authorities put the safety and welfare of the Norwegian people—the ones who are citizens, and vote, and have struggled for their democracy—after those of foreigners? A peaceful life should not come at their expense, of course, but it shouldn't come after, either.

And how can the aspirational ideals of good Norwegians be allowed to eclipse the data? Good, hard data? How can we be this foolishly optimistic about the world only sixty years after having been occupied by the Nazis?

Or maybe it's a generational thing, which explains why older people are voting for the more conservative parties.

It's enough to encourage a trip to the Wine Monopoly.

Sigrid isn't political—except when the politicians irritate her —but it strikes her that there are two ways you can act: on faith or on evidence. And if it's going to be faith, then liberals and conservatives alike have to be grouped in the same camp as people who govern from their heart and not their head. The only decision to be made about them is whether their views give you a warm feeling. And on the other side are those trying to make things better by facing things the way they are, and working from there. It doesn't seem like a coincidence to Sigrid that doctors and engineers bicker less than politicians.

Enver Bhardhosh Berisha, KLA fighter. Allowed into the country by Immigration on the basis of legitimate threats to his life in Serbia, and with a son living in the country.

The Kosovo Liberation Army was a paramilitary group that first received Western and NATO support because of its armed struggle against Serbian ethnic cleansing, but eventually lost the backing of the West because of its drug running, and the executions, mass murders, and other atrocities they committed that undermined any moral standing the group might have had. It all confounded the rest of Europe, and without a clear good guy or bad guy, people just changed the channel.

Sigrid puts down the file, rubs her eyes, and shouts, "My light bulb's burnt out," which for some reason causes laughter among her staff. So she adds, "I need a new light bulb," and this only makes them laugh more.

The thing about military people is that they have social standing. You work your way up, and people recognize your status. When a soldier's group breaks up, he loses the one thing that was precious during the rebellion: respect.

Would a man like Enver—a senior soldier with confirmed kills but with no family, no money, no roots—turn his back on his own status and reputation and suddenly flee the fight and go to a Scandinavian country to become a peaceful family man? What kind of woman would have a man like that anyway?

Sigrid's thoughts leave the station and go to her father at their kitchen table. She recalls a conversation they had once when he explained something useful, which she has since had a hard time explaining to others.

"It's all artifice," he'd said with uncharacteristic seriousness.

"You mean it's all meaningless?"

"No," he said, "I don't mean that at all." He paused for a long time before he spoke again. Her father was not an affected man and did not indulge in dramatic pauses. Rather, he was motivated to be precise. And sometimes, he said, that requires time to collect one's thoughts. If people are impatient, and walk off in the meantime, then clearly they are not interested in the answer.

"What I mean," he'd continued, "is that the buildings, the desks, the great structures are all products of ideas. So it isn't the buildings that matter. It is the ideas. But because the buildings are shiny and expensive, and the ideas are more elusive, we tend to become dazzled by the buildings—that is, the artifice. In fact, they distract us from the ideas that fill them. People stand on the steps of great buildings and feel awe before they enter. Why? The ideas don't know where they are being expressed. When I read history, I don't read about the great buildings; I read about the ideas of empires. They all asked similar questions, but came to different answers. It is a fact that when we compare worlds, those worlds are different.

"The interesting bit is this. For those worlds to hold together, the ideas must be shared. So I like to look to the ideas that are being shared. Who is involved? What are they thinking? What do these ideas make possible? What, for them, is obvious, and what is impossible to imagine? What is permissible, and what is not?

"And if you can't start with the ideas, because they are hidden, first start with who is talking to whom to get things done. Patterns always emerge. If things are getting done, there is a pattern behind it. You can be sure that it's more than mere motive. There is . . . a logic that holds the conversation together."

Sigrid had nodded and considered what her father had said.

After some time she said, "You live on a farm and converse with the animals. What am I to make of that?"

"Ah," her father had said, "but which animals? And what do we talk about?"

# CHAPTER 11

S HELDON DID NOT dream of the woman who was killed. For the first time since he could remember, he also did not dream of his son. He dreamed instead of a young boy sitting with his back to him, playing with colored blocks. Stacking them precariously, higher and higher and higher.

Sheldon slept well because he had no worries about getting caught in the house. Something groundbreaking had happened sometime around the millennium, when he turned seventy-five. He found he could pretty much get away with anything, and people would chalk it up to Crazy Old Man.

*Not my house? No kidding!*

So why worry?

Better to concentrate on real problems, like how to get to Glåm-lia without taking public transportation or a taxi, or hitchhiking.

Paul is hard to wake, but Sheldon knows he's been sleeping since at least nine o'clock last night, and eight hours is plenty for anyone.

"Good morning," he says to Paul, leaning over his bed.

As Paul awakens, Sheldon can see that he is—like any other

child—uncertain of his surroundings and taking stock, his eyes adjusting to the light. When he finally focuses on Sheldon, he wordlessly puts his arms around Sheldon's neck and holds him.

It is not a hug of affection, but the grasp of the drowning around flotsam.

"Come on," Sheldon says to Paul. "Back to the funky toothbrush, and then to breakfast. We need to look around a bit and think. No one says we have to go to the cabin. Which is good, seeing as I can't think of a way to get us there. We could take that little boat out there all the way to Sweden if we wanted to. Only I don't want to. One day on the water is enough for an old man. I need to be near a toilet, see? You don't see. You pee like a racehorse. You're so young, you don't know how to hold up a toilet seat that's committed to falling down all the time. The trick—and I'm telling you this to save you a lot of trial and error—is to stand to the side of the bowl and prop it up with your thigh. Oh, I know what you're thinking. In the fullness of time you would have figured it out yourself, a bright boy like you. Probably true, but after how many embarrassing moments? And wait until you get to England and find they put carpets in the bathrooms, as if that isn't the grossest idea in Western civilization. One New Year's party over there and you'll never walk barefoot again. What were we talking about?"

In the kitchen, Sheldon raids the cupboards and makes them both a breakfast of instant coffee, hot tea, chocolate chip cookies, frozen fish sticks, Wasa bread, and moose jerky.

Between courses, Sheldon nibbles at pistachio nuts and hunts for the bits in his gums with a butter knife.

"Let's go rummage through the closets and see if we can't find you something to wear."

After a halfhearted, admittedly male effort at cleaning the kitchen, Sheldon takes Paul to the master bedroom and starts searching the closets.

In a plain cedar armoire with mirrors on the front doors, they find men's and women's clothes for all seasons. Conservative clothes for people who can afford a house on the Oslo Fjord and don't feel bothered about having to occupy it. People, Sheldon decides, with clothes to spare who wouldn't mind passing on a bit of their good fortune.

"I'm not saying that we're doing a Robin Hood or anything. And I'm not going to mince my words. We're stealing. The boat was more of a temporary thing. The clothes are for keeps. All I'm saying is that the owner can probably live with one fewer tweed jacket. And, to be fair, I'm leaving behind an excellent orange jacket that anyone would want."

Sheldon keeps his own trousers, but takes clean underwear and socks. He also takes a starched, white-collared shirt that looks as though it has been waiting for its owner's attention for at least a decade. It is too big for Sheldon, but he tucks the tails deep into his pants and pulls his belt tight.

Unexpectedly, on the woman's side, on the top shelf, Sheldon finds a blond wig. While his first thoughts turn to sex and all-too-present—and all-too-out-of-reach—memories of playing make-believe, one more glance back at the tweed jacket and the old shirt gives him a new thought. One that is less cheery.

"Cancer," he says. "Probably explains why no one comes here. Now that I think about it, that moose jerky was pretty tough."

Paul reaches up for the wig. Sheldon looks at it, then down at the boy, and hands it to him. Paul touches the blond hair and examines the curls. He turns it inside out and sees the white mesh of its artificial scalp. Sheldon gently takes it back and places it on his own head.

Paul's eyes light up, suggesting playfulness. Though perhaps this is just the imagination of an old man who needs to believe it.

"OK, let's see you, then."

Sheldon takes it off and puts it snugly on Paul's head. Closing the armoire, he points at Paul in the mirror.

Paul looks back.

"Huck Finn dressed in drag, too, when he was checking out the scene from Jackson's Island. There's a strong literary history of boys dressing up like little girls when the going gets tough, so don't give it a second thought. In fact, with the long white shirt, I'm starting to get an idea."

From the woman's side of the closet, Sheldon takes a thin brown leather belt and puts it around Paul's waist.

"We need a hat. Maybe a woolen cap or something. Oh! That. Up there. That'll do nicely." Sheldon takes down a brown cap and sticks it on Paul's wig-clad head.

"OK, OK. This is taking form. I need the hat back. Now I need a hanger and some tinfoil. Back to the kitchen!"

Spry, and loaded up on caffeine and sugar, Sheldon leaps for the kitchen and starts opening and closing cabinets. As if divinely prepared, tinfoil drops from the cabinet above the refrigerator. Humming now, Sheldon takes hold of a paper-towel roll and begins pulling furiously at it. The paper spins and spins. "Help me!" he says to Paul, handing him an armful of paper.

Taking his cue, Paul gets behind Sheldon and pulls and pulls and pulls as though hoisting a sail on a mighty frigate. Together, dressed like outpatients, they manage to get all the paper off the roll, and only then is Sheldon satisfied.

"Now. Now we've got something to work with."

Sheldon takes the cardboard towel tube, the wire coat hanger, and the woolen hat, and sets to work. With the kitchen table drafted into service as his laboratory, Sheldon uses a steak knife to slice the tube in half. Wincing from a pang of arthritis in his knuckles, he manages to straighten the coat hanger and then bend it into a giant, curvy W. Giving a wink to Paul, he weaves one end of the coat hanger through one side of the woolen cap and out the other. Pulling the hat into position, he centers it on the bent wires, forming ram horns. He slips the cardboard tubes onto each horn and then very, very liberally wraps each one with the tin foil.

The result looks like what the Vikings might have worn in outer space.

Satisfied, Sheldon slips the whole contraption on Paul's head and pulls him over to the mirror again to get a gander at himself. With the expression of someone trying to sell a motorcycle to a pregnant woman, Sheldon smiles *big* as he presents Paul to himself.

"Paul the Viking! Paul the Completely Disguised Albanian Kid Who Is Not on the Run Through the Norwegian Hinterland with an Old Fool. What do you think?

"Oh! But wait! One more thing. What's a Viking—or *Wiking*, if you listen to Norwegians pronounce it—without a battleax or something equally destructive? If I had a copy of the Republican Party's platform, I could give you that, but in its absence I'm thinking . . . wooden spoon."

Back to the kitchen one more time, where Sheldon finds a nicely worn wooden spoon and slides it into Paul's leather belt.

Then he stands back and looks.

"One last touch." And, with that, Sheldon draws an ancient symbol on Paul's Viking chest with a black marker he noticed earlier in one of the kitchen drawers.

Sheldon is proud of himself.

Paul, with a newfound sense of purpose—and no longer looking like Paddington or any other stowaway—goes into the master bedroom to pose in front of the mirror.

Sheldon takes the lull in his childcare obligations to fill his satchel with bottles of water, some crackers, and the last of the moose jerky.

Leaving the back door open, he goes out to the yard and down to the pier to check on the boat they borrowed in Oslo. The sun is already high above the horizon, despite its being only eight o'clock. There is a chill in the morning air, but this only suggests a high front and continued good weather. He could turn on the television and find out the proper forecast easily enough, but he worries that the murder will be on the news. Every moment that Paul does not see his mother's face, or can find a respite or even a distraction from the wider reality, is a blessing that Sheldon does not want to forsake.

With his hands on his hips, Sheldon walks to the pier and scopes out the spot where he moored the boat last evening. Softly shaded and well protected from most angles, it's the kind of place a person might go for a picnic with a loved one, and lay out a blanket and throw stones into the water. He can see all this very well now, because the boat isn't there blocking his view.

*Huh?*

It's possible it was borrowed by some teenagers, or that it floated off on the tide. Whatever the cause, the effect remains the same. They now have one fewer option than they had a moment earlier.

"All the better," says Sheldon quietly as he turns away from the river for good.

From the pier, and with less to demand his attention than there was last night, the old scout-sniper notices something else that had escaped his eagle-eye vision—namely, two massive tire tracks leading from the edge of the water to the back of a garage beside the house.

With no plan in mind, Sheldon follows the tracks. The garage looks like a small American barn that should be red, but instead is the same bright blue as the lonely house belonging to the couple with cancer.

The garage doors are painted white, and there are windows at eye level. Sheldon presses his nose against the glass and peers inside. He sees windows across the way on what he suspects are identical doors on the other side, but they do not illuminate the otherwise dark interior. All he can really tell is that it is filled with something long and large.

Sheldon tries the handle, and is surprised to find the doors locked.

This brings him to his drill sergeant's lesson two.

*If you can't use a hammer, try to find the key.*

Nothing was too obvious not to deserve a formal lesson in the United States Marine Corps.

In the kitchen, in the drawer where he'd found the marker, there is a ring of keys with labels on each one. The labels are in Norwegian, but as chance would have it, one of the keys fits the padlock of the garage doors facing the street.

So, without much optimism, Sheldon opens the padlock, places it back on the door in the open position, and swings the doors wide in a dramatic gesture, for no other reason than because it feels good.

What he sees inside gives Sheldon the first genuine reason to laugh since Rhea told him about the miscarriage.

Leaving the garage door open, he shuffles back to the living room and finds the lower half of the Viking coming into view from under the vintage three-seater sofa. Sheldon addresses the boy's bottom.

"Whatcha doing under the sofa?"

Hearing Sheldon's voice, Paul slides the rest of the way out and holds up a large ball of dust and hair.

Sheldon pulls over a curvy Danish chair and sits in it. He considers first the boy and then the dust bunny he's raising overhead like a trophy.

"That's a mighty impressive hairball you've got there."

Paul considers it.

"You know, this is a good sign. You see, before Huck and Jim hit the road, Jim had a hairball. His could talk if you put a coin under it. I don't have a nickel, though. And this one probably speaks Norwegian. I think we should go now."

Sheldon takes a pillowcase from the bedroom and places the dust bunny in the middle of it. He folds the four corners over it and ties them together. From the hall closet he takes a broom and unscrews the handle from the plastic head. He slides the handle through the knot on the pillowcase and puts the whole rig on Paul's shoulder.

"Now you're a Norwegian-Albanian Dust-Bunny Hobo Viking. Bet you didn't know you'd be one of those when you woke up this morning."

Their battle Wellingtons on, the dishes washed and put away, the beds stripped, the sheets piled on the floor, and the toilets flushed again for good measure, Sheldon snaps his fingers a few times to signal that it's time to go. He shoulders his satchel and adjusts the strap so it rests more comfortably on his thin shoulder, and walks with Paul out into the light of a new day to show him his special discovery.

"Come, come, come. Now, you stand there. And don't move. OK?"

Paul has no idea what Sheldon is talking about, but, horns and all, he stands at attention as Sheldon disappears into the garage.

There is a long silence. Paul looks down to the fjord, where beautiful sailboats skim over the surface of the cold and salty sea. Where seagulls glide, high and free in the morning sky. Where . . .

A thunderous noise startles the boy, who steps away from the garage.

Smoke billows from the open door and slips in from under the closed one. The windows undulate, and the birds all fly away. And out of the darkness comes Sheldon Horowitz on a massive yellow tractor, pulling a huge rubber raft on a two-wheeled boat trailer with a Norwegian flag affixed to the stern.

"River Rats!" he shouts, flapping his map high above his head. "Let the journey commence!"

All around them the world is alive and in bloom. The road winds and twists, and the wilderness is close enough to touch. The birches and spruce stand tall and gallant amid the beech and pine. Birds, relishing the long summer days, sing full-bellied songs that dance through shimmering leaves and pipe above the gently swaying tops of trees.

Paul's rubber-clad feet flip and flop inside the rubber boat as he waves his spoon at passing cars, carrying on almost like a normal child.

Sheldon shifts the tractor into the wrong gear about a dozen times before figuring out—to a point—how the thing works. Once he gets into a groove, at about twenty kilometers an hour, he holds his course and counts his blessings.

He pulls out onto Husvikveien and then onto the 153, which also seems to be called Osloveien, if he's reading the map correctly. His first marker is Riksveg 23, which he hopes will be announced by some kind of sign, and is about thirty minutes away at their current pace. He figures he can settle into the trip for a bit and try to adapt to this unfamiliar place.

It doesn't feel so unfamiliar, though. It feels like the Berkshires in western Massachusetts, where white-steepled churches keep vigil over saltbox houses with their black, blue, and green storm shutters, and schoolchildren carry tin lunch boxes with cartoon characters on them, and policemen stop traffic on Main Street to make way for ducklings as they walk across the road with their stubby orange legs and curious little faces.

The last time he was in the Berkshires was in 1962, when Saul was ten. It was the perfect time to take the family "leafing," to see the magnificence of the New England tapestry unfold all around them and envelop them in the seasonal bliss of autumn and the coming of Halloween.

They were staying in a bed-and-breakfast near the town where Sheldon was born. Saul had run down the carpeted stairs, absurdly early, to launch an untethered attack on the breakfast table as he and Mabel idly wondered what it might have been like to have had a girl.

"Quieter," Sheldon figured.

"For you. I was tough on my mother," she'd said.

"Mothers and daughters."

"Right."

"But we might have slept later."

"Maybe."

"I can go down and keep him company," Sheldon said. "Wanna stay in bed a bit?"

And so Mabel slept for another hour as he watched Saul consume twice his body mass in cranberry muffins, blueberry pancakes, hot chocolate, eggs, bacon, maple syrup, and butter.

It was mid-October, and Sheldon was reading about the Cuban missile crisis in the *Boston Globe*. The Soviets were trying to get missiles into Cuba, and Kennedy had set up a blockade to try to keep them out. The standoff almost resulted in a nuclear war. This would have ruined Halloween entirely.

"If they drop the bomb, you know what you're supposed to do, right?" he'd asked Saul.

"Ruff and rubber."

"Don't talk with your mouth full."

Saul swallowed and then said, "Duck and cover."

"Right."

Parenting done, Sheldon refilled his coffee mug and decided that today would be an excellent day to pick the remaining apples at a nearby orchard. And after that, he'd play the front nine at a local golf course. Mabel could do some leafing with the kid, and he'd give himself a break. Take a deep breath in his native state, and get the car fumes of New York out of his lungs.

The apple-picking went well. They paid ten cents for a big basket and set off into the rows of trees.

Mabel was in a red skirt and a white blouse. Remembering it now, he marveled at how tiny her waist was, how shapely her calves. How she wobbled ever so slightly in her shoes over the uneven ground. He walked behind her and smiled as the heels speared the fallen leaves and followed her around like a stack of receipts on a spike back at the repair shop.

It was a pity that day was ruined.

In the afternoon, Mabel came down with a headache, so Sheldon decided to take Saul to the golf course, to teach him to hold the putter properly. What ten-year-old kid wouldn't want to caddy for his dad?

There was an old country club with a low and long white colonial clubhouse at its center, and the course stretched out behind it like puddles of emeralds. The blue of the sky lit out to the heavens, and a string quartet was playing on the terrace, on account of some fancy catered event. It was a delightful place.

Sheldon and Saul walked into the lobby and smiled at the man who waited like a maitre d'. The man smiled back.

"Hi. My son and I want to play a round of golf. Just the front nine. He'll caddy. We won't hold anyone up."

"Your name, please?"

"I'm Sheldon Horowitz, and this is my son, Saul."

"Mr. Horowitz."

"Yes. So, who do I pay and where do I get some clubs?"

"I'm sorry, sir, but the club is for members only."

Sheldon furrowed his brow. "You're the only course in town. I asked at the B & B. They said everyone plays here."

"Oh, no, no. They were mistaken. It's members only."

"How can the guy be mistaken? He lives here and runs a tourist business."

The man used the old technique of raising his eyebrows and leaving the question unanswered, in the hope that the other conversant would see where the conversation was headed and, not wanting to pursue it, leave off there. This technique was not designed with Sheldon in mind.

"Sounds like you didn't hear me. Allow me to repeat. How can the guy be mistaken? He lives here and runs a tourist business?"

"I'm sure I don't know."

"Fine. I come up here pretty often. How much for membership?"

"It's very expensive. And there's a selection process. You need to be nominated by a member."

In a gesture that surely harked back to the Greek chorus, Sheldon looked around for witnesses to the insanity he was experiencing.

"What kind of thing is that to say? Are you trying to attract new members or repel them?"

Out of habit, which can overpower learning, the man tried the same technique again, upon which Sheldon decided that the man had some screws loose, and so chose to speak slowly. As one does to foreigners and small animals.

"Do you or do you not want to sell people memberships to your clubhouse so we can play on your shiny green fields with little white balls and then drink your drinkies in the bar?"

"Mr. *Horowitz*," he said with emphasis. "Surely you understand. And there's no need to shout. We don't want a scene."

Sheldon, genuinely trying to do the math, squinted as he looked at the man. Then, perhaps for moral support, or to be reminded of the face of normality, he looked down at his well-fed ten-year-old son. And, on looking at his son, his eyes fell upon the gold Star of David that Mabel's sister had given him for Hanukkah last year.

Then Sheldon turned back to the man.

"Are you saying you won't sell me a membership to your country club because I'm a Jew?"

The man looked left and right, and then whispered, "Sir, please, there's no need to use language here."

"Language?" Sheldon shouted. "I'm a United States Marine, you pipsqueak. I want to play a round of golf with my son. You will make that happen *now*."

It did not happen, then or later. A security guard, larger than Sheldon and with darker features, made toward him.

At this moment, Sheldon was undecided, and he looked back at Saul. He should have walked away. He should have accepted that the world was a big place and that change happens gradually. He sincerely did not want to do anything scary that could upset or traumatize his son. He didn't want to get arrested and upset Mabel. A higher wisdom was, even then, available for consultation.

But it was not convincing. Because what he saw on his son's face was shame. And Sheldon, being no intellectual, made his decision. And the decision was based on what he felt was the least shameful way to respond, given who he was and who he wanted his son to be. The line from this moment to Saul's death in Vietnam was to be, for Sheldon, immutable and absolute.

As soon as the guard was within range, Sheldon sprang into the space between them and swung his right elbow like a punch into the man's lower jaw, dropping him immediately. Then, for good measure, he jabbed the other guy in the nose and watched him vanish from behind the desk like a clown in a tank of water.

This is when Sheldon took Saul's hand and led him from the

country club, certain he would not be pursued and that the cops would not be coming for him. The only thing worse for an anti-Semite than a Jew is being beaten up by a Jew. The fewer people who knew about it, the better.

When they were good and far from the scene of the scene, Sheldon spun Saul around and wagged his finger at him and said this:

"This country is what you make it. You understand that? It isn't good and it isn't bad. It's just what you make it. That means you don't make excuses for America's bullshit. That's what the Nazis and commies do. The Fatherland. The Motherland. America isn't your parent. It's your kid. And today I made America a place where you get your nose broken for telling a Jew he can't play a round of golf. The only one allowed to tell me I can't play golf is the ball."

Saul was wide-eyed, and clearly had no idea of the gravity of what his father was saying.

It was, however, a moment that Saul would never forget.

And, unlike the Cuban missile crisis, it ruined the whole day.

# CHAPTER 12

SIGRID HAS RECEIVED so many calls since the murder made the newspapers that she has donned a headset with a microphone in order to get some work done. The calls, she has decided, have nothing to do with her job.

In Norway, the police operate under the authority of the district offices of both the Prosecuting Authority and the National Police Directorate, allowing people like Sigrid to get slapped on both sides of her face at the same time.

This slap, for example, comes from the chief of police for her district. She takes it with her eyes closed, as one does a colonoscopy.

"How's it going?" the police chief asks.

"Fine, thank you," says Sigrid.

"Need help?"

"No. It happened yesterday. I think we're doing fine."

"Pretty political, all this."

"Yes, I suppose it is."

"You have a suspect, right? This Serbian?"

"Kosovar. We suspect him, but we don't have any direct evidence of his involvement. So I can't charge him. And, besides, I also can't find him."

"Muslim, right?"

"Probably, but I don't think religion is relevant to the case. Nationality may be. I'm not sure yet—it's too soon to establish motive."

"Do you have any other suspects?"

Sigrid opens her eyes and looks around. Then she shuts them again. Something about being blind feels appropriate to the conversation.

"There is someone we're listing as a 'person of concern,'" she said.

"What is that?"

"It's a new category I made up."

"Can you do that?"

"I think so."

"Who is it?"

"His name is Sheldon Horowitz."

"Albanian?"

"Jewish."

There is a pause on the other end of the phone.

A Very. Long. Pause.

The chief whispers, "Jewish?"

"Jewish," Sigrid says, not whispering.

"An Israeli spy? Mossad?"

"No. Not Israeli. Jewish. He's American. He's an old Marine who may be suffering from dementia. Or sadness. Or something. He's in his eighties."

"The Israelis are hiring old American Marines?"

"This has nothing to do with Israel, and no."

"You said this has nothing to do with religion, but then said his name is Jewish."

"Yes, his name is Jewish."

"But you said religion doesn't matter but nationality does. So I said Israel."

"He's not Israeli. He's American. An American Marine."

"But . . . Jewish?"

"And . . . Jewish."

"Why do Jews have Jewish names?"

Sigrid stares at the burnt-out light bulb.

"Is this a trick question, Chief?"

"No, what I mean is . . . Norwegians don't have Lutheran names; we have Norwegian names. And the French don't have Catholic names; they have French names. And the Catholics don't have Catholic names either, and the Muslims don't have Muslim names. As far as I know. Though I suppose Mohammed is a Muslim name. So why do the Jews have Jewish names?"

"Mohammed is a first name. Not a last name."

"That's a very good point."

"If I had to take a guess," Sigrid says, wondering why she should guess when surely someone else knows the answer to this, "I'd say . . . because the Jews were a tribe at least a thousand years before Norwegians, French, or Catholics ever existed. Maybe things were more combined back then. Like . . . with the Vikings. So if there were still Vikings, and they lived in different countries, they'd have Viking names. I guess."

"Do you think there were any Jewish Vikings?" asks the chief.

"I suspect that if there were Jewish Vikings, it would have surfaced in conversation by now."

"Are the Palestinians involved?"

"In what?"

"The murder."

Sigrid looks to the ceiling, eyes now open, for the hand of God to rescue her from this moment. All she sees is cracked and peeling paint.

"There are no Palestinians involved in this crime. There are no Israelis. There are no Arabs. None of it has anything to do with the Middle East. At all."

"But there are Jews."

"There is one single, solitary, old, probably confused, and definitely American, Jew. Who didn't do anything wrong, may I add."

"Who concerns you."

"Who apparently concerns us all."

"The world is bigger than Oslo."

"I've seen the pictures, Chief."

"So if you need help, you'll ask."

"I have your number right here."

"Catch the bad guy, Sigrid."

"Yes, Chief."

Eventually—and Sigrid can't say for sure when, because she's lost track of time—the conversation ends.

Rubbing her eyes, Sigrid emerges from her office into the main room. This is not the morning she had in mind. Last night, she ate poorly, went to bed late, and woke to find only decaffeinated instant coffee in the cabinet above the refrigerator. She simply didn't have the spiritual gumption to walk three blocks to stand in line for ten minutes at United Bakeries for a twenty-seven-kroner cup of coffee that has been carefully engineered, to be served lukewarm because—according to the turtleneck-wearing elite barista—"it makes the coffee taste better."

*Try letting your customers tell you what tastes better.*

Perhaps, though, it is the morning she deserves. Despite it being obvious to everyone connected to the case that the woman was killed by the Kosovar, they have no direct evidence, which is irritating. They have a shoe print on the front door, but no fingerprints. The woman was strangled with a cord, so there are no prints to take off her body. The murder weapon is missing—though they do have the knife—and no one saw anything. Unless someone was in the closet, and saw something.

Sigrid takes a few steps further into the room, where she is generally ignored by her colleagues, who all seem remarkably busy and professional.

This is comforting, because she feels neither.

The hunt is on for the killer, of course, but Sigrid's real concern is for the boy, and perhaps also for the old man. If the boy was in

152 · DEREK B. MILLER

the closet, and the killer was his own father, he must be terrified beyond words. Ideally, she'd like to have him in custody and turned over to Social Services, but there is a niggling—though very un-likely—loophole. If there really is nothing connecting the boy's father to the murder, what's to stop him from walking in and de-manding the boy?

There must be grounds for preventing this from happening. It's morning, and there is insufficient caffeine in her veins, which is why she can't think of the plug for the loophole. It still amazes her that her own father used to wake in the morning and take a shot of *akevitt* before going out to the barn to get on with the milking and other duties. He was never a heavy drinker, but times have changed. The Oslo intellectual types don't go in for that sort of manly ap-proach to facing the cold and dark of a northern morning. And surely they're right. It's unhealthy and old-fashioned; we all need to take better care of ourselves now.

*Or maybe we've become a nation of pussies.*

"You," she says to a young cop she's never seen before.

"Mats," he says, surprised she is speaking to him.

"Mats, go get me a cup of coffee."

*Admit it, though. Wouldn't a shot of* akevitt *be better?*

"And everyone else, I need your attention. Gather round. Pull up a chair."

It takes a minute for the room to wind down and for the of-fice chairs to roll into position. When the circle has formed, Sig-rid—sitting now, and still decaffeinated—addresses the troops.

"Thank you all for working so hard. I know it was a long night. I see that we still don't have any direct leads on the boy, the old man, or the suspect. So, to summarize, we have no CCTV footage of anything useful, no reports from other police stations or patrols, no leads from the flat itself that could point us in a direction, and no active theories about how everyone is slipping through our iron grip."

They're all staring at their own shoes, which Sigrid reads to mean that her summary is accurate. There are seven of them. Seven droopy dwarfs. And she is Snow White, awake from her long sleep. And not a cup of coffee to be found. Just a roomful of hairy midgets.

"OK. So let's think beyond our case. What has happened recently in Oslo that, by some creative act of imagination, we may be able to connect to the current problem?"

A woman in her twenties with blond hair raises her hand.

"You don't actually need to raise your hand. We can just talk."

"Ah. A couple was arrested for swimming naked in the fountain in Frogner Park."

"Anyone else?"

"No, just the two of them," the young officer added.

"That's not what I meant."

Flipping through his notes, another cop raises his hand. Sigrid points to him.

"A man stole a shopping cart from a Kiwi supermarket. His friend pushed him down Ullevålsveien. He was going forty kilometers an hour. The officer said the man was issued with a speeding ticket."

Sigrid does not look pleased.

"Serious things happen in this city."

"Not yesterday," the officer adds, immediately wishing he hadn't.

"OK. I want anything else unusual brought to my attention. Anything at all. The way Petter does. Understood?"

They are quiet, and Sigrid nods.

A man in his forties speaks up. "It would have been easy for the suspect to leave in a friend's car. We can't track that."

"No," says Sigrid. "I've been thinking that, too. Does anyone know whether this Enver has a car registered in his own name?"

"He doesn't," says the same cop.

Petter Hansen speaks up. "A boat was stolen from the pier by Akershusstranda."

"What kind of boat?"

"A little boat."

"Do you see a connection?"

"Well, I've been thinking about the line from Mr. Horowitz's note about River Rats, but he's an old, frail man. How's he going to steal a boat with a little boy?"

Sigrid nods. The connection and the rejection of it both make sense. But her father's voice speaks to her and offers another view. She listens to this, and shares it with the others.

"Another way to see it is that a former U.S. Marine who fought in Korea sees himself on a last mission to protect a small boy who reminds him of his dead son. And this Marine, in a foreign environment, has successfully evaded every trap we have set for him in over thirty-six hours, and no one—including his immediate family—has any idea where he is. So let's change our frame on this. What if we're not tracking down a senile man, but instead we're up against a wily old fox with a noble cause? And what if we're not simply inept—though we are—but in fact we're competing, and he's winning?"

They are quiet as they think about this. Then Petter says, "Why doesn't he turn the boy in to the police? He'd be safe with us."

"I don't know. Maybe he doesn't think so. Maybe he doesn't trust us. Maybe he saw something that made him think otherwise. I can't say. All I can hope is that if he's able to evade us, he can also evade the suspect and his associates. Because I have a feeling that the father wants the son back."

"Go find that boat," Sigrid says. "It can't have gone far."


At the Åpent Bakeri, across from the Oslo Literature House, Kadri talks with his mouth full of frosted cinnamon bun as a former KLA colleague and a young recruit strain to understand what he might be saying.

One lights a cigarette and squints his eyes so he can hear better.

Kadri swallows and says, "Are these delicious or what?"

"I'm not hungry," says the one with the cigarette.

Kadri takes another bite and says in Albanian, "Hungry has nothing to do with it."

The second one says, "Kadri, what are we doing here?"

Kadri—though Enver has begged him not to—wears gold chains around his neck, over a black shirt that looks as though it was found in a 1970s disco memorabilia shop. Kadri's mobile phone is on the table next to his Marlboros, and he sips from a big bowl of caffe latte.

"You don't like caffe latte?" he says to them.

They shake their heads.

"Does it give you tummy troubles?"

They shake their heads again.

"Look. We're in Norway. You want everything to be like home? Go home. You want to be here, you take advantage of what they have here. Here they have caffe latte and cinnamon buns, pretty girls in fuzzy boots, and old American cars that come out in the summer. It's not so bad, really."

"Kadri, we have things to do. Can we get on with it?"

"Senka is dead."

"We know."

"The boy is missing."

Burim, who slouches lower in his chair than Gjon, says, "We know this, too."

"Enver is looking for the boy. That means you're going to look for the boy."

Burim pulls on his cigarette. "I don't know where the boy is."

Kadri swallows the soft center of the bun and says, "The middle is the best part, all sweet and sticky. You don't know what you're missing. Look, shithead, if you knew where he was, I'd say, 'Hey, shithead, where's the boy?' And you'd say, 'Oh. He's right here in my pocket, with the lint and the chewing gum.' But you don't know, and I know you don't know, which is why I say you're going to look for him."

Burim scowls and says, "If Enver is following the couple to get to the old man, and the old man is with the boy, what do we do? It sounds like it's done."

Kadri holds up a finger and says, "Because we may be wrong.

Maybe the boy isn't with the old man. Maybe the old man isn't even connected to the people who own the flat. Maybe he is just some Norwegian pensioner who was standing on the street watching the car go by, and that's who Enver saw. Maybe the old man isn't going to meet up with the couple. Maybe Senka stashed the kid someplace else and fooled us by running the other way. We don't know. We are . . . ," and he put his finger in his mouth, sucked on it, and then put it, wet and glistening, into the light breeze, "speculating."

Gjon, who sips an espresso with a great deal of sugar, says, "If not the old man, who? Kid's about seven years old. Can't stay on his own. Maybe he's with the police?"

Kadri wipes his finger with a napkin. "Maybe. Maybe not. If they put a missing-person announcement on the news, I'll know there's still hope."

"Then who?"

Kadri doesn't look up. He just shrugs and casually says, "Maybe the Serbs."

At this, Burim and Gjon both moan and wiggle in their seats.

"Look," says Kadri, licking his lips. "Senka was Serb. She has Serb friends. She doesn't want the boy going to Kosovo with Enver. She knew he'd come to take him away. Kosovo is free now. A new state. A new beginning. Time to start afresh. Take the boy back where he belongs. Reap the spoils of all our labor. As soon as Norway recognized Kosovo in March, it was all over—the universe was conspiring against her. So maybe she hides the boy with the Serbs for protection. It makes sense, no? And maybe now is a good time to get that box back, no?"

"Why not ask Zezake? Put him on this?"

Kadri becomes very serious. "Because Zezake is a killing machine. He's not Colombo. Are you even old enough to remember Colombo? Never mind. Point is, you use a knife for knife things. Now we are reaching for a magnifying glass to play Sherlock. Not the same thing at all. No such thing as an all-purpose tool. This is what my father taught me."

Burim and Gjon look at each other for support, for a way out, and Burim says, "OK. It makes sense. But, what? I give a call to the Serbs? *Hey, you seen the boy? Mind if he comes back with his father to Kosovo now that we won the war? Meanwhile, sorry about your sister.*"

"People know people," Kadri says. "Start asking around. Just be discreet, OK?"

Burim and Gjon both nod. Then Gjon says, "How?"

Kadri sighs and rubs his face. "Do I have to spell it out for you?"

"I think so, yes."

"Romeo and Juliet. Find a boy and girl from different sides who are fucking. Get the Serbian one to find out if the community is protecting the boy. In return, we don't tell their parents. And their parents don't kill them. Makes sense, no?"

Gjon, who is older than Burim and remembers the old country well, takes one of Kadri's cigarettes and lights it. He leans back in his chair and takes a long drag. "What about me?"

Kadri digs deep into his back molar. He takes his finger out and looks at it, disappointed. "I wouldn't mind recovering the contents of the box."

"What's in it?" Gjon asks.

"Things Senka collected from Kosovo. Things we don't want remembered. It's time to forgive and forget, you see. Not to wake sleeping beasts."

Gjon says, "This could get out of hand fast. Like you said, people know people."

Kadri nods. "There have been four hundred murders in Norway in the past ten years. That's forty or fifty a year, in a country of five million. Which isn't high. The cops quickly solved over ninety-five percent of them. Eighty percent of them involve a man between thirty and forty years old killing a woman with a knife, and most of these people know each other. Enver strangled the girl. It's already out of hand. And they'll catch him if we don't help him. What we need to do now is make sure it plays out nice and smooth. Get the boy back. Get them over the border. Take a private boat to Estonia.

From there, it's like sliding into a Ukrainian whore. If we can keep our noses out of any mess, we get to stay here." Kadri smiles. "With the sticky buns. And the fuzzy boots."

Burim puckers his lips and sucks on his front teeth. He says, "Why did Enver kill her?"

Kadri's face goes very stern. He raises a finger, and his eyes are fierce. "Enver is a legend. He does what he wants. You don't question him. You do what he says, and remember that it is because of men like him you have a country now to call your own. You stay here with the fuzzy boots if you want. Or you go to Kosovo. But you have a choice because of Enver.

"Besides, I already explained how the times were conspiring against her. She failed to negotiate with them. She met her fate. It could happen to any of us."

He sits back in his chair and opens his palms.

"I want to clean the mess. And as much as I love him, I wouldn't mind if Enver went away. You know the Norwegian police? They're a bunch of pussies. They don't carry guns, just like the English. But they stay after things for years and years, nagging and nagging. They're like herpes. You think you're rid of them, and then, when you're a little stressed out, boom! There they are. In the end, they catch all the killers. They exhaust their prey into submission.

"So we need to stick together. We band of brothers! Huh? Right? In twenty-four hours, this is all over."

Kadri reaches even farther back into his mouth. He gets most of his hand in there. He comes out with a piece of dental floss. He holds it up.

"Because victory, victory is wonderful!"

Gjon nods, but Burim says nothing.

# CHAPTER 13

B URIM GETS OFF the metro at Tøyen Center and walks the few blocks to his building in the intense sunlight. He climbs five flights of stairs, pants a bit, and hears that the music in the hallway is coming from his own flat.

The music is old-fashioned and airy, and the woman is singing in an operatic voice in English. As he turns the key and opens the door, he knows it can mean only one thing.

Adrijana bursts into the hallway, barefoot and in what must be a new shirt from Zara, and yells in English, "Pink Martini is coming to Oslo!"

Before Burim can reply, Adrijana says, "Take off your shoes."

She kisses him on the cheek and walks back into the kitchen, where she's boiling some water for tea.

Burim takes off his shoes and puts them under the shoe rack in the hall, leaving his knapsack on a hook by the front door next to the umbrellas—one with smiley faces against a black background, and the other from the World Wildlife Fund, in green with a panda bear on it.

"Isn't it a little hot for tea?" Burim asks in lightly accented English.

"Iced tea. You use English breakfast with a bit of honey and put it right into the fridge."

In the kitchen, he sits on a pine chair from IKEA and watches her make the tea.

"We have a problem," he says.

She stirs honey into the tea as he slouches in the chair and puts his elbows on his knees. He scratches his shoulder and rubs his face.

Drawing a deep breath, he holds it for a moment and, finding the courage, says, "I just saw Kadri."

And, like pushing a button, Adrijana does exactly what he expected her to do.

First she turns toward him. Then she says, "You said you'd stay away from him."

To which Burim has no choice but to say, "They called. And I couldn't say no."

And then she gives him Lecture Number Nine.

"Kadri is dangerous. He's still part of that mob. He's a gangster, and he's crazy. You promised you'd stay away from all those people. They are not your friends. And if you get pulled into their world, especially now, you will fall down a well and never get out. And I'll leave you—I swear I will."

"Especially now" was new. Burim decided to try it.

"Why especially now?"

"Why? That's a good question. Let me see if I can think of the answer." Since starting her law studies at the University of Oslo, Adrijana has become a more formidable prosecutor. She always had the talent to persuade, but her courses have unlocked her potential by teaching her that reasoned argumentation is a weapon worth unleashing on the feeble.

Feigning a conceptual breakthrough with a wide-open mouth, she waves the wet tea bag for emphasis, which sprays Burim, ruining his T-shirt.

"Oh, I know. Could it be that we now live together and our futures are permanently intertwined, and part of your being a man in this relationship involves making small compromises like . . . oh, I don't know . . . I do the laundry and, in return, you stay away from heroin-trafficking psychopaths and a dead Serbian woman three blocks from here?"

"I'm not involved in any of that. You know that."

"No. What I know is that you said you're not and I've chosen to believe you. I don't really know what you're doing and what you're not doing."

"You know me."

Adrijana softens her tone, but the focus remains the same.

"And I know them, too. And I also read the newspaper. Please tell me they had nothing to do with that woman getting killed. Please tell me that."

Burim opens his hands, and Adrijana slumps.

"We should go to the police."

"Enver is my cousin. And I'm sure they already know."

"How do you know? You can't read Norwegian. How do you know what the papers say?"

"There's an English-language website. I looked."

Adrijana shakes her head. "Why did you go?"

"I'm afraid, OK? I need to know what they know."

"About what?"

"About us!"

"What about us?"

"You're Serbian!"

"I'm Norwegian."

"Oh, please. Not this again."

Adrijana now raises her voice, as she does every time she is forced to defend her identity and those she identifies with.

"I am Norwegian. I have a Norwegian passport. I've lived here since I was eight years old. I have Norwegian parents. I go to the university. It is my best language. I am not Serbian!"

And Burim raises his voice, too. He cannot believe that she can fail to see how little any of that matters.

"You were born in Serbia. Your name is Serbian. You escaped during a war and were adopted here. Your mother tongue is Serbian. Your blood is Serbian."

"So what?" she yells.

"It doesn't matter what you think you are," shouts Burim. "It matters what *they* think you are!"

"Who?"

"All of them!"

And with that they both fall silent.

Pink Martini plays a glowing song of melancholy and remorse, and eventually they look at each other. And then—the irony too rich to ignore—they smile.

She says, "I love you."

And he says, "I love you, too."

"You may not see this, but I really am Norwegian. I trust them. If you think we're in some kind of danger because the crazies don't approve of our relationship, then I'm going to tell someone. I'll tell the police. Because the Norwegians won't tolerate that sort of thing. I can love whoever I want. You're a slob, and you smoke, and you keep terrible company."

Burim frowns and looks up. "But."

"But what?"

"You're supposed to list all my bad traits and then say 'But' and tell me all the reasons you love me."

Adrijana pouts. "I've never heard that."

She puts the tea in the refrigerator and straightens a black-and-white postcard of a Flamenco dancer that slipped from its magnet.

Burim says, "I really am worried, though. Kadri said something that makes me think he knows about us. They're trying to find a little boy." He looks at her carefully as he says this.

Adrijana is expressionless and says, "What little boy?"

"The son of the woman who was killed."

"Why would they want to find a little boy?"

"I can't say." He pauses and takes out a cigarette, which Adrijana immediately takes away, rinses under the faucet, and throws in the trash. "You don't know anything about it?"

"What are you talking about?"

"Are you sure your parents are OK with us?"

"No. They think I can do better than you. As I said, you're a slob and you smoke and your friends suck, and you need a better job, and I'd like you to go to college. But they don't care that you're from Kosovo, if that's what you mean."

"What about me being a Muslim?"

"You're not a very good Muslim."

"That's not what I mean."

"They don't care."

"Why not?"

"Because they don't care what you are, Burim. They care *who* you are. If you act like an asshole, they'll hate you. If you act like an asshole because you're a Muslim, well, that's your business. What's with the little boy?"

"Can I trust you?"

"About what?"

Sigrid receives a call from the garage informing her that the part they ordered for her car had been damaged in the mail and that it would be another three days before she could pick it up, so did she need a loaner? Next, the chief calls again to ask if there is anything he can do to help. And by then the morning energy has been sucked out of the room and turned to vapor, so Sigrid throws in the towel and announces, perhaps a bit too loudly, that she is going to visit the crime scene—where the phone doesn't ring—to find a lead.

Anything to put her in a better mood.

She goes out the front door and turns right along the building to a parking lot behind a chain-link fence. In the lot are three squad cars—a Volvo S60, a Saab 9-5, a Passat—and one BMW custom police bike. The fleet is a rather odd mix.

Sigrid takes a deep breath of the late-morning air and listens to the sound of no phone ringing, no superiors cajoling, no theories deduced from a smattering of facts, no journalists asking when the police will know the answer.

She was actually asked this yesterday, and the reporter wanted to use Skype for a video chat. Because, apparently, talking on the phone using words isn't enough anymore.

The journalist looked young and . . . generic.

"When we're finished with the investigation," she'd told the young liberal from *Dagbladet* as gently as she could.

"And when will that be?"

"When we know the answer."

"But that's circular. You're avoiding the question," the pipsqueak had had the nerve to say.

It was tough being in command sometimes. It wasn't so much the rules—like the rule that you can't grab journalists by the ears and lead them out of the building like bad children—but rather the need to set a tone for the other officers.

More to calm herself than to accomplish anything valuable, Sigrid offered a riddle she once heard as a little girl.

"Why is something always in the last place you look?"

It was clear to the girl, and to Petter, and to the three other officers who pretended not to be listening but were, that she was being condescended to. But what choice did she have? Reject the question? Sigrid was the chief inspector.

"I don't know. Why?"

"Because you stop looking once you find it."

Then, because the girl had insisted on video to really *connect* with her subject, Sigrid winked.

Oh, how'd she love to take the motorcycle! Put on a white helmet. Open the visor. Take in the smell of summer pines and cut grass. Feel the splendid isolation, the momentary step into timelessness.

Maybe she should get a license. Learn to ride. Find a new hobby and settle into the reality that she might never meet a man and would certainly never have a family.

Have the maturity to face the life she actually has.

She takes the Volvo. It is comfortable and has leather seats. She closes the windows, turns on the air conditioner, and rolls out into traffic that is unusually heavy for the middle of the city. The radio occasionally crackles with news, but otherwise the day is quiet and bright. Again there is no sign of rain, no clouds between the Volvo and eternity. Sigrid turns on talk radio for company as she waits for the traffic to clear.

She is listening to a radio show called *Doktor*, in which people from all across the country can ask questions about their health. It is a national program, and it takes Sigrid out of Oslo, back to the farm, as the calls come in. Her mind wanders.

One caller, an old man from a remote village, has a terrible cough. He is alone and has no family. He lives with three cats he loves very much. They are his only friends. He tells the doctor that he can't stop smoking, though he knows he should. His health is getting worse, but he doesn't have the strength. Recently, one of the cats has started to cough. He thinks it is his fault. Sigrid hears his voice crack with guilt and remorse, underscored by terrible loneliness. Can the doctor help them?

Sigrid turns off the radio and runs her hands over the steering wheel. She reaches for the radio again, but does not turn it on. She sits in the car for several minutes, in heavy traffic, doing nothing.

Then she calls her father.

The phone rings at least a dozen times. Then the phone — an old and heavy one — is removed from the cradle and bumps a few times before arriving at her father's ear. Before saying hello, her father says, "Sigrid. What's wrong?"

"Nothing. I just wanted to call."

"Anything on your mind?"

"I want to make sure you're OK."

"My daughter. All sentimental."

"I'm as hard as you made me."

Her father laughs, which makes her smile, and then he coughs a bit, which takes her smile away.

"Next time you come, I need heavy work gloves. I don't like the ones they sell here. Go to Clas Ohlson, they have good ones. And I want some more books. There's a history of the Chinese I read about in *Aftenposten*. It was translated this year from the French. Bring me that."

"OK."

There is silence on the line for a few moments that neither finds awkward. Eventually, Mr. Ødegård says, "Have you met a nice man yet?"

Sigrid nods. "I'd been meaning to tell you. I got married and had three sons."

"That's wonderful news."

"Huey, Dewey, and Louie. They're delightful, but have speech impediments and very short legs."

"The school years may be challenging."

There is more silence on the line as Sigrid flicks the turn signal and approaches the block of apartments where the murder took place.

"Where are you?" he asks.

"I'm going to a crime scene."

"Who else is there?"

"No one. It's closed off."

Her father says, "Has it been busy until now? The crime scene?"

"Yes. I suppose. We go back periodically when we need to reconsider something. Why do you ask?"

"Do you have your gun?"

"Why would I need a gun?"

"Do me a favor. Carry your nightstick in your hand."

"Now who's being sentimental?"

"Do it anyway."

"Why?"

Mr. Ødegård says, "A reporter says to a bank robber, 'Why did you rob that bank?' The bank robber says, 'Because that's where the money is.'"

"Willie Sutton denied saying that."

"The point remains."

"Bye, Papa."

"Goodbye, Sigrid."

Sigrid sees an empty space a half block up the street from the building, where she parks, takes her nightstick from the trunk, and locks the doors. She carries it lightly and walks without haste so no one gets the idea that anything might be wrong.

Anything *else*, at any rate.

She opens the front door of the building and proceeds past the crime scene to the left, up the staircase to the second floor where the woman lived with her son. She steps through the tape, unlocks the front door, and goes inside. Sigrid removes her shoes, turns on the lights, and visits each room, looking for anything interesting—anything that might not have appeared in her report.

According to the rental agent, the apartment occupies sixty-seven square meters. From the front door there is a short entry hall, with a bathroom straight ahead. The bedroom is to the left, and she goes there first.

The apartment, which has been taped off, given its centrality to the investigation, has already been closely examined by an officer named Tomas and a new forensic specialist named Hilde. Thus far she'd been doing a good job, despite a nervous sort of officiousness that comes with too much respect for authority, which can interfere with one's work with data—not good for a forensic specialist.

She has a folder containing copies of the photos taken here at the scene, and summaries of the reports already filed, which were thorough enough. But Sigrid wants to see it all for herself—to get a feel for the space where this small family of two once shared each other's company, talked of small things, enjoyed small pleasures.

The bedroom has a queen-size bed pressed into the far corner, and a single pushed into the opposite corner. The beds are unmade. The room is untidy, but not unclean. To the right of the hall is a narrow galley kitchen that has not been renovated since the 1970s. The cabinets are cheap, and there is a small, two-person table at the far end where Sigrid presumes the mother and son would eat together and talk about his school days. The table is flimsy, but the surface is clean. Dishes are stacked in the sink.

The second door on the right leads to the living room.

Her officers seem to have done well. She kneels on the carpet to look closely for remnant footprints from standard-issue boots, but does not see any. Petter and the boys don't seem to have tracked in any dirt, either. There are evidence numbers on items around the room, and they all look familiar from the photos.

The bathroom contains only things that a woman or child would use. The larger containers—shampoo, bubble bath, talcum powder—are from the bargain end of the cost spectrum. The smaller ones are higher-end samples. In a basket there is a pile of perfume testers that have been torn from women's magazines.

Behind the toilet she finds very little grime and dust. The soap dish had been rinsed after its last use. She notices a plastic bin of Q-tips with the lid removed, and a boy's toothbrush in fairly new condition. The paste has been consistently squeezed from the bottom.

In the kitchen, there is no candy and only one box of sugary cereal. There are no soft drinks, but lots of fruit-flavored syrups. Boxes of pasta and cans of tomato sauce. In the freezer, she sees a large container of inexpensive ice cream and one pint of Häagen-Dazs cookies and cream.

Sigrid reaches in and takes the pint out. It is almost full. Five small valleys have been dug out by an experienced hand. By someone who loves this but can't afford the pleasure, and so rations it with discipline and solitary pleasure as her son eats the other stuff.

She places it back in the freezer.

*You were a good mother, and you loved your son. Whatever else, this is true.*

Sigrid puts her shoes back on, turns out the lights, and closes the door behind her—feeling, though, as if she's forgotten to do something.

The staircase is made of treated hardwood. The edges are worn from hundreds of people having stepped on them thousands of times since the building was renovated in 1962, when it was converted from a cooperative into condominiums.

She turns on the landing and steps down the second flight to visit the crime scene itself. The names Rhea Horowitz and Lars Bjørnsson are on the black-plastic insert above the doorbell.

The police seal is broken. Sigrid removes her hand and stares at the door handle. She stares at it for quite some time.

The door should be closed. If any of her officers were posted inside, she'd have been notified.

Did she not post a guard at the door? There are officers in a van outside watching the premises, but no one at the door. This might have been a good idea, in retrospect.

She thinks of several plausible explanations for the door being open.

*Perhaps the old man has returned. One assumes he has a key. Or perhaps the whole family has returned. They shouldn't have, but people act impulsively. It is illegal to enter a crime scene, but that doesn't mean it doesn't happen. Given the turmoil in their lives, it would be understandable, if not permissible. Or someone else has been in the flat.*

*Or someone is in the flat right now.*

She shakes her head. She knows right away that her father would never approve of this. Not only the action, but the logic that supports the action.

*There's also a possibility that the landlord is in there right now, wearing women's undergarments. Or a drug addict is inside stealing jewelry. Or a boatload of recent Chinese immigrants without a television are watching Russia play Finland in hockey and placing bets over beer.*

*You have no idea what's behind that door. You can't just pick the options within your field of vision. Reality comes from everywhere. At best, you can narrow down the likelihoods. But in the end, it's not a matter of deduction. It's a matter of fact. One bullet will kill you if you're stupid or unlucky. So at least don't be stupid.*

This is what her father would say.

Sigrid removes her radio from her belt and calls in the intrusion. She does this very quietly. The radio crackles and then returns to silence.

Sigrid presses her ear to the door and listens.

She just isn't sure. She stands outside the door for a few minutes, playing with things on her utility belt. She's always liked the utility belt. It carries a lot of weight, but rests rather nicely on her hips.

The button on the canister of mace has a crisp click to it. The handcuffs don't jiggle, but stay snug in their black pouch. Everything is well designed. These are the little things that people do to make the world a bit better, but for which they never receive thanks.

If she had a gun, it would really throw off the weight. She figures that's why cowboys tied their six-shooters to their thighs.

"Right. That's it."

Sigrid opens the door wide.

The crime scene is familiar to her. It has been described in all the poorly spelled reports she's received. She has seen dozens of photos and watched a video walk-through—a new tool they have started using. One industrious cadet has even rendered the apartment in a CAD program so police can track the steps of victim and perpetrator and imagine various scenarios.

But she has not experienced the actual murder scene before. There is no explaining why we see things differently in person, but we do. She traveled to Florence once. She saw the *David*, a figure so visually familiar, but in person it left her speechless.

The floors have been refinished with wide Danish planks. Walls have been knocked down, creating a cavernous space through the living room and kitchen, which is tastefully appointed in stainless steel and maple. There's an oversized American refrigerator and an island in the middle with a built-in grill. The stove is fueled by natural gas. This is a rarity in Oslo, as the city is not equipped for it. Lars must go trekking out every few months for a new gray canister.

Sigrid does not go inside. Instead, with the door open, she steps back and looks through the space along the fringes for anyone who might be waiting with a knife.

She looks at her watch. She has been standing in the hall for eight minutes. It is, she thinks, long enough.

Sigrid steps into the room. It feels as though she is drawn in by a whisper from the dead and the promise of a revelation.

She removes her shoes, leaves them out in the hall, and flicks on all the lights as she passes them, surveying the room. It is fresh, bright, and feels lived in by people who are worldly and cosmopolitan. Also somewhat foreign. There is a wine rack of some twenty bottles, with the reds higher up than the whites. Four different olive oils sit beside the stove. On a magnetic strip beside the sink hang an assortment of utensils from IKEA and expensive cutlery from Japan and Germany. There are American appliances from Kitchenware. There is a bowl full of fresh apples, pears, lemons, and limes that will soon rot.

There is a *Penthouse* coffee mug beside the sink. It is unwashed and well used.

This apartment is much bigger than the one upstairs. Maybe one hundred and twenty square meters or more. There's a master bedroom to her right, and between that doorway and the refrigerator is a short staircase leading down to where the old man stays and to the closet where they found the urine stain.

She opens the folder and takes out the photos. She walks to the spots where each was taken, and compares what she sees with what the camera saw. She wonders whether anything is out of place, and what someone might have been doing here.

Sigrid goes into the bathroom and pokes around. It contains finer cosmetics than upstairs, subtle fragrances, loofahs. In the cabinet under the sink are "marital aids," and Sigrid closes the cabinet respectfully, though perhaps enviously.

There are a few novels by authors she has not heard of: Philip Roth, James Salter, Mark Helprin, Richard Ford. There are copies of a periodical called the *Paris Review*.

Nothing odd in all this, but there are many things she does not understand. These three people have crafted an existence that is not natural to any one of them.

The effort, and even the result, is admirable.

In the mirror above the sink she sees the shower curtain. It is closed.

Turning, she takes out her nightstick. The curtain has moved since she came into the room.

Her backup should be on the way. The police station is not far.

Sigrid takes her flashlight from her belt and, rather than push the curtain away, she steps back to the bathroom door, switches off the light, and shines the flashlight at the white ceiling above the bathtub, illuminating the white curtain.

There are no shadows cast. There is no one inside.

Switching the light back on, she moves the shower curtain to the side just to be sure, finds the tub empty, then leaves the bathroom, switching off the light behind her.

The living room has been carefully preserved by her detectives. She sees evidence of a struggle everywhere. The fragments of fragile objects are clustered close to where the violence occurred. The woman's final moments were spent suffocating and with a knife in her chest, lying on her back on the coffee table in front of the sofa. Her blood dripped down the sides and soaked into the white floorboards.

He had the leverage here. Once she was on her back, he pressed his knee on her. The hatred was personal and remorseless.

The downstairs room is less a cellar than another room of the apartment. The building itself accommodates the slight drop in the land.

The room is orderly. The bed is made. On a red chair there is a black suit, a white shirt, and a gray tie, as though waiting to be worn by a mourner. She opens the wooden dresser and finds a few sweaters, pairs of pants, and pieces of underwear.

On the nightstand by his bed there is a lamp, and at its base is an antique silver picture frame—two frames, connected by tiny hinges. In the left frame is a black-and-white picture, taken maybe fifty years ago, of a woman who was almost Sigrid's age. She is petite, with dark hair and the sort of eyes that women had only in the

1950s. She is sitting on a stone wall with one leg up. A white sneaker rests on top of a park bench below her along the wall, and she's laughing. It looks like autumn. It is probably his wife—the one who died in America and prompted his move here.

In the right frame is a young man, probably a teenager. He is slender and has the same eyes as the woman. This one is a color photograph and is slightly out of focus. It may have been taken quickly or with a cheap camera, like a Polaroid Land camera or even an old Minox. His arms and legs are crossed as he leans against a 1968 Mustang. It is baby blue, and he is smiling as though he designed and built the car himself.

The only other item on the night table is a jacket patch, propped carefully against the base of the lamp opposite the photos. It is drab green with thin red trim, and looks worn. On it is the motto of the U.S. Marine Corps: *Semper fidelis.*

Always faithful.

"Where the hell have you gone to, Mr. Horowitz?" Sigrid says aloud to herself. "Why are you missing and what are you doing?"

Just before leaving Sheldon's room, Sigrid drops to one knee and looks under the bed. And, for the first time, something seems off.

There is a large pink jewelry box with a silver lock on the front. The midday light reflects off the floor, and she sees it easily.

She reaches under and pulls it out.

Staying on one knee, she fiddles with the lock. It doesn't open. With her Leatherman knife she could easily pry it off and open the box, but right now that isn't the point.

Sigrid looks again at the woman in the picture frame—at her white sneaker, her wristwatch, her white collar tipping out of a V-neck sweater. She has a wide smile. Her universe is full of possibilities. It must have been taken in the late 1950s. Sheldon was back from Korea. Her son was probably five or six then. She had her figure and her grace. The bad things in her life hadn't happened yet.

Would this box belong to her?

Sigrid takes out a small black notepad and flips to the interview with Rhea and Lars. She flips a few more times.

There. Her husband was a watch repairman and antique sales-man.

She looks again at the pink box.

*No way.*

And then it occurs to her what she'd forgotten to do upstairs. She'd forgotten to look for a match to the key that Senka had in her pocket when she died.

Had all the officers forgotten to do that? If they had, she'd raise hell at the office.

If the match to that key was here in the apartment where she was murdered, it means she must have brought it downstairs. It could have been stored here, but that would have meant Sigrid had been lied to and that Senka, Rhea, and Lars did know each other. Which seems unlikely. More likely is that Senka brought it here before she was killed. She hid it. The killer wanted it. It is part of the reason for her death. She protected herself and its contents. She fought to the death as her boy hid in the closet across from it.

Whatever is in the jewelry box must be important.

This is Sigrid's very last thought before a hard object strikes her on the head and she collapses to the ground.

# CHAPTER 14

KADRI HOLDS THE huge Maglite in his hand and looks down at the woman cop he has just bludgeoned. He doesn't like hitting women—though it doesn't especially bother him, either—and she certainly hadn't done anything to deserve it. But he needed that box, and he was pretty sure that asking her for it wouldn't have done the trick.

"You should have checked the closet," he says to her in English. "You check the shower, but not the closet. Who would stand in a shower? Everyone gets killed in a shower. Don't you go to the movies? *Psycho*. Dead in shower. The Mexican in *No Country for Old Men*. Dead in shower. Michelle Pfeiffer in *What Lies Beneath*. Almost dead in shower, or in the bath, anyway. But she did that thing with her toe and got out OK. Still the shower, though."

He looks at his feet. Then he says, "Glenn Close in *Fatal Attraction*. Dead in shower. John Travolta in *Pulp Fiction*. Very dead in shower. But never closets. I can't think of anyone shot in a closet. This is why I hide in closets."

Kadri scratches his stomach. "So, look. I'm taking the box and going for a coffee. Get well soon."

Kadri checks her pulse, confirms that she's alive, picks up the box, places it under his arm, and walks out the front door. He strides up the street past the police car, gets on his Vespa scooter, and heads directly to the nearest Kaffebrenneriet for a bun.

It is good to see the process working as it should. Burim is infiltrating the Serbs with more than his penis, and will come back with valuable information. Gjon is collecting the guns that Enver asked for. The box—whatever is in it—has been recovered.

The sun is shining, and the air is dry and bracing. If you wave your hands in front of your face, you can pull the summer into your lungs and feel its peace and serenity. Just what an accomplished man needs.

And peaceful it is. There is no history here. No weight. No echoes or whispers of tragedy on the breeze. It is odd, really. Because for Kadri, when he leaves Oslo and meets colleagues in other towns to talk politics, play cards, or buy and sell drugs, he can feel the expanse of Scandinavia—the big sky, the vastness of the land—reveal itself. It is as though the lonely inhabitants cannot fill that much space. It taunts them, spreads them too thin.

They should sing, as they do in the Balkans. And dance. Something in the people here prevents them from expressing the few words that could free them, connect them, rejoin them to each other and the heavens. They should live life. And laugh at death.

But they don't. Their Lutheran cloaks smother them and take their voices away.

Whatever is causing it, though, it is not history. There is no history here to speak of. Some old boats and a wooden church—that's not history. This is the part of Europe without a history. No Romans. No Christians. No Crusades. No religious wars. Only old gods and trolls and blondes wearing fur. Really, what's to be depressed about?

*How I miss our sad songs sung together for joy!*

But now is not the time for sadness. Or joy. It is the time for coffee.

Kadri impatiently rocks back and forth on his toes as a Swedish girl—here in Norway for the summer because of the higher wages—delicately pours the steamed and fluffed milk into his latte, leaving on top the signature flourish of the café.

Kadri plops his forty kroner on the table and stares deeply at the coffee.

The girl stares at it, too.

Kadri looks up at her and says, "Why did you put a vagina in my coffee?"

"What?"

"Vagina. In my coffee. In the foamy bit."

"It's a leaf."

"A leaf?"

"Yes. A leaf."

"You ever seen a leaf like that?"

They both consider the design in the coffee foam again.

"It's my first day," she says.

"You were trying to make a leaf?"

"Yes."

"So it's a leaf."

"Thanks."

"Keep the change."

A middle-aged couple pushing a lime-green pram stands to leave one of the wrought-iron tables, and Kadri springs for it. He gives a little chuckle as he wiggles into the chair.

Ah, life. So many twists and turns. So much unexpected, and so little of it preventable. We do what we can to find balance. And to stay calm, we retreat to the simple pleasures. Like coffee and a good smoke.

Once he's well seated, Kadri whips out his iPhone and jabs at the little icons. He waits for Enver's phone to ring.

It rings a few more times than expected. Hell, who knows what

Enver is doing from one minute to another? Besides, Kadri is going to do his part, be a good soldier, pay his respects. But he isn't going to take the extra step and make any of this his own problem. It isn't his kid. Kadri didn't kill anyone. Not in Norway, anyway. The sooner this all ends, the better. Let Zezake step into the picture, if it comes to that. Kadri has the box. That's enough for now.

Enver picks up the telephone. He is breathy and humorless as ever.

They speak in Albanian.

"So, I got the box with the stuff in it."

"Was there any trouble?"

"I hit a woman cop on the head, but she's there, and the box and I are here. She's alive. So, that's pretty much that."

Enver is silent. He does this when he's thinking. It makes Kadri cringe. If you know your mind, why not speak it?

"They take that sort of thing seriously here."

"Look, Enver. Whatever, OK? I was behind her. *Thump.* Like the good fairy asked the bunny not to do to the field mice. She knows nothing. Can I open the box? It's an ugly box. I'd like to get rid of the box."

"No."

"No? No what? No, I can't open it, or no, it's not ugly? Because, believe you me, it's ugly. It's all pink with little silver—"

"Don't open it. I don't want you losing anything. I assume it's locked. I expect to find it locked when you bring it to me."

"Where are you?"

"Glåmlia."

Kadri scratches his chest where the gold chain occasionally pinches some hairs.

"Any chance that's near Paris? I'd like to go to Paris."

"It's near the Swedish border. Look it up on that stupid toy of yours."

"There's something you should know."

Enver says nothing.

"The box? It wasn't in her flat. It was in the one where it happened. And I was right. An old man lives there. And I had to hide in the closet. And it smelled bad. Like somebody peed. Maybe an old man. Maybe a young boy. I'm thinking he peed because something scary was happening outside the closet. If it was a boy, then maybe the old man got him out of there later. So I think I was right about the old man. I think maybe he knows something. And I think maybe he has the boy. It doesn't tell us where to look. But it tells us where not to look, you know?"

Enver hangs up without saying goodbye.

*Yes, please, go back to Kosovo. Take your sullen attitude with you. The war is over.*

Just before he can take a sip of his coffee, Kadri feels a tap on his shoulder.

He looks up and sees a uniformed police officer in his mid-thirties.

"What?" Kadri says in English.

"You're under arrest."

"What are you talking about? I'm drinking coffee at a coffee shop. I'm smoking a cigarette outside, like everyone else."

"Like movies?"

"What do you mean, do I like movies?"

Petter has been holding his walkie-talkie, and now he raises it to his mouth and says, in Norwegian, "Is that the guy? Is that the voice?"

"That's him," crackles Sigrid through the radio.

Petter tells Kadri he is under arrest, but Kadri begins to laugh.

"You don't have a gun. Why should I come with you? Because you have nice manners?"

"Because *they* do."

Petter signals behind Kadri, and Kadri turns to see two very serious men in black flak jackets holding Heckler & Koch submachine guns.

"That's the *Beredskapstroppen*."

"What's that?"

"Delta force."

Petter sees Kadri's smug face melt.

"They'll shoot me here, in the café?"

"No," says Petter. "They'll shoot you there, in the chest."

Then Petter leans in closely and whispers, "They are Santa's little helpers. They know if you've been naughty or nice. And you've been very, very naughty."

"You're maybe a little crazy, you know that?" says Kadri.

Petter walks back to the squad car and buckles himself into the driver's seat. He adjusts the rear-view mirror so he can see Sigrid lying in the back, her head with an ice pack on it and a foul expression on her face.

"I'm supposed to take you to the hospital. You might have a concussion."

"I can't. I've got work to do."

"Don't be stubborn."

"I'm not being stubborn. I have to make calls and get this wrapped up. It would take me longer to explain it to you than to do it myself."

"You should probably call your father before this makes the newspapers."

"Oh, Christ. Does it have to be in the papers?"

Sigrid sees Petter shrug. "The police chief inspector was assaulted in connection with a murder," he says. "But I suppose you're right. We can pretend it didn't happen. Or, if it is in the reports, I'm sure *Dagbladet* won't care very much."

Sigrid moans.

And then her father calls.

Sigrid looks at the phone. "Papa" flashes on the screen. It is not merely a headache. She's in terrible pain—a throbbing, pulsing, pounding, relentless jackhammer to the cerebral cortex.

She curls into the fetal position in the back seat.

"It's my papa."

She sees Petter shake his head. "Better answer it. He never leaves the farm, but he always seems to know everything."

"He does have a way. Push the answer button for me. I can't find it."

He hands her the phone.

"Yah. Hi, Papa."

"So?" he says.

"So what?"

"What happened?"

It occurs to Sigrid, though she is unsure why, that the American saying "adding insult to injury" surely derived from someone's literal experience.

"I got hit on the head."

There is a pause on the other end of the phone.

She waits for it to end. But, oddly, the pause continues.

"Papa?"

"Yes?"

"You have nothing to say?"

"Now that you ask . . . Why didn't you bring a gun?"

"I told you. I was hit on the head. I didn't need a gun. I needed a helmet."

"Well, there's no arguing with that, I suppose."

"Can we take this up again later, Papa? We need to regroup at the station, and try to see straight through this. And right now I need to throw up."

The search for the missing boat on the Oslo Fjord required a helicopter, and required paperwork and phone calls that Sigrid was not able to file or make when she returned to the station. Petter had to take over the office management. Most of her energy was spent insisting that she didn't want to go to the hospital.

She either had a concussion or didn't have a concussion. If she had one, she shouldn't sleep. At the police station she would not be able to sleep. So, clearly, being at the police station with a concussion was good for her health. If she did not have one, she did not need to be at the hospital. With aspirin and a cold pack, Sigrid was able to make a convincing argument—to herself—that her office was the only logical place for her to be.

With the helicopter airborne, she was now receiving regular reports. The biggest decision had been whether to send it directly south toward Nesodden, or southwest toward Drøbak and along the route to Denmark.

In the end they chose Drøbak. If they took the more easterly route, they would fly to Nesset or thereabouts, then turn west, go overland to meet up with the coast, then travel south, backtrack, and take it north all the way back to the helipad. That would burn a lot of costly fuel, so the decision was to gamble on the Drøbak side, take it as far south as the fuel on board a small boat could be expected to last, and, if they found nothing, fly overland to meet up with Nesset and head up toward Kjøya, Nebba, and other hamlets in that area.

The copilot was in regular contact with Petter, who had now returned from lunch and resumed his duties of keeping Sigrid awake. The mission took several hours, because of the distance, the tree cover along much of the coastal route, and the bewildering range of fishing and leisure craft on the water. Trying to tell whether a small boat was moored, adrift, derelict, in use, or even fitted the description was tiring and time-consuming for the pilots.

By four o'clock that afternoon, they had managed to find it. With the change of tide, it was more than a nautical mile from the little blue house. When the house was finally inspected by local people, they found no signs of Sheldon or the missing boy.

"Where is it?" Sigrid demands.

"It was adrift off of Kaholmene. Near where they sank the German ship."

"I know where it is, Petter. Everyone knows where it is."

Petter is getting increasingly concerned about Sigrid's general welfare, and her blood pressure in particular, but thinks it wiser, and perhaps safer, to say nothing.

"Call the local police there. I think Johan is still chief. Tell him what we're looking for. Maybe they'll come up with something."

Enver's crotch vibrates again. He reaches deep in his pocket and takes out the mobile phone to read the text message.

"At the car," it reads.

It is late afternoon. Enver takes one last look at the house through the binoculars and decides that the man and woman aren't going anywhere. Secretly, he's thrilled for the chance to get up and stretch.

But he doesn't stand. He crawls on his stomach until he's over a small knoll, and then slinks low to stay out of the cabin's line of sight.

It takes twenty minutes to walk back to the car, through the woods, out to the road, and around the bend where he'd made an effort to hide it, but wasn't as successful as he'd hoped.

Gjon and Burim are leaning against the trunk of the white Mercedes. They are smoking and talking quietly when Enver reaches them.

Both look up when he steps onto the dirt road, brushing off his trousers and straightening his hair.

When Enver is close enough, Gjon whispers, "You heard about Kadri?"

"What have you got to eat?"

"Huh?"

"What do you have to eat? What did you bring? A sandwich? What?"

Gjon and Burim look at each other and then at Enver. "We don't have any food. Why would we have food?"

"You were supposed to bring food."

"Kadri was arrested. I don't know what he did," says Gjon, "but he was a few blocks from the apartment when he got picked up."

"How do you know this?"

"I was waiting for him outside the flat," says Gjon. "He went in to look for the box and told me to —"

"Told you to what?"

"Well . . . I suppose he told me to pick up a few sandwiches."

"Right."

"Yes. But then I ate them."

Enver says nothing. He just stands and looks at the two of them.

The impulse to stand up straight, to stop leaning against the car, comes over Burim, but he suppresses it.

"I didn't know they were for you. I figured one was for Kadri and the other for me. And then the police went inside and, when he came out, he walked right past me. So I ate them both."

Enver still says nothing.

"I called him first and told him that the woman cop was there," Gjon adds.

"Who else is coming?" Enver asks.

"And then Kadri was the only one out."

"Who the fuck else is coming?"

Burim speaks for the first time. "No one."

"Give me the rifles."

Burim and Gjon look at each other and hesitate, too long.

"There are no rifles," Enver says. "You didn't bring those either. No food. No weapons. No soldiers. Why did you bother coming at all?"

"Enver, it isn't like back in Kosovo. You don't find AKs under every pile of hay. In '97 we looted millions, billions, of rounds of ammo. Here, you need to take classes and get a license to shoot ducks."

"There're rifles behind the counter at Intersport, on the main street."

"But you need a permit to touch them. And if you buy one, they can track us, because we need to register them."

"So instead of doing your job, you decided to protect yourselves from possible future paperwork. And the men?"

"You've crossed a line, Enver," says Gjon. "You killed the mother of your child. Some think you're cursed."

"But you're here," Enver says to Burim.

He was here, but Burim had not wanted to come. He'd explained to Adrijana about the missing boy and the old man, and she'd listened. She didn't raise her voice or begin a new and complex lecture. She just listened, and when he was finished, she said, "I don't know anything about this. If someone I knew had them, or was even looking, I'd have heard."

"But you'll ask your people about it," Burim had said.

If Kadri was really threatening to expose their romance, he wanted it over. He wanted the threat lifted.

"I can't believe you just said 'your people.' Is that really where we are?"

"We're in danger."

"I'll see what I can do," Adrijana had said.

When Burim got the call from Kadri, he knew he had no choice but to go and pretend that everything was fine. Show that he didn't suspect he was suspected.

Burim reasoned that there was only one way through this, and that was for Enver to leave the country. Kadri was a punk and a drug trafficker, but as far as Burim knew, he wasn't a murderer. Though maybe he was. Stories from the old country blew north like leaves on a wind. There was no telling one from another. No way to know where each one came from.

There was another way, of course. It was for Enver to be arrested—to be locked in a cage where he belonged and where he'd leave everyone alone. But they'd still keep calling in favors. Keep saying that Burim's family owed him. That Burim was a soldier and needed to step up and serve the country.

And there was a final way. Enver could die.

Burim was afraid even to harbor these sorts of thoughts. He never had. It was just that one small favor, one peculiar but insignificant request, had morphed into larger ones. They grew and expanded, until last year he was holding half a kilo of heroin in a box that he'd placed in the middle of the kitchen table and stared at it. It was worth tens of thousands of kroner, this brown lump from Afghanistan—a country where a bunch of tribesmen grew poppies in open fields as helicopter gunships sniped at them by day and the Taliban came by at night for their cut. And there it was on his kitchen table, by the salt and pepper shakers, embraced in a cute little pink-and-blue hug that Adrijana had bought at some fancy kitchen store at Oslo City.

Then, a few days later, Kadri called and asked for the box. So Burim brought it to the Åpent Bakeri in an orange JanSport backpack that Adrijana would eventually find missing, and wonder how she could have been so dumb as to lose. He handed it to Kadri and, as though a malignant tumor had been excised, the Brick of Brown Doom was gone.

Later, there was not a trace of it except for the fifteen thousand kroner that Kadri eventually gave him. So Burim went to Paléet and bought some books for Adrijana, subscribed to eMusic.com for two years at their discount price, bought a new winter jacket for himself, and put the rest in their savings account.

Burim remembers walking out of the bank that afternoon near Majorstuen, arms laden with purchases, wondering what had just happened. He didn't quite understand, but some part of him knew that he'd signed a deal with people who didn't keep their promises. And the idea had filled him with dread.

Gjon gets down on one knee on dry dirt and opens a small green sack. He removes three large bowie knives with wooden handles and brass hilts.

Enver is on the phone. He does not tell them whom he is calling. When the call is over, Enver looks back at the man who was once his friend.

Gjon hands the knives to Burim and Enver. Both regard them with some confusion, each for different reasons.

Enver asks the question that Burim is also thinking. "What are we supposed to do with these?"

Gjon stands up, unlocks the trunk of the Mercedes, and puts the green bag back in place beside the spare tire and the bucket of cleaning materials.

Burim then hears Gjon answer in a way he'd never heard before.

"Whatever the hell you want, Enver. This is your mess! I want this done with. And then I want you and your bastard kid to fuck off and never come back."

Burim takes a step back with his knife.

Enver is motionless. Then he nods. Just nods. Then he asks Gjon for a cigarette. Gjon's shoulders droop slightly, and he reaches into his pocket to take out the soft pack of Marlboro Reds that was almost empty, and taps the pack against the first joint of his left hand to shake one loose.

American soldiers, he'd noticed, used to pack their cigarettes. They'd take one out and bang the filter against a table, or a rock, or a friend's helmet so the tobacco would compress and the white cigarette paper would form a hollow funnel at the end that burned fast and bright before the soldiers took their first drag.

Russian soldiers did the opposite. They rolled the cigarettes between thumb and forefinger so the tiny leaves separated and crinkled. Whatever the weather, the Russians cupped the match between their two hands from the bottom, shielding it so the wind wouldn't blow out the precious flame.

He hands one to Enver, who puts it in his lips.

"Light it for me," he says.

Enver is holding the bowie knife in his right hand.

Gjon slides his own blade into his belt and takes the Swedish matches from the pocket of his blue jeans.

He strikes a match along the side of the pack and immediately cups it like a Russian. He holds the flame in his hands as though he were cupping a small bird before release.

"Hold it higher for me," says Enver.

Gjon steps in closer and raises his hands closer to Enver's face. Close enough so that, even in the shadowed daylight, the flame glints off Enver's tired eyes.

As Enver leans forward to place the tip of the cigarette into Gjon's cupped hands, Burim sees the tip of the knife angled up to Gjon's torso.

Then, as the cigarette is lit, he sees the two men look hard at each other.

There have been so many conversations about what they call home. The smell of the land. The taste of the food. The values of the men and the memories of the women. They talk about those who are lost and what it is we owe the dead. What the Serbs did to them. If every recollection, every so-called fact, is not real, then at least the emotions are, and they come from memories that have been torn from life.

Burim had looked into history to find out what was true and what was myth. He had followed Adrijana to the library, and spent hours on the Internet looking up the names of villages he's heard them talk about. Bela Crkva. Meja. Velika Kruša. Djakovica. There had been Serbian massacres in every one of them. But Burim has never been to these places. Never experienced the killings. His debt to Enver, in particular, and to the cause of Kosovar independence — and dignity — is abstracted and distant.

Here in this tree-covered lane, two thousand kilometers from the whispered stories and the louder silences, Burim watches these two men stare into each other's eyes, and he sees for the first time how close death really is. What it is that terrifies Adrijana. What she smells on his clothes when he comes home at night. And what he brings into their bed with him. What stalks them is History.

Enver lights his cigarette and lifts his head. Gjon opens his palms and drops the burning match. It taps the ground and burns for a moment before being snuffed out.

Gjon does not look down at the knife. He does not step back, either. He just says to Enver, "What now?"

Enver takes a long pull on his cigarette and feels the hunger fade. Then he nods to Gjon. "Last night they sensed me, but they saw nothing. Today they rested, and we all waited for the old man and the boy. Tonight we take the house."

Last night in the cabin, Rhea stared into the woods for a good long time. Then she went outside and walked to the wood line. She couldn't see Enver watching her through the binoculars, staring at her, eyeing her black leather trousers, black boots, vintage leather jacket with steel zippers, bright blue eyes, and long black hair.

Watching her hips as she approached.

Far enough away to feel safe, but close enough to look carefully, she crouched down on the ground and started picking up small stones. And some not so small. She stood and pitched them into the woods. She wasn't aiming exactly in his direction. Instead, she was making a sweep.

But nothing happened. No flock of birds flew off. No deer rushed out. No dog with a limp hobbled out, looking for love. Just silence.

Rhea turned around and saw Lars, shrugged, and walked back to where he stood. She slapped him a few times on the chest. "Thanks for putting up with me."

And then, unexpectedly for Lars, she began to cry. It lasted only a minute before she wiped her tears, smiled, laughed a bit, and slapped him on the chest again.

"What a day!" she said.

Back inside, he fixed her a simple meal of pasta with tomato sauce from a jar. After dinner, he took off her clothes and helped her into a pair of striped pajamas. He shook out the duvet and pulled it up over her as she snuggled into the fetal position. He tucked in the edges to protect her against the cool night air and stroked her hair. He read her a short story from an ancient issue of *The New Yorker*. Then he opened the window a little so the room would be fresh, turned out the light, and retired to the living room to clean up and make sketches for a new video game he had in mind—one where you wander the famous sound stages of Hollywood with a giant gun, offing zombie versions of actors and other celebrities.

In the morning, Rhea awoke topless in bed with the covers pulled down as the rising sun warmed the cabin. Lars got up naked to make coffee on the iron stove. There were no neighbors for kilometers, so he went outside and ground the beans on the steps while looking out into the forest.

It was easy for Lars to imagine why Rhea got spooked. The path to the house is more than five hundred meters long, through a thicket that Rhea once likened to the ride of Ichabod Crane fleeing the headless Hessian. But Lars grew up here. He knows the trees, the animals, the sounds they make, and their rhythms by day and night. They change with the seasons, and the seasons come, one after the after, with all their unique pleasures and challenges. Things are not spooky by themselves, Lars decides; they need us.

They spend the day quietly. Lars insists.

*You had a miscarriage. And the next day our neighbor was murdered in our apartment. And your father is missing.*

*He's my grandfather.*

*He might as well be your father.*

*I suppose.*

*There's nothing we can do now but wait and rest. You need your strength. Your focus. We can play Scrabble in English. You can make up words and convince me they're real.*

*Why don't they release a missing-person report on him? Why don't they put his face all over the news?*

*Sigrid said it's because his name is the same as yours, and your name is on the door, and it's possible that if the killers know he is missing, they'll start to look for him, too. Maybe they'll wonder if he saw something. And they say the boy might be with him. If the killers are looking for the boy, and they know that Sheldon is missing, they'll know the police don't have him.*

*It all sounds a little convoluted.*

*It's like chess. This woman . . . Sigrid. She's cautious.*

*Does she think we're in danger?*

*No. The crime seems unconnected to us. And there is no way the kill-*

*ers should know about this house. All the same, the police in Kongsvinger know we're here. We should be safe.*

They wait for calls throughout the day, and rest.

At six in the evening, while the day is still inviting and warm, Enver Bhardhosh Berisha walks through the front door of their house with Burim and Gjon and heads directly to the refrigerator.

# PART III

# New River

# CHAPTER 15

THERE IS A NORWEGIAN poem in Sheldon's room, far away in Oslo. Rhea found it at an antiquarian bookshop in New York, and was struck by its power and its early use of free verse in translation. She photographed it, framed the print, and gave it to Lars as an anniversary present.

It hangs above the lamp by Sheldon's bedside table. When he sits on the bed and looks at the photos of his lost family, he sometimes turns away. When he does, his eyes fall on the poem.

It was written in 1912 and translated into English by a professor at the University of Minnesota. The university published it, in an obscure collection called *Poems of Modern Scandinavia*, seven years after Norway secured its independence from Sweden.

> *Norway. A gift*
> *to the wandering tribes who pressed*
> *ever northward into the sea-split orchestral tumult*
> *of salty shores and cragged earth*

*sheltering the gods that time forgot.*
*Wine spilling like children*
*through empty halls echoing*
*waiting, neverly for distant guests,*
*the fire and song rising,*
*still and bright into the ever darkening sky.*
*A proclamation to the eternal night.*
*A chorus of candles and spice.*
*We . . . they say. Children of the norlands,*
*with fathers buried in this earth's cradle.*
*All memory conspiring to a single story—*
*This . . . they say.*
*This is our land.*

This world is all around him now. He has never seen it before. They have been on the move for several hours. With a panoramic view from high on the tractor, he can recall the pictures that the poem created in his mind. He doesn't remember the exact words, but does sense its mood and the flow of its metaphors. It comes back to him now, because the wind blows against his face as the chassis shimmies beneath him, with Paul and the raft in tow. This land around him—so silent before—now begins to speak as Sheldon gazes out on it. He begins to sense that silence itself is a kind of language. There is more there than death and memory. More than the voices of the lost. There is something in Europe's silence that he has not heard before. But he will not live long enough to fully understand it. And so he holds this new insight as loosely as a poem found by accident. One with no title and no author. One experienced and never found again.

Defying age and gravity, he stands up straight and tall on the moving tractor and lets the world slip by underneath him. He watches the trees approach him, slowly at first, and then speed past.

He takes them on to Husvikveien, then Kirkeveien, then Froensveien. He turns them toward Årungveien and Mosseveien, and eventually out to the Rv 23 and the E18, where there is nothing between them and the gentle land that sways like the sea and says so much that Sheldon cannot comprehend.

Mario was putting a cloth to Sheldon's head as he opened his eyes.

"Donny, you OK?"

"I don't feel so good."

"A medic bandaged your leg. And put a note on your shirt."

"What does it say?"

"'Shot but OK.'"

"That seems clear enough."

"How did you get here?" Mario asked.

Donny thought about this. He had been shot on the water as he approached the seawall. He shot back. Then he'd passed out. Now he had a headache. Can a wound migrate?

"I got here by boat."

"What boat? By LST? I didn't see you on the boat."

"No. A little boat. A life raft. I borrowed it from the Aussies. I must have washed up. Or someone pulled me. Who knows."

"That's why you're wet?"

"Yes, Mario. That's why I'm wet."

"Can you stand up?"

"I think so."

Donny wasn't sure what time it was or how much time had passed since the troops had secured the three beaches. T-34 tanks were in formation, crouched still and low on the beach, cooling and hungry. A MASH unit had already been set up. Above him, he could see the Korean lighthouse at Palmi-do. It was high tide, and the sun gleamed off the hulls of the landing craft. Men were smoking. It was all rather calm.

Mario pulled Donny up until they stood eye to eye, and both smiled.

"It's nice to see you," Mario said.

"Don't get all sappy on me."

"We should take a picture."

"Of what?"

"Us."

"Why?"

"We're brothers in arms! We take a picture and show our sons someday, so they'll be proud of us."

"You actually think we're going to meet girls?"

"Me, yes. You . . . maybe a nice cow. Or a duck. They say ducks make excellent lovers."

"Do they?"

"Yes," said Mario. "And when the relationship sours, you can eat them."

"Where's the camera?"

Mario took off his backpack and pulled out a Leica IIIc. It was stainless steel and shiny, with a sharkskin grip. He handed it to Donny.

"I don't know how to use it."

So Mario taught Donny how to adjust the shutter speed, take the white balance, and set the aperture. All the while, the American, Canadian, and South Korean forces hustled to clear the debris of battle from the beach and the water. They hammered at supply centers and heaved hard at the docks. As the two young men talked about the intimate clicks and clacks of the camera, behind them Inchon was being transformed into a northern operations base against the communist forces.

"You get it now?" Mario asked.

"I suppose."

"Take one of me first."

They heard gunshots in the distance—some vague sense that fighting was continuing over the hills, engaging the last of the local resistance, as Mario walked backward to his mark. Donny's hands were sticky from the oily sea, and he wiped his sandy fingers on his wet pants so he wouldn't ruin Mario's camera.

When he put the camera up to his eye, it occurred to him that he had never looked through a camera before. Perhaps on some distant day he might have fooled with one. But he had never looked. Every time he'd looked through a viewfinder, it was the scope of a rifle.

The first time was a target at New River, North Carolina, where he trained with the Marines near Camp Lejeune, and he always had an itch he was trained not to scratch.

*It'll give away your position and get you killed. Any questions?*

His class of Raiders consisted of fifteen volunteers. They shot targets for five weeks. They learned scouting, patrolling, map reading, demolitions, camouflage, and how to shoot with a scope. They learned immobility, misdirection, balance, resistance to impulse, breathing, and control. Sheldon was taught to slow the beating of his own heart.

They learned range and wind and light. They talked about rifles and ammunition and gunsmithing and girls. They debated jazz and car engines. They fought over cigarettes. They learned to swear and how to insult each other's ethnic and religious groups, and invented a highly specialized vocabulary to describe character types.

Snarf: A boy who sniffs girls' bicycle seats.

Twerp: One who inserts false teeth between cheeks of his ass.

They practiced killing people, in preparation for the time when such knowledge would prove handy.

For the sniper, the index finger was an instrument of death. But with the Leica he was being asked by his buddy to hold steady and use his training to find a composition in the image he saw, not a target. To use his finger to make that composition immortal, not to destroy it. To bring a moment into being, not to force its end.

Holding that camera in his hands only hours after killing men over a dawn sea, Donny felt transformed.

The sense of wonder, of humility, and of simple pleasure in setting the lens to take a photo was all immediate. Mario had once talked to him about the transubstantiation, when the wafer and the wine become the body and blood of Christ. Until holding the camera in his hands, he had always mocked Mario for the absurdity of it. Now, looking down the barrel of the lens, he believed such a thing might be possible.

He smiled at Mario. "Let's make it a good one," he shouted.

In the upper left-hand corner, in what would eventually be a black-and-white photograph, was the lighthouse. Mario was slightly lower, to the right. The shore and the dark sea were to the left, and on the extreme right were the dunes, extending back to the rise that eventually led to Palmi-do. Everything seemed set, but the composition didn't look quite right.

"Take a few steps back," Donny said. "I don't want your feet cut off."

Mario gave this no thought. He didn't pause, didn't push back against Sheldon's presumption that he should be the one to move. Why should he? Mario was a soft-hearted and kind person who didn't see his friendship with Donny as a competition for dominance. He was an Italian boy on a distant shore at a victorious battle with few dead, and here was his lost friend holding his undamaged and favorite camera, ready to commemorate the moment.

For sixty years, Sheldon will ask himself a question. He will ask it when he repairs watches and when he is on his near-nightly rides with the Riverines after Saul's death. He will ask it when Mabel leaves a restaurant table for the powder room and he fiddles with his cutlery. It is a question he will not be able to answer until now, here in Norway, as memories, once safely cloistered, assert themselves and change their character. As they emerge from secret places in a hall closet and demand to be disclosed. All of it reminding him that, soon enough, he will have to face it all.

The question he will ask himself is why he told Mario to step backward rather than doing so himself.

Someone had to move; that much was clear. The lens on the Leica didn't zoom at the press of a button. There was no telephoto lens. He couldn't twist his wrist and bring the world closer or send it farther away. Back then, his relationship to the world was fixed. It was seen as it was through a 50-millimeter lens. Back then, we captured what we experienced.

That someone, however, did not necessarily have to be Mario. Donny himself could have stepped back a few yards. If he had been the one to move, Mario might have been perfectly framed. And if Mario had stepped back, the result would have been the same.

So why did he ask Mario to move, rather than do it himself?

*I was sticky and uncomfortable and edgy, and had a wound in my leg, and I didn't want to go anywhere.* This was one answer. He tried using it for years, but it lacked conviction. *I was always somehow the elder with Mario. Always playing the wise one. Maybe it was part of our game that he should move and I shouldn't, that he should obey my instructions, rather than me taking the steps for him.*

All of this was true. But none of it mattered. It may have made the request more natural, but this wasn't the source of the impulse. Donny had nothing to prove with Mario.

The lighthouse at Palmi-do was small and stubby and white, offset against the gray and overcast sky. It was calm and unmoving against the bustle of foreigners creating a new world around it. It was steadfast in a world of change. It soothed him. It was . . . beautiful.

He did not want to move. He did not want anything ever to change.

The beauty of that eternal moment, passing through Donny, killed Mario.

No one knows what Mario stepped on. It was probably unexploded ordnance. Whatever it was, it needed only his gentle footfall to upset it.

The explosion blew Mario into the air. Whether it was coincidence or the startling impact of the shock wave, Donny will never know. But whatever the cause, it was just enough for his finger to depress the shutter at the very instant of the explosion, catching something horrible on film and forever.

In 1955, he opened Mario's camera, found the film, and developed it. This was the year that Sheldon set off around the world with the Leica. There was only one photograph on the roll. It was not a photograph he ever published. He never showed it to Mabel. He never so much as hinted at its existence, or explained the power it had over him—how it set him off to wander through Europe, to visit the capitals and the camps.

Rhea does not know it, but the photo is here in Norway. It is in a thick manila envelope at the top of his closet, along with forty or fifty others that no one has ever seen. Most are photos of Saul as a baby, a toddler, a preschooler. Some are of Mabel.

One, beneath all the others, shows his old friend Mario being pushed off the earth, his two legs already disconnected from his body, a white lighthouse in the corner, and a smile still on his face.

# CHAPTER 16

O H, CRAP," says Sheldon.

In the tractor's left side mirror is the least intimidating police car that Sheldon has ever seen. It is a white Volvo station wagon with single red-and-blue stripes down the sides. It exudes no sense of doom. It commands as much respect as a high school hall monitor would.

And yet, inside it is a cop with a radio.

Sheldon considers his options. He cannot outrun the police officer. He cannot hide. Fighting would be both impossible and completely inappropriate.

The eternal wisdom of the United States Marine Corps immediately returns to him in the voice of his drill sergeant.

*When you have only one option, you have yourself a plan!*

The nemesis emerging from the police car is a slightly overweight gentleman in his late fifties, with a pleasant face and a relaxed composure. He does not carry a weapon and does not look especially bothered.

Sheldon hears the man say something polite to Paul, but from this angle he can't see Paul or hear his response, if there was one. Most likely, he has just sunk lower into the raft without replying.

Sheldon takes a breath and gets himself into character as the officer comes up to the side of the tractor.

The policeman speaks Norwegian.

Sheldon does not. Nor, however, does he opt for English.

*God ettermiddag*, says the polite officer.

*Gut'n tog!* replies Sheldon, enthusiastically, in Yiddish.

*Er du fra Tyskland?* asks the officer.

*Jo! Dorem-mizrachdik*, says Sheldon, hoping that this still means "southeast," as it did fifty years ago when he last used the term, while also assuming that "Tyskland" means Germany in Norwegian.

*Vil du snakke engelsk?* asks the officer, who apparently does not speak German, or the language that Sheldon is pretending is German.

"I speak little English," says Sheldon, trying not to sound too much like either Wernher von Braun or Henry Kissinger.

"Ah, good. I speak a little English too," says the officer. He continues in what he surely has no idea is Sheldon's native language. "I thought maybe you were American," he says.

*Amerikanisch?* answers Sheldon in what might be Yiddish. "No, no. German. Und Swiss. Ya. Vhy let zem off da hook. In Norway wit mine grandson. Only speaks Swiss. Dumb kid."

"Interesting outfit he's wearing there," says the police officer.

"Wiking. Likes Norway very much."

"I see," says the officer. "Interesting, though, that he has a big Jewish star on his chest."

"Ah, yeah. Studied Jews and Wikings in school ze same veek if you can tink of a reason vhy. Vanted to be both. I am grandfather. How to say no? Last veek Greeks. Next veek maybe Samurai. You have grandchildren?"

"Me? Oh, ya. Six."

"Six. Christmas is very expensive."

"Oh, ya. The girls only want pink things, and nothing is the right size. And how many cars can you buy for a boy?"

"Buy the boy a watch. He'll remember. The Christmas and you. Time is against us old men. We might as well embrace it."

"That's a fine idea. A fine idea indeed."

Sheldon asks, "Am I driving too fast?"

The officer smiles. "Not too fast, no. Have a nice day."

"*Danke.* Nice day for you, too."

As the Volvo drives off, Sheldon puts the tractor in gear.

"Hold on back there," he shouts to Paul. "We're going to find someplace to bunk down for the night. And we need to ditch this rig."

Saul returned from his first tour of duty on a Pan Am commercial jet from Saigon to San Francisco. He was twenty-two years old. Eighteen hours before boarding the plane in civilian clothing, with a novel by Arthur C. Clarke in his jacket pocket, he had shot a VC with his M-16. The man, dressed in black, was in a squad of three who were setting up a mortar. The engine on Saul's boat was off, and they were drifting. The Monk saw the VC first and nodded in their direction. Saul wasn't a sharpshooter like his father, but he was the first to distinguish the shape of the men from the shadows of the trees and the light from the canopy. He fired a burst of three rounds, and one of them hit the unknown person in the stomach. The other men scattered. The Marines went ashore afterward and collected the mortar. They found the VC that Saul shot. He had a second bullet in his head, put there at close range.

The boat puttered back to port after the mission. There was a small farewell celebration for Saul, involving beer, rock music, and dirty jokes. After dropping off his gear and rifle, filling out a pile of paperwork, and slipping into the clothes he'd come with to Vietnam, he was taken by bus to the airport and sent off to America.

Or a kind of America.

He read his book on the plane and fought sleep. There could be no peaceful sleep, because he had not known a truly peaceful sleep in two years. He often had nightmares about the things he'd seen and done. He suffered from the way his mind tried to make sense of it all. The hum of the plane's cabin was seductive, and lulled Saul into a reverie, which was a dangerous place. Because reverie is the land where monsters dwell.

He watched other men drink the free vodka and cognac. He thought to do the same, but his Jewish DNA conspired against him. The alcohol would only make him sleepy without bringing release.

Saul looked at a man across the aisle for some kind of recognition. He had a strong chest and neck, and wore gray slacks and a wrinkled blue shirt. Three tiny bottles of gin sat on the tray in front of him, and he had no reading material. He felt Saul looking, and looked back. Their eyes met briefly, but then he turned away.

The America he landed in was San Francisco in 1973, filled with colors and music, interracial couples, and flamboyant homosexuals. No one spat on him or called him a baby killer. But as he walked past them with his crewcut and duffle bag, and they walked past him with their long hair and tinted glasses, each regarded the other as some kind of odd and exotic animal, as distant and unfamiliar as a creature from a mystical zoo.

The only experience he could liken it to was landing in Vietnam two years before. He'd met the riffraff of conscripted America at boot camp, but it didn't prepare him for the layers, patterns, and perplexities he found in Vietnam. For the interweaving stories and motives, moods and memories, of all these people.

He didn't understand the Navy. He didn't understand Saigon. He couldn't make sense of the silent shopkeepers or the treasonous VC. He was confused by the communists and their Buddhist families.

He tried to see some glint of familiarity in the eyes of a woman —a teenager, really—as she shot at him, a month after he arrived, from beside a thatched hut in a muddy village, and just before she was burned alive in a torrent of fire spewed from the flamethrower carried by the Monk.

Custom dictated that Saul thank him after this took place. He had opened his mouth to try, but the Monk just turned away.

He understood—vaguely, and with partial information pieced

together from the papers and the military and former soldiers and rumors and newsreels—what the war was about. But he had no idea what these people were about. Somehow the war was the product of what all these people were doing when they woke up each morning. But what they did seemed insane, and so the war—the term used for the theater piece he was involved in—became an abstraction, just as it became more vivid and tangible.

Unable to understand the big picture, he tried to take in the small story lines. The relationship with a buddy. The reason the colonel was rumored to cry himself to sleep. What his father might make of all this.

On the plane ride home, he imagined different ways he might discuss these things with his father, who had spent years in Korea with the Marines. They'd be more than father and son when he returned. They'd also be veterans of foreign wars: American vets who'd seen action—boys who'd passed through a looking glass. They were both altered, and permitted by ancient and universal tribal law to speak in new ways, and to command respect and authority that are not permitted to those who haven't been baptized in the fires of war.

Over time, Saul was able to sort out the people he met in Vietnam, and learned to place them in categories. These are on my side. And those are not. These can be reasoned with. And those cannot. Eventually, a category emerged that he could slot himself into. It was a box that was built by his father, and it was labeled—on the outside at least—*Patriotic Jew*. Inside, it was filled with stuff that neither of them could ever have imagined. Sheldon had stocked it with ideas from a past war and a past era. Saul just filled it with nightmares and impressions.

Saul was in San Francisco for only one night before heading back east. He took a cab to a cheap motel near the airport, and watched TV all night while drinking Coke and Fanta from the minibar. Between eight and eleven, he watched *All in the Family*, the second half of *Emergency*, *Mary Tyler Moore*, and *The Bob Newhart Show*, and then fell asleep in the middle of *Mission: Impossible*. He had crossed the International Date Line, and it was only the second time he'd experienced jet lag. He slept with his shoes on. The dirt from Vietnam soiled the motel bed covers.

He was out-processed the next day in a surprisingly brief visit to the base, and before he could realize that he was now a civilian with nothing to do and no one to report to, he was already on a plane to New York.

When he arrived at the front door of the apartment in Gramercy, the sun was high and the city smelled good. He looked at the doorbell with his parents' name on it—a name he momentarily forgot was also his own—and considered whether to press it.

Without knowing why, or stopping to question the impulse, he turned and went away.

"He should be here by now," Sheldon had said to Mabel, who sat on the living room sofa with both feet tucked underneath her, reading the *New York Times* Sunday magazine. It was already very late.

"We didn't set a time."

"We set a day. According to my perfectly serviced watch, that day is going to be over in less than an hour. And then he'll be late."

"He's been through a lot."

"I know what he's been through."

"No, Sheldon. You don't."

"What do you know about what I know about?"

"Vietnam isn't Korea."

"What's not Korean about it?"

"All I'm saying is that you can't presume to know what he's been through just because he walks through the door looking the same."

"That's what you did to me."

"You were a clerk."

"You don't know what I was."

Mabel tossed the magazine on the floor and raised her voice.

"Well, what the hell were you, then? First it's one thing and then it's another. You want my respect? You want my sympathy? You want me to understand why you shout 'Mario' in your sleep? Then tell me."

"I did what I was told to do. That's all you need to know."

"Because that's how men act?"

"You wouldn't understand."

"I'm going to bed."

"I'm staying up until he gets home."

"Why? So he can come home from a war and you can tell him, first thing out of your mouth, that he's late?"

"Go to bed, Mabel."

"Aren't you looking forward to seeing him?"

"I don't know."

Mabel was angry, and walked to the bedroom door.

"I don't even know what that means, Sheldon. I really don't."

"I don't either."

While his parents were arguing, Saul was on the last number 5 train from Union Square out to Beverly Road in Flatbush, Brooklyn. He stared down at his hands during the whole trip.

The woman who would eventually become Rhea's mother lived on the second floor of her parents' house, on a plot of land so small that residents in the bathrooms of the adjacent homes could have handed each other rolls of toilet paper without getting up.

Saul's clothes were a little too big for him; he'd lost twenty pounds on the Mekong River. He stood in front of the dark house staring up at the window, the way he did when he was a teenager hoping to get laid. They'd met on a bus four years ago. In the fumbling way of adolescents, they neither chose nor rejected each other. As the relationship continued, they were unable to pull one another close or let go because it all seemed so *significant*. So they kept at it. They cheated and repented. Then he went to Vietnam.

Saul picked up a pebble and tossed it at the window. It could just as well have been a grenade. There'd be an explosion in the window and then he'd return to the boat. But it wasn't a grenade. It was a pebble.

She opened the window almost immediately and looked down.

*I guess all the guys do this*, he thought.

"Well, I'll be damned," she said.

"Probably," Saul said.

She was wearing a ripped T-shirt from a band he'd never heard of that hung loosely off her body. Her face looked especially pale. From the light of the street lamp he could make out the contours of her breasts.

"So you're back."

"Whatever the hell that means."

"What do you want?"

"I want to see you."

"You mean you want to fuck me. Big soldier back from the war with a hard-on. Right?"

"Baby, I don't know what I want until after it's over."

For some reason, this made her smile.

"Come in the back."

And so he did.

When he was on top of her, and inside her, and his hands were gripping her thighs and his eyes were closed, he heard her say, "If I get pregnant, it's yours, you understand?"

In that moment, he thought she meant that the baby would be his and not someone else's. That she hadn't been with another man recently. That there was still something between them. That the past was secure.

In a few months' time, as the baby grew, Saul would be dead. He would never understand that she had not been talking about the past. She had been explaining the future.

The old watchmaker was asleep in his living room chair when Saul came in the next morning at seven-thirty. He'd been kicked out of her bedroom early, so her parents wouldn't know he'd spent the night there. She insisted that, since she paid rent, she could do whatever she wanted in her upstairs apartment, but her father used vocabulary from a different age. He talked about what happened "under his roof" and how "no daughter of mine" would bring "shame to the family."

There was no engaging this language with the vernacular of 1973. So they played the game and talked past each other, and hoped that the consequences would be manageable. With the pregnancy, all that would change. Nothing was manageable anymore. Some of this dynamic with her parents—had Rhea known it—might have explained what she would eventually hope to learn but never would. This enigmatic woman had been a stranger to Saul, and would remain one to Rhea.

Saul stepped quietly into the apartment so as not to wake anyone. He carried his green canvas duffle bag on his left shoulder as he struggled—as he used to—to free the key from the deadbolt. The trick was to turn it slightly off-center clockwise and give it a jiggle.

As he worked the lock, the smell of the house worked its way into him and made him suddenly nauseated. A thought he hadn't articulated until now came to him as powerfully as the scents of his childhood.

*I can't do this.*

Just then, as his mind was able to put words to the sensation, his father spoke.

"Welcome home."

The key was freed, and Saul closed the front door. He stepped to his right and looked into the living room, which was unchanged from the last time he had stepped into it. His father wore shapeless, colorless clothes, and his face was drawn and tired.

Saul put the duffle bag down by the umbrella stand and stretched his shoulders. He took a deep breath, pulling the past into his lungs, where it didn't belong.

"Thanks."

His father did not get up.

"You look OK," he said.

"Yeah," said Saul. "I do."

"You hungry? Want some coffee?"

"No, I don't think so."

"You don't think so, or no?"

"I don't know the difference."

"Sit down." Sheldon gestured to the sofa, where Mabel had been curled up with her magazine.

His father's calm was reassuring, as though he understood what might have happened over there. But he never understood what his father had done in Korea. He'd asked before, and all his father had said was "I did what I was told to do," which wasn't much help. It was more important now to learn what they might have in common. What his father understood. What was understandable at all.

"How are you doing?" Sheldon asked.

Saul slumped back into the overstuffed sofa cushions, but still visibly shrugged.

"I don't know. I'm not completely here yet."

Sheldon nodded. "I took off with the camera when I got back. You might need to do something."

"I guess."

"You thought about it?"

"I haven't even started thinking about it." Saul paused, and then asked, "What do you think of it?"

"I don't think about it."

"It's not a choice. I saw stuff, Dad. I did stuff. There's no putting it in a box. I need to figure it out."

"You did what you did, and you saw what you saw, because your country asked you to. You did your service. You did what men do. And now it's over. You try and get back to it all. That's all there is."

"I know what burning people smell like."

"And now it's over."

"It's still in my clothes."

"Then wash them."

"That's not the point."

"It has to be the point. You know what's going on out there? There aren't many like you. You need to step out of Vietnam and step into America and get into character."

"There are tens of thousands like me."

"Not Jews."

"What the hell does that have to do with anything?"

"Everything. We fought like hell in World War II. We tripped over ourselves to sign up. But in Korea, not as many. And now? Every Jew is in college. Out there, protesting the war. Civil rights, rock-and-roll, smoking pot. We're not pulling our weight. We're getting weak. We're losing the ground we made."

"Dad." Saul rubbed his face. "For Christ's sake, Dad. What do you think's going on out there?"

"What's going on? America's at war. And rather than get behind our country, we're talking like the communists."

"Dad. Dad, this country's a mess. There are different ways to try and make it better. And besides, we have nothing to prove anymore. I was born here. You were born here. Your parents were born here. How American do we need to be?"

"There are still firms on Wall Street that won't hire us. There are law firms that don't want us."

"In the South they're still killing black kids."

"This country has a lot of ground to cover. I know that. But we've still got ground to cover ourselves. Ground to hold."

"What happened to you in Korea?"

"I did what I was told."

"Mom says you were a clerk."

"That's what I want Mom to say."

"So, basically, men don't talk about it. Who *do* you tell? What about Bill?"

"Bill was there, too."

"Not with you."

"No. He was Armor. He was somewhere else. We met afterward. On the street. Near the shops."

"You talk to Bill?"

"I talk to Bill every day. I can't get him out of my shop. I have to lock the door. And when I do, he just calls me."

"Maybe he has a crush on you."

Sheldon snorted. "That's the kind of thing your generation says."

"It happens."

"You take things and turn them into things they aren't, and then insist you're right and that everyone else is blind. That's what the communists do."

"I don't know who the communists are, Dad."

"They were the ones shooting at you. Who want you enslaved to their own view of the world. Who put people in the Gulag for independent thought. For being free. For not upholding the imperatives of the state and the revolution."

"Everyone was shooting at me. I don't know why."

"You sound like Mario."

"Who's Mario?"

"Doesn't matter."

"Who's Mario?"

"A friend."

"Anyone I know?"

"He died before you were born. You don't need to know about it."

"I saw a lot of stuff, Dad. I did a lot of stuff."

"I know. You hungry? You want coffee?"

"I think I want to tell you what I did."

"I don't want to know."

"Why not?"

"Because you're my son, that's why not."

"I want to tell you because you're my father and you might understand."

"Your country is grateful, that's all that matters."

"My country isn't grateful, and it doesn't matter at all. I need to figure out how to sit here."

"You need a distraction."

"Like repairing watches?"

"That's so awful?"

"You can't fix time, Dad."

"You should eat something. You've lost weight. You look sickly."

"I am sickly."

Sheldon said nothing.

"Where's Mom?"

"She's sleeping."

Saul hoisted himself up from the sofa cushions and walked up the stairs, two at a time. Sheldon didn't move. He sat for ten minutes, waiting for Saul to return. He assumed that Saul was going to see his mother. He wouldn't learn for many years that he had simply gone upstairs to sit. To look over the banister as he did as a child to see who just rang the doorbell or what kind of mood Dad was in when he came home from work.

When Saul came back downstairs, he sat across from his father in the wing-backed armchair where his mother often sat with a book or to watch television.

"How have you been?" he asked his father.

"Me? I've been working hard. Minding my own business. Trying to stay out of trouble."

"Yeah, but how have you been?"

"I just told you."

"What did you think about when you came home from Korea?"

"Why?"

"Because I'm home from a war, too, and I want to know what you thought about. I want to know if it's the same."

"When I came back from Korea, I thought about Korea. Then I thought about thinking about Korea, and realized it was a waste of time, so I stopped."

"How long did that take?"

"Don't be a sissy, Saul!"

"You took a camera and went to Europe."

"Yes."

"What did you find there?"

"It was nine years after World War II. You know what I found there."

"You didn't just go there to take funny pictures of them, did you?"

"Sure I did. And I was good at it."

"You hated them, didn't you? Each and every anti-Semitic one of them, didn't you? You went to look into their souls to see it for yourself. To document it, because you couldn't put them in a rifle sight and shoot them."

"Where do you come up with this stuff?"

"I had time on the boat."

"You want to know what I found in Europe? I found silence. An awful, dreadful silence. There wasn't a single Jewish voice left. None of our children. Just a couple of meek, shell-shocked hangers-on who hadn't left or been murdered. And Europe just closed up the wound. Filled that silence with their Vespas and Volkswagens and croissants, like nothing had happened. You want psychology? OK. I probably pissed them off to let them know I was still there. To get a reaction from them."

"What did this have to do with Korea?"

"Everything! It made me proud. It made me proud to be American. It made me proud to have fought for my country. It reminded me that the tribes of Europe will always be just that. Tribes. You want to call them nations? Go ahead. But they're a bunch of petty tribes. America isn't a tribe. It's an idea! And I'm part of that idea. And so are you. How have I been? I've been proud that you're fighting for your country. That you're defending the dream. My son is defending the dream. My son is an American. My son has a rifle in his hand and is facing down the enemy. That's how I've been."

Saul did not answer right away. Sheldon did not fill the lull.

"Where are the pictures?" Saul asked.

"What pictures?"

"All the pictures you took."

"They're in the book."

"Those are the ones you picked. Where are the rest?"

Normally, his father had his response ready, fired out the second there was an opening. This time, Saul had caught him off-guard.

*Yes, there are more pictures. Important pictures. Pictures that are never far from me.*

"I'm the photographer. I decide what's a picture and what isn't."

"If it isn't a picture, what is it?"

"Did you do any work on that boat at all?"

"I want to see the other photos."

"No."

"Maybe someday?"

"I didn't say there are any more."

"Has Mom seen them?"

"She hasn't been sitting on a boat long enough to come up with the question."

"What made you come back?"

"You were the one who was away. Why are you asking me all these questions? I feel like I'm on *The Dick Cavett Show.*"

"You took a thousand photographs across a half-dozen countries. Then, one day, you come home. Why?"

"Because the war was over and everyone was dead. I couldn't go back to the war, and my friends weren't coming out of it. So I grew up and moved on."

"Which war?"

"Enough, Saul, please."

Saul tried to fill in what his father couldn't or wouldn't express. "They weren't coming back from Korea," he began. "But you also mean the ones who went off to fight in 1941. Who left you behind in America. You watched it all happen when you were a kid. The older brothers of your friends. Your cousin Abe. You were the youngest, and you were left behind. And so you signed up to go to Korea."

"Saul," said Sheldon, growing quieter. "I didn't go off to the wrong war. I went off to the next right one. The communists killed millions. Millions and millions of people. When I joined up, Stalin was running the Soviet Union and developing nuclear weapons to be aimed at us. The only reason we don't think of Stalin with the same hatred as we do of Hitler is because we were subjected to a massive propaganda campaign during the war, trying to convince us that 'Uncle Joe' was a hero for giving us a second front. But Uncle Joe had signed a secret pact with Hitler, and Russia was only on our side because Germany attacked it. They weren't our eastern front. We were their western one."

"Mom said you used to cry sometimes when she held me as a baby."

"You're really going too far."

"Why?"

"Who taught you to talk like this?"

"People my age talk. Just tell me why."

"Because when I looked at your mother holding you, here in America, I could see the women in Poland who clutched their children to their naked chests in the gas chambers and told them to breathe deeply so they wouldn't suffer. Infants who still smiled at their executioners. Squeezed their fingers in line to their own deaths. And it filled me with rage."

"You came back from Europe because there was nothing you could do," said Saul.

Sheldon nodded.

"What do I do now, Dad?"

"We're alive because of this country. All its madness. Its history. Its problems. It's still our champion and our future. We owe it our very lives. So we protect it from harm and help it grow up right."

"I know," said Saul.

"And this country is at war."

"I know."

"I'm not sure how to honor our dead if we don't protect the only place that gave us shelter. If we don't work to make it a better place."

"I'm gonna go to my room now."

"OK."

"I love you, Dad."

Sheldon just nodded.

Less than a week later, Saul was gone, and shortly after that he was dead. He'd left a brief note on the kitchen table saying that he'd signed up for a second tour of duty and was going to be reassigned to the same crew. He'd write, and it was wonderful to have seen them both. He loved his parents. He hoped his father was proud of him, and he looked forward to the day when the war was over.

# CHAPTER 17

I KILLED MY SON, BILL. He's dead because he loved me."

"He loved you very much."

"I've always remembered that morning as a fight. I guess it wasn't."

"No. He wasn't looking for an argument. He didn't have a side to argue."

"I don't know how to talk without arguing."

"It's part of your charm."

"What should I have done?"

"You mean, when he came in? Started questioning you?"

"Yeah."

"You should have hugged him and said how you felt."

"I did say how I felt."

"No, you didn't."

"What do you know?"

"Who do you think you're talking to?"

"So how did I feel?"

"You felt love and relief. You loved him so much you had to keep your distance."

"You talk like a girl."

"That feeling—in your hands. The one that makes you clench your fists sometimes. Do you know what that is?"

"It's arthritis."

"You never touched him. That last time. In your living room. He was right there. And you never held him. Never touched his hands. Never put your palm against his cheek like you used to do when he was a baby. You never pressed your cheek against his. That's what you wanted to do. He was such a beautiful boy. Can you remember? He glowed with the eternal. And you didn't touch him. And you can't get the feeling of it out of your hands."

"What feeling?"

"The emptiness. You told him about the silence. You never told him about the emptiness."

"You're a real killjoy, Bill. You know that?"

"The lake is coming up. Now's your chance to hide the tractor."

"Yup."


They have been traveling for fifty kilometers. There on the left, and coming up slowly, is Rødenessjøen. It is a small lake in Akershus, and it is Sheldon's planned destination for the day. They have been on the road for hours. The boy is probably hungry, and he's certain they both need to pee.

What Sheldon is planning to do would best be done at night, under the cover of darkness. The time of day when most *farkakta* ideas get a second look and start to seem better than they did a few hours earlier.

With an aching back and stiff hands, Sheldon pulls the tractor to the side of a quiet, wooded street and turns off the engine. He waits a full minute before gingerly stepping down the full meter to the pavement.

Paul is napping in the raft. He has not taken off the Viking helmet, and his right hand clutches the long wooden spoon. The magic dust bunny is safely tucked under one of the bench seats. Sheldon smiles and chooses not to wake him.

Standing back from the rig, he notices how tall the tractor really is. The top of it must be a good two meters high. The tires alone come up to the middle of his chest. It isn't an easy item to hide — you can't put an orange tarp over it and hope it goes unnoticed.

This is farm country. He does not know the people, their mentality, their ways of getting through the day. But the trappings of this place resonate, and he suspects they are not as foreign as their language. People here probably know one another. There are likely to be only a few schools, and they'd cater to a wide age range of children. Families would be familiar with each other's children. Cars and maybe even livestock would be known to belong to particular locals.

They are not far from Oslo, and this is not a desperately rural terrain. It is, however, a place where people form tighter bonds and speak, not of "real estate," but of the land.

So the cover of night would have been better. Because this is definitely the kind of place where people would notice a tractor that didn't belong here. It is probably also the kind of place where they'd talk if they saw someone drive one into the lake.

Once again, as has so often happened in Sheldon's life, there really does seem to be only one reasonable course of action. As Paul rests in the boat, Donny stares at his amphibious recreational unit and considers the situation. The most important fact is that he was pulled over by a local cop. He was asked if he was American. There are two good explanations for that. One — which he doesn't believe for a second — is that his fake German-Swiss accent wasn't good enough to fool Barney Fife back there. No chance on earth he could sense that Sheldon was from New England.

None.

The other explanation is more troubling, and more plausible.

For Paul's sake, he has not turned on the television, so he does not know whether the Oslo police have issued a missing-person alert on him—assuming that such things exist here. But it's possible that they have, and that Rhea is behind it. Even if they haven't, they could certainly have alerted other police stations about him and the boy. It's possible that he was stopped because he fitted some profile.

Like, for example, "Foreign old man with young boy."

But maybe he got lucky. Maybe they said, "American old man and young boy missing." In that case, he and Paul didn't fit the profile.

Who knows? In any case, it all points to the same conclusion: this tractor is going to be trouble, and needs to go in the drink.

He steps back to the raft and releases it at four points from the trailer frame. He checks carefully to be sure nothing is connected or would obstruct it from detaching itself when the time comes.

When he is satisfied, he starts up the tractor again. As the beast coughs and gurgles, Paul wakes up. Sheldon can tell because he can see silver horns in the mirror. He turns around and waves. Paul, he is delighted to find, waves back.

He pulls back onto the road now and, staying in first gear, drives along slowly, looking for a parallel, secondary path along the lake. This does not take long. The absence of power steering makes the hard-left turn a challenge, so he leans into it like a bus driver on a city street. The tractor falls right in line, and soon they are chugging along the western side of the small lake.

In five minutes, a nice open space emerges, and Sheldon executes a sweeping left-hand turn away from the lake, then swings the wheel all the way to the right, bringing her in face-to-face with stage two of Operation Hide the Tractor.

It is all working perfectly. All he has to do now is drive straight into the lake. If it is deep enough, and the tractor lives long enough, it will disappear below the surface where it belongs, and the raft will gently drift off the trailer onto the clear and bright water, where Paul can start the engine and sail off into the distance alone, because Sheldon will end up at the bottom of the lake, behind the wheel of the tractor.

This is not a perfectly devised plan as such.

A stick would do it. He could wedge the stick under the seat and onto the gas pedal. That would probably work.

The trouble then—which has been the same trouble he's been facing for three days—is that he is eighty-two. How exactly is he to get on the moving raft? Outrun it? Dive onto it as it rushes by? Have Paul hook out an arm and wrestle him up like a rodeo cowboy?

Once again, logic dictates the final conclusion: *I'm going to get very, very wet.*

Over the course of five minutes, Sheldon stands on the ground talking to Paul, the Balkan Jewish Viking in the raft. They both have their hands on their hips. Sheldon points and gestures. He explains and draws pictures on his palm. He makes quizzical faces and explains the odds.

Paul nods.

Sheldon smiles.

It is all going to work out just fine.

So he starts the engine and wedges the stick under the seat—and if he'd been a Christian, he would have made a cross, or kissed one—and off goes the whole contraption toward the water.

It can all end badly. Someone might notice and think there has been an accident. Helicopters and TV people arriving would be counter to the spirit of the operation. Sheldon might swim after the raft and, having not swum in thirty years, drown. None of which would be ideal.

Perhaps, if Bill showed up, he could drive the tractor. But Bill does not show up. The man's timing is self-serving and capricious.

As it turns out, it does not go badly. In fact, it goes surprisingly well.

Not only does Paul laugh, thereby making his first sound since the death of his mother, but as the raft detaches from the trailer, it floats *backward* a little, on account of the waves made by the tractor.

By wading in up to his knees, Sheldon is able to grab hold of a tow line and pull the raft back toward shore, where, with only minor difficulty, he hoists his leg over its side and flops into it.

The tractor fights against its watery grave, but to no avail. Steam rises from the lake, which bubbles and burps, but eventually digests its meal whole.

Sheldon lies panting at the bottom of the raft. Looking up into the sky, he is shocked by how tired he has become. Really, what just happened? Not much by a young man's standards, but apparently more than usual for him.

"Old people really should be in better shape," he says.

Sheldon sits up and looks around. It is truly lovely here. The lake reminds him of East Pond, near Waterville, Maine, where Rhea used to go to summer camp in the early 1980s. Like Rødeness-jøen, East Pond had a simple, common tranquility. It was not over-whelming or unique. It was not a destination on someone's winding itinerary. It was a refuge. And this is what he and Paul need more than anything—to motor to the northeastern corner and find a quiet and safe place to hole up for the night. It will be their own Jackson's Island, where Huck and Jim first met up and set forth as the world closed in on both of them.

This is the plan now. Though still early, he wants to set up camp as far from the tractor as possible, in case someone noticed him disposing of it. They'll eat their rations from the bag, and pee in the woods, and Sheldon will dry his socks and try to make everything comfortable.

It is surprising how cozy the dry forest can be with a little know-how. It is especially nice when there are no Koreans skulking about in the undergrowth. For once in quite some time, this seems to be a reasonable certainty. If they manage to find him here, then they probably deserve to.

Tomorrow morning they'll hitchhike the rest of the way. It's a little risky, but there is no thread connecting them to Oslo now. So unless there is a national manhunt for them, with any luck they'll get a ride for the last ninety kilometers.

Paul is in a rather different mood from Sheldon. He is still in full regalia and energized. His little feet are pattering up and back on the raft, and he's looking overboard at the misbegotten tractor, pointing and smiling. It's a pity he doesn't have grandparents here to see this. They can be an excellent source of whimsy.

They can also be useful when you have a dead parent, as in Rhea's case, and the other one turns out to be useless.

Rhea inevitably learned that there was supposed to be a generation of people between her and her grandparents, and in her twenties she went looking for her mother. Out of college—brazen, rash, and excitable—she kept talking about Truth. Finding her mother became a quest, and Rhea was now old enough to embark on its perils.

He'd tried talking her out of it. He told her that people aren't usually lost. They aren't socks. They aren't wedged behind doors, hoping that someone will find them. They hide. And not from everyone. They hide from particular people. In this case, her. He'd explained that his own watch-repair and antique shop hadn't moved since it opened, and all her mother needed to do was send a letter or call. The connection between mother and daughter was a phone call away. But only one side could enter the magic code to unlock the conversation, and Rhea didn't have the code.

He knew this before she was old enough to understand it. Crushing her hopes was the only humane thing to do. But college and education have a way of instilling the most foolish ideas in the brightest of people, and Rhea went forth to turn hers into reality.

It went about as badly as Sheldon had expected, perhaps worse than Mabel had predicted, and it forced Rhea into a position that until then she couldn't have imagined.

It didn't matter where Rhea found her. It didn't matter what she was wearing, or what she'd been doing only moments earlier. What did matter was the expression of utter indignation on her mother's weathered and joyless face when she opened the door and met her adult daughter. The memory of that encounter—what they were holding, how they stood, what smell lingered longest in the air—dissipated into irretrievable fragments the moment it was over, because the words her mother used blotted out the rest. Her words were so definitive, so clear and concise and without equivocation, that they grabbed Rhea by the heart and shook apart every dream, every illusion, every rationalization she had created and cherished for twenty years, so that nothing of the present or the past remained but the harsh reality of the new world.

*I was done with you!*

And so Rhea walked away from that door, and came home to New York to be with Sheldon and her grandmother.

She didn't talk about it for a long time. It was four months before Sheldon broached the topic, with an oblique "Anything on your mind?"

By the 1990s, the shop had changed with the taste of the times. Sheldon stocked what people liked, figuring that this was a reasonably strong business strategy. During the Clinton years, with property prices booming and the definition of sex on the national agenda, people were returning to Midcentury Modern. Sheldon haunted estate sales and hunted auctions with an eye for quality, beauty, and price. When Rhea was in her early twenties the shop was filled with Max Gottschalk's leather chairs, Poul Kjærholm's delicate woods and steels, and Eames's classic lounges and ottomans. Wall Street was booming, and retro was back.

In the shop, Rhea sat in an egg-shaped Danish chair suspended from the ceiling by a chain. Whatever was on her mind was about to hatch.

"Why was Dad attracted to her?" she finally asked.

"Oh, Rhea, that's a question for your grandmother, not me."

"I'll ask her later. For now . . ."

Sheldon shrugged. There was nothing left to protect her from, except lies.

"I don't think he was. I think they had what counted as a fling in the seventies, just before he went to war. Why? She was curvy and outgoing and fun, and was so obviously not a fit for him that she suited all kinds of bills. She was hardly the only girl he had flings with, by the way. When he got back, I think he ran for the nearest safe haven, so to speak. Why her and not another girl, I can't say. Things get lost to time. Stories dry up."

"So I wasn't conceived in love."

"That question is self-pitying, and it isn't worthy of you. You know perfectly well that your grandmother and I adore you. For my two cents, being conceived in indifference but raised in love is better than the inverse. I'm sorry this woman is a disappointment to you. Truly. But you didn't miss out on anything, because there was nothing there to miss."

"I'm never going to have kids," she'd said.

Sheldon put down the Tudor Submariner watch he'd been working on and frowned.

"Why would you say that?"

"What if I don't love them? It clearly happens, right?"

"It wouldn't happen to you."

"How do you know? Maybe it's all hormonal and stuff. They say everything changes when you have kids."

Sheldon sounded sad when he corrected her.

"Everything doesn't change when you have them. Everything changes when you lose them."

Rhea rocked on the chair, and Sheldon said *Don't rock on the chair*, and Rhea stopped.

From out of nowhere, at least to Sheldon's mind, Rhea asked, "Why don't you go to synagogue anymore?"

Sheldon leaned back in his chair and rubbed his face.

"Why are you punishing me?"

"I'm not. I really want to know."

"It's not like I made you go. I'm entirely fair."

"I want to know why. Is it because of Dad?"

"Yes."

"You stopped believing in God when Dad died?"

"Not exactly."

"What then?"

How many of their conversations took place right here? Right in this very spot over a period of twenty years? All of them? It seemed that way. It was as though there were no apartment upstairs. No kitchen. No den or bedroom. Sheldon sat here, year after year, being interrogated by various women. The antiques changed, the women aged, but Sheldon was always here, fixing timepieces, answering questions. The only conversation he remembers having in the apartment was the one with Saul.

"You know what Yom Kippur is?" he'd asked.

"It's the Day of Atonement."

"You know how it works?"

"You ask for forgiveness."

"You ask for two kinds of forgiveness," Sheldon explained. "You ask God to forgive you for your trespasses against Him. But you also ask people to forgive you for your trespasses against them. You do the second because, according to our philosophy, there is only one thing God can't do. He can't forgive you for what you do to other people. You need to ask forgiveness from them directly."

"Which is why there is no forgiveness for murder," Rhea said. "Because you can't ask forgiveness from the dead."

"Right."

"Why did you stop going to synagogue, Papa?"

"Because in 1976, the year you arrived on my doorstep and a song about a sinking ship was on the radio, I took you to temple on Yom Kippur, and I waited for God to apologize to us for what he did to your father, and he never did."

# CHAPTER 18

I T WAS A GOOD night. They found a dry, secluded spot a short
distance from the shoreline, out of view of the road and nearby
houses. It was best not to light a campfire, which was a pity, but
they managed without it.

Paul was willing to take off the horns, but would not give up the
world's most unusual crusader outfit. This seemed to Sheldon the
least weird decision of the day.

Lying close together, Sheldon whispered, "You wake me if you
hear any trouble." And then they fell into a glorious, restful sleep.

By six o'clock the sun was so high that its warmth stirred them.
The fresh air had probably done them both some good, but the
ground had not been kind to Sheldon. He was stiff and sore and
grumpy. It felt as though rigor mortis was getting an early start
on him. Worse yet, there was not a drop of coffee to be found
anywhere.

It did not take them long to break camp. There was little to
gather up, and they hadn't left much of a footprint in the forest.
They weren't being tracked, after all, and since they'd made it

through the night without being caught under searchlights, it likely meant that no one had witnessed the tractor's final moments.

Within an hour they have made their way through the thicket of evergreens to a reasonably large road that holds the promise of passing motorists. After about twenty minutes of walking on that road, Sheldon feels winded.

"Wait a minute, wait a minute. I need a rest." Sheldon eases himself down in the high grass by the side of the road. Paul, who is up ahead, turns back toward him.

"Don't get old," he says to Paul. "If Peter Pan shows up, just go."

Paul is standing tall with his wooden spoon, magic dust bunny, and woolen hat. He looks good. The way a young boy is supposed to look.

Sheldon looks at his watch. It has bright white hands, and insists that it is only eight o'clock in the morning.

"Come here," says Sheldon. He waves Paul over and the boy comes. "Do this." Sheldon sticks out his thumb to hitchhike.

Paul doesn't quite get it, and his thumb angles off toward Germany, over his extended index finger. "It's more . . . sort of toward Finland. Like this." He reaches over and fixes Paul's thumb, tucks in his extra appendage, then tilts the whole hand-and-thumb arrangement backward and down the road a bit. "Good. Let's hope this isn't an obscene gesture up here."

Paul stands looking down the road for a couple of minutes, and nothing happens. In the meantime, Sheldon catches his breath and stands up again. He walks over beside Paul and says, "Right, now we start walking backward. If we're lucky, we'll go backward in time, before yesterday and the day before. Before you were born, all the way back to at least 1952, when Saul was born.

"We could stop for lunch in 1977. I knew an excellent sandwich shop in 1977."

They cover several kilometers on a road that winds northward. There are few signs of civilization other than the perfect ribbon of road running alongside the green strip of grass that edges the forest.

Sheldon has placed two pencils in his lips, insisting he is a walrus. To entertain Paul, he has started walking like one. Before long, however, Sheldon stops.

"Big walrus thirsty. Little walrus thirsty? Big walrus also needs to pee again. Big walrus is old and has a bladder the size of a lima bean."

Sheldon makes the universal symbol of an old man chugging a beer.

Paul understands and nods. Yes, he says, he too would like to be an old man chugging a beer.

"Right. Then it's time to scare up a ride. Enough of this playing around. Here's what I'm going to do. I'm going to count down from ten, and when I do, a car will show up and offer us a ride to a place that has ice-cold Coke in a bottle. OK?"

Sheldon nods for both of them.

"Right. Here we go." He stops, looks down the road, and starts to count.

"Ten."

Paul stops and looks at him.

"Nine."

Nothing happens.

"Eight."

A bird poos right in front of Sheldon, which makes Paul laugh, but Sheldon raises a finger and says, "Concentrate."

"Seven."

A cool breeze blows off the river, accompanied by a chilling cloud that makes Sheldon close his eyes for a moment and blissfully forget the world.

"Six."

Nothing.

"Five."

Sheldon sticks his thumb out higher and with more confidence.

"Four"

He closes his eyes and concentrates. Really focuses his mental energies. On what, he's not sure. He tries to imagine the Swedish women's volleyball team slowing down and asking directions to heaven. He is sure that Bill has put this vision in his mind.

"Three."

A nap would be very welcome now. Who is going to explain to the boy that his mother is dead? How much longer should he wait until going to the police?

"Two."

Is there any way the killer could know about the summer house? He must be missing something. *Am I missing something?*

"One and a half."

Will they try for another baby? Or is this it? The end of days for the family?

"One."

And then, if not on cue, at least on time, a pickup truck filled with hunters and their rifles comes around the bend, slows, and comes to a halt.

A scruffy man in his early forties wearing a T-shirt hangs out the passenger-side window and, in a friendly tone, says something to Sheldon in Norwegian. Paul, it seems, is about to speak when Sheldon takes the pencils from his mouth and says, expansively and in English, "Boy, am I glad to see you boys. My grandson and I broke down a few kilometers back. We're trying to get to a cabin outside Kongsvinger. You couldn't give us a lift, could you?"

The scruffy man is about to speak when Sheldon rubs a handkerchief across his forehead and says, "Yes, indeed. Some nice cold beers, some chilled white wine, and a big pile of pork. That's what I could use this afternoon. In fact, I have to go to the Wine Monopoly in town before going out to the cabin. I couldn't interest you boys in a little barbecue before you go back in the forest to shoot bunnies, could I? Speaking of which, I don't see any game in the truck. Didn't you kill anything?"

A large man in the bed of the pickup slumps a little and turns sullen. His friend across the bench pokes a finger at him. "Tormod missed."

Tormod nods. "I missed."

"Poor Tormod," Sheldon says. "Better luck next time. So, how about it?"

Today is the fourth day. The event took place, and they had fled. They had bedded down at the hotel, made for the water, slept in the blue house by the fjord, traversed land and lake by tractor and raft, and made camp at Jackson's Island. Now they were up again and, with luck, on the final stretch.

That's a good amount of time to be on the run with a boy. Any minute now, the tumblers could fall into place in Paul's mind, and the enormity of what he has experienced could swell his soul. If he started to encounter the past now, he could become inconsolable. Once that happened, what could Sheldon do? Paul would go from being his companion to being his hostage. And that is not what friends do.

Hitchhiking was dangerous. But strategy changes with circumstance. And now was the time to catch a ride and hope that the police have made some progress in capturing the killer.

Sheldon sits as comfortably as he can on someone's duffle bag in the bed of the Ford F-150 as it glides along the well-trimmed road by the tiny lakes and ponds that pop in and out of view. The hills undulate as they round each bend. The road twists and meanders and then straightens again for long stretches past farmland and forest. Sheldon pulls the scent of cut grass and pine trees into his lungs.

"I should have spent more time outside," he says to the young man in the hunting vest sitting beside Tormod.

When Sheldon first moved to Oslo last month, Lars had told him that the Norwegian mountains form a continuous chain across the sea to Scotland, Ireland, the Appalachians, and on through the Berkshire Hills of Massachusetts. They run across the seas and oceans from when the world was one piece and the continents lived together. The land was called Pangaea.

Sheldon didn't know if it was true, but he smiled at Lars for his kindness.

Now he is sitting next to a young man named Mads. Mads is

having the devil's time trying to light a cigarette in the bed of the truck. Sheldon watches as he tenaciously burns through some eight or ten matches before sitting bolt upright and looking around wide-eyed for some reservoir of patience.

Sheldon smiles to himself and snaps his finger to get Mads's attention. He points to a spot in the center of the truck directly behind the cab.

"Sit there."

"Why?"

"The air flows over the cabin, and at this speed it creates a vacuum behind it. There's no turbulence in there. You can light up like you're in the kitchen."

Mads appears to be in his early twenties, though these fair-skinned kids can be a bit older than they look. He's a little more slight than the other four men and has a hapless charm that Sheldon finds endearing. He is the kind of boy who could grow into either a malcontent or a leader of men, depending on the winds of fortune.

Mads looks at the spot behind the cab and then skirts over there and sits. He strikes the match, and smiles as it flickers before the orange point singes the tobacco and white paper.

"Cool," says Mads. "How'd you know that? You an engineer?"

With the warm breeze blowing around him, Sheldon locks his blue eyes on Mads with the affected look of a hilltop sage. "I used to design search-and-rescue aircraft for the Canadian Mounties, 1961 through 1979. You ever hear of the wreck of the *Edmund Fitzgerald*?"

"No."

"Good. Lake Gitche Gumee. Or at least that's what the Chippewa called it. It was November, and the gales were blowing. Ship was loaded with twenty-six thousand tons of iron ore, more than the good ship weighed empty. A hurricane-force west wind came in, and the ship was in peril. Then . . . then there's something about Wisconsin and Cleveland I can't remember. So we came in by air from Whitefish Bay, but the hurricane gales were slashing and it was freezing rain. If the *Fitzgerald* could have put fifteen more miles behind her, we could have saved those twenty men. But it wasn't meant to be. No sir, it wasn't meant to be."

Mads nods and takes a pull off his cigarette. He sits silently after that.

Sheldon rubs his hands together. He isn't cold, but circulation at his age isn't always dependent on temperature. Seating position alone is enough to make anything go numb. Anything that still had feeling to begin with.

"The Wreck of the *Edmund Fitzgerald*" was a song by someone named Gordon Lightfoot. It was playing incessantly on the radio in August 1976, a month after Rhea showed up. The same four chords went round and round in a mournful, monotonous, drunken hymn. A cargo ship had, in fact, sunk on Lake Superior in 1975, killing twenty-nine men. The song made number two on the charts a year later. Meanwhile, fifty thousand American soldiers had died in the jungle, including his son and Eli Johnson, and Sheldon couldn't find a bumper sticker on the streets of New York during the bicentennial remembering them.

But that goddamned song played on and on as the teenagers wept.

After being struck on the head yesterday, Sigrid had allowed the medics to examine her, but otherwise refused, refused, refused to go to the hospital. Instead, she vomited in the police station's bathroom, cleaned herself up, and—once she found it—sat behind her desk with feigned dignity.

As a concession to the medics, she slept in the office, so she could remain under some supervision, in case she needed emergency aid. The station was busy all night, and an officer on each shift was assigned to look in on her.

Today, Sheldon and Paul have been on the road for several hours before Sigrid finally sits up on her sofa. In front of her is a large, shapeless mass making cloying, guttural sounds, both off-putting and strangely insistent.

As through a sea of molasses, Sigrid wades to her desk, where she takes a piece of salty licorice from the drawer and pops it into her mouth.

With each heartbeat, she is being slammed in the back of the head by a semi.

"He's still in custody?" she asks.

"Your assailant? Yes. Still here."

"Is he the killer?"

"We don't think so."

"In that case, can I just smash him over the head with a fire extinguisher?"

"Unfortunately, no," the shapeless mass answers, in a voice much like Petter's.

"We didn't shoot him in some struggle, did we?"

"Again, unfortunately, no."

"We should interrogate him."

"We should open the box."

"What box?"

"The pink box. The one on your desk. That you think belongs to the dead woman."

"Yes. That's a good idea. I can use my gun. Where's my gun?"

"No," says the someone, who is evidently Petter. "We want to use the key. We don't just want to open the box. We want to know whether it belonged to the woman. So we want to use her key."

"Right. And if the key fits the lock, it'll establish the connection between the key, the box, and the woman."

"That's the idea."

"And it might explain something about the murder."

"Yes, it might. We're hoping it will give us the legal grounds to arrest the father."

"Legal."

"We're upholding the law."

"Which is how we fight crime."

Petter smiles. "You're feeling better."

"Burn after reading."

"No, we don't want to burn anything."

"George Clooney shot Brad Pitt in *Burn After Reading*. In a closet. I knew that guy was wrong."

"He probably didn't see that one."

Changing the subject: "Norwegian law isn't good enough. Not for this case."

"What do you mean?"

"Between throbs last night, I was looking at their records. None of them, not one, is in the Schengen database."

"Not so surprising. If there's no criminal record . . ."

"Well, see, that's the thing about war crimes. No 'able or functioning' courts in a war-torn country means no trials and no convictions, so no record in the SIS, which means almost no grounds for rejecting their immigrant status. The International Criminal Tribunal for the Former Yugoslavia was supposed to fill some of that gap, but it's a big, big gap."

"There are many things to fix in the world. Can we open the box now?"

"What box?"

"Here's the key."

Petter hands her a small silver key less than two centimeters long, with a tooth that splits into two. The rudimentary lock is designed to do little more than deter siblings, parents, and other perpetrators just long enough to be arrested by their own sense of guilt.

Sigrid takes the key.

"The problem is that all the things that aren't fixed allow the flotsam and jetsam of Europe to flow into our little Norwegian boat here. The politicians are so excited about uniting Europe that they set the little boat to sea before its hull is patched up and ready for the voyage. And that means it will take on water and sink before we set off. And we sink because of the unfounded optimism of a bunch of people we elected to office. And the ones who have to bail them out are us. The cops. Want to know what's wrong with Norway? Ask us. We know."

"That's very lucid of you. Can we please open the box?"

Sigrid holds up the key and moves it toward the lock.

"It's awfully small."

"I'll do it."

Petter takes the key and turns the box around so it faces him. He puts the key in the lock, looks up at Sigrid, and twists it.

It opens.

"OK, then."

Petter flips open the lid and looks in. "What are those?" he asks.

Sigrid isn't sure. She opens the drawer of her desk and takes out a pair of latex gloves. She puts them on and removes the contents of the box.

"Letters and photos."

"Of what?"

She doesn't know. The letters are written in a foreign language. Serbo-Croatian, perhaps—when it was still the same language. Maybe Albanian. The photos are of a village. Or what once was a village.

They are carefully ordered. On top of each photograph there is a small piece of paper with the name of a person, a place, and other information she can't discern. The top photo shows a person in an everyday snapshot. At a table, waving. By a car. Carrying groceries. Lifting a child. Raking leaves. All are typical events captured on 35-millimeter film, and usually placed in albums so we can remember who we and our loved ones used to be.

Under this stack of photos are photos of each person's murder.

The images are gruesome. Some of the people have been shot. Others have been sliced open. Throats have been cut. Children have been shot in the back of the head. Some have been shot in the face. Children too young to fear their killers.

Sigrid is holding evidence of a massacre that someone has courageously documented and hidden, and possibly fought to the death to protect.

"We need to contact Interpol, Europol, the Foreign Ministry, and the Ministry of Justice and Police. We need to photograph all of this immediately, so there is a copy of everything. I am beginning to see what might have happened here.

"Let's call everyone together. I want a briefing on what happened around Oslo yesterday. Anything out of the ordinary. We need to find these people."

With her officers in a circle around her, Sigrid sips a cup of coffee despite the instructions of her medic, who insists it is a diuretic and will increase dehydration, which is not what she wants to be doing right now.

Evidently, he is wrong.

"Anything," she says. "Anything at all. Did anyone phone in?"

A few calls did come in—domestic abuse, drunks, an attempted rape. Nothing that seems connected.

"So you're telling me that we received no calls of any kind about an old American accompanied by a young boy from the Balkans. We issued a very clear description. I want to be sure I'm hearing this correctly." She pauses. "Fine. Start calling around. If the information isn't coming to us, we start asking for it."

As Sigrid returns to her office, a junior officer comes to her with a young woman in civilian clothes.

"Inspector, I think you need to hear this," says the officer.

"Hear what?"

"Inspector Ødegård? My name is Adrijana Rasmussen." She hesitates and then adds, "But I was born Adriana Stojkovi. In Serbia. There are some very bad people looking for a small boy and an old man. And I think they're in trouble."

Adrijana speaks Norwegian with an upper-class, west-end accent. Everything about her, other than her Slavic features, bespeaks the qualities of a native Norwegian. Her clothes are stylish, but slightly toned down so as not to make other women jealous of her looks. Her hair is carefully styled to look natural. She's not self-consciously trendy or rebellious enough to be from Grünerløkka, but she isn't bedecked in watches and jewelry that she hasn't had the time to earn, either, and therefore suggesting old money from Frogner.

Perhaps out in Skøyen or St. Hanshaugen. Maybe a nice part of Bislett.

She tells her story quickly and with such narrative confidence that she exudes integrity and purpose. And a certain level of youthful immaturity as well.

"He's not a bad person," she says to Sigrid. "He's a good person. He's just stupid. Stupid like a piece of fruit. Stupid, stupid, stupid . . ."

"OK. I see. What did he do?"

"Well, he didn't come home last night, for one thing. He asked me about this old man and kid, and I didn't know what he was talking about, and I told him to explain it, and he wouldn't, and he said I should ask around 'in my community' . . . and what does that mean, anyway . . . so I got upset and told him that the Serbs aren't 'my community' any more than the Japanese are, and then he started getting high and mighty like he had some deep insight into the human condition."

"Where is he now?" asks Petter, trying to gain a foothold.

"Now? Like, right now? I have no idea. He disappeared. So I assume he's with his dangerous friends. Gjon, Enver, Kadri . . ."

"Enver Bhardhosh Berisha? Kadri . . ."

"Yeah, yeah, them. You know them?"

"Yes. Where are they?"

"I don't know. But Burim said they're looking for an old man and a boy. I think they saw something. I think the old man is hiding with the boy. I think you need to find them."

"Can you stay here for a few minutes, please?"

"I didn't do anything wrong."

"No, no, it's not that. We're very grateful you're here. Just don't go away. I need some of my colleagues to ask you for a few details."

"I love him," says Adrijana. "He's stupid, but he's kind, and he's gentle, and he's a moron, and he acts like an abused puppy, but . . ."

"I understand," says Sigrid. "Just stay here."

Out in the main room again, she waves to get everyone's attention. When she feels she has it, she calls out loudly.

"Anything. Anything at all. Any information on Horowitz. Just shout it out."

A quiet policeman named Jørgen raises his hand. Sigrid opens her palms to signal that she is prepared to catch anything.

"I spoke to an officer from Trøgstad. He said he pulled over an old German man yesterday. The man was driving a tractor pulling a raft. He had his grandson with him."

"An old German and a young boy."

"Yeah. He said he remembers it clearly because the boy was dressed like a Jewish Viking."

"A Jewish Viking."

"Yeah. A big star on his shirt and horns on his head."

"An old German was driving a tractor pulling a Jewish Viking on a raft, and no one thought this was worth bringing to my attention?"

"The bulletin we sent out said the old man was American. Since this man was German, he didn't see the need to mention it."

Sigrid sits down in the nearest empty chair. She can no longer pinpoint the source of the pain in her head. This morning she was sure it was coming from the outside of her skull. Now she is not so certain.

Petter is still standing. He says, "It looks like the woman was right."

"What woman?"

"Ms. Horowitz. She said being Jewish mattered. Perhaps we should have mentioned it in the bulletin."

"You think?" Shaking her head, she asks, "Are we the most naïve people in Europe?"

"Actually, there was recently a survey . . ."

"I don't want to know."

"If we consider when the boat was found, and then draw a line to the tractor sighting, we can see them moving northeast from Drøbak."

"In the direction of the summer house."

"More or less."

"Any sighting of the tractor?"

Jørgen shakes his head.

"Call every unit between Trøgstad and Kongsvinger, and tell them to get on the road and look for it. And start with the ones in the north, not the south, OK? We tighten the grip from the top, not the bottom."

Petter puts his hand on Sigrid's shoulder.

Sigrid looks up at Petter. She gives him a smirk.

"You have to admit, the old fox is kicking our ass," Petter says.

"I'll take my hat off to him when we get the boy back safely."

"He should have turned the child over to us."

Sigrid knows better.

"I don't think this is a man defined by trust," she says.

# CHAPTER 19

SIGRID SITS IN the passenger seat of the speeding Volvo V60. The lights are flashing, and Petter's face is grim. They have called Rhea and Lars. They have not received an answer. The police radio is on, and the local precinct has been notified. The *Beredskapstroppen* are coming from three different locations to converge on the summer house, and are well armed and briefed. Sigrid has taken command of the operation, and everything is on hold until she gives the word for an assault.

"We're out on a limb here," Petter says after thirty minutes of silence on the highway.

"I'm right. The old man is going to the house with the boy, and I'll bet you a whiskey that Enver and his clan are waiting to take the boy, if they haven't already."

"We really don't know any of this."

The nausea remains, but her focus has returned. Sigrid is angry, and the anger heals her. Petter is not wrong, but he isn't right, either.

"The man and the boy live in the same building," she says. "The box from the boy's mother was under the man's bed. She went in there with her son to hide. He hid them because he's that kind of a man. He heard his neighbor at risk, and he stepped up to help. But something happened. Bardosh broke in, and Horowitz and the son hid in the closet. The boy urinated, and somehow they both got out. Bardosh and his gang learned this, one way or another, and they've been hunting for them. Horowitz has kept a step ahead of all of us. He probably thinks they don't know about the summer house. And maybe they don't. But maybe they do. After all, the movie buff was skulking around in the old man's room. If they learned about the summer house, surely they'd send someone there to look around.

"I can't get Rhea and Lars on the phone. So I'm going to take a risk and assume they can't pick it up. If I'm wrong, we scare them with a big entrance and I become the laughingstock of the police force for a few weeks. If I'm right, we're showing up to a fight, well armed. Unless," she says, "the fight is already over."

The speed limit on this stretch of road is 80 kilometers an hour, and Petter is driving 130. They should be at the staging point in under an hour if the traffic stays light.

She takes a key from around her neck, opens the glove box, and removes a 9 mm Glock 17 pistol. She releases the magazine and pulls it from the gun, which she places on her lap. Then she presses her fingers down hard on the bullets to check that the magazine is fully loaded. She puts it between her thighs and picks up the pistol. She pulls the slide all the way back until it clicks open, and peers into the chamber to make sure it's empty. She checks the magazine receiver for any debris or lint. Satisfied, she returns the magazine to the pistol. With a flick of her thumb on the release, the spring rams the slide forward, chambering the first round, "American style."

She engages the safety and holsters the gun.

Petter looks at her, and she looks back.

She turns her head fully to him and says, "What?"

"Nothing," says Petter.

The radio crackles. Sigrid can picture the operations room back at the police station, and imagines the computer display that tracks all the vehicles as they converge on the summer house.

It is a rushed mission, and she knows it, but the *Beredskapstroppen* officers are ready. Like her, they have already seen the satellite images of the approaches to the cabin, and noted that there is only one road. They'll have checked the angle of the sun against the available natural covers, to position sniper and assault teams. The Kosovars are probably armed. There are a great many unregistered weapons across the country, and criminals are getting bolder in exploiting that weakness faster than the state can guard against it. The Kosovars may also have found the two hunting rifles registered to Lars Bjørnsson. Unless Lars got to them first. Or Horowitz has. In which case, everyone is armed, and the situation is even more volatile.

Sigrid taps her fingers anxiously on her knees and checks their speed.

"Can't we go any faster?"

"Yes, but we shouldn't," Petter says.

She taps faster and looks out the window again.

*River Rats.* The old man's letter was a quote from *Huckleberry Finn*, the American antislavery novel by Mark Twain, where Huck and the runaway slave Jim make their way down the Mississippi River, evading capture for wrongs they never committed. Sigrid had typed it in on the Internet, and it popped right up. Horowitz's spelling of "sivilize," with an "s" and a "z," made it a distinctly American misspelling that was unique to the novel.

Sigrid keeps tapping.


It was probably pity that motivated the hunters to drive Sheldon and Paul all the way to Glåmlia. It must have been out of their way, even if they had been heading north. The ride has taken more than an hour, and now that it has finally ended, Sheldon is staring straight at his biggest fear.

The Ford pickup approaches a white Mercedes parked on the shoulder of the dirt road behind a yellow Toyota Corolla from the mid-1990s.

Standing in the flatbed, Sheldon slaps the top of the cab and yells to the driver, "Stop the truck."

The pickup crunches to a halt behind the Mercedes. Only a meter away, the car looks like a sleeping white panther waiting for its tail to be pulled.

Sheldon walks carefully on the corrugated floor of the truck. He touches each man's shoulders for support. At the end, he eases himself down to the ground, walks around to the passenger side of the cab, and gets in.

"Is this the turn?" the driver asks him.

It is a good question. Sheldon looks down the road. He's never been here before—he just knows the picture.

"Do you see a white Mercedes?" Sheldon asks the driver.

The driver is about thirty-five years old and has dirty-blond stubble on his tanned face. He's a smoker and an outdoorsman. The question does not surprise him. Instead, he looks out the window and then back at Sheldon. He has become familiar with such questions from his own grandfather. He answers gently.

"Yes, I do."

Sheldon hasn't seen a Korean in weeks. Not a single one in the shadows. And now the white car is here at his granddaughter's summer retreat. After all his attempts at evasion, they not only knew where to find him; they got here first.

*I can't be trusted. I have to give up the boy.*

"That's more disappointing than I can explain," he says.

"Is there anything I can do for you?"

Sheldon wonders the same thing. The driver looks weathered, but he does not look tough. His coarse skin and calloused hands come from peacetime activities, like taking off his gloves in the winter to get a better feel of the rifle; lying on packed snow with a flashlight between his teeth to find the hook to winch his friend's car from a ditch; walking barefoot to the sauna; letting the rope slip too soon when coming about in his boat and getting his hands burned on the sea.

Walking up to the window of the truck, as though he'd been waiting for Sheldon to arrive, is his friend Bill.

Bill leans in and says, "What are you thinking about, Sheldon?"

"I'm thinking that from here on, I go alone."

Sheldon gets out of the cab and holds the cool steel side of the truck for support as he walks to the back. Paul is sitting Indian-style in the bed, with Mads and Tormod on either side of him. There are two other men that Sheldon hasn't properly met, sitting on their hunting gear.

"Any of you have girlfriends?" Sheldon asks.

One of the two men Sheldon doesn't know raises his hand tentatively.

"Well done. Have lots of sex. Now, what I want to say is this: you can't come up to the house. I can't tell you why. But it has to do with the white car. I need you boys to take young Paul here to the police station in the middle of town. And don't stop for anything. Don't stop for a drink. Don't stop for a pee. Don't stop if one of you falls overboard. Just bring him to the police and give them this." Sheldon hands the one without the girlfriend a piece of paper with the license plate of the Mercedes, as well as his driver's license from his wallet.

"You tell them you saw this car. You tell them you saw me. You tell them this is the son of the woman who was murdered in Oslo."

There is silence in the truck.

"Are you all getting this? I can't tell when your race is processing information and when it isn't. It's nothing but blank stares with you people. I need you to get this. Are you getting this or not?"

"OK."

This is said by the big one who failed to shoot the bunny.

"OK what? Repeat it."

He'll go to the police with the boy and the license-plate number and the old man's driver's license, and say that he's the son of the woman murdered in Oslo.

"And tell them to get over here. And bring guns. Speaking of which, I need a rifle."

No one moves or answers.

"Rifles are the thunder sticks you all use to scare bunnies with. I need one. With a scope. An adjustable scope. My eyesight is off. And bullets. Don't forget bullets."

There remains no movement or speech.

"OK, boys, what's the matter?"

"We can't give you a rifle, sir."

"Why the hell not? You've got plenty."

No one says anything.

"You think I'm nuts."

"It's just that it's against the law, and we aren't hunting anymore."

"Speak for yourself," says Sheldon.

Without asking, he unzips one of the hunter's duffle bags and rummages through it.

He pulls out ammunition he can't use and tosses it. He pulls out flashlights, whistles, a pair of shoelaces, and a woolen hat. He discards them all. He finds a pair of binoculars and puts them in his satchel.

"Um, sir . . ."

"I need them more than you do. I'll give them back if I'm not killed. OK?"

The man only nods. What else can he do? Perhaps if Sheldon were forty years younger and sane, he might have acted differently. But no other response was possible. They'd already cashed in their chips by saying no to the rifle.

"Any of you fish?" Sheldon asks.

The other hunter sitting next to him raises his hand. He is, however, reluctant. He is very fond of his fishing rod.

"Give me the fishing line. And hurry up. Now, who's got a knife?"

There is no response.

"Each and every one of you weenies has a knife, and I know it. Now give me one."

Tormod, his lower lip visibly extended, reaches so deeply into his pocket it looks as though he might extract an organ. He pulls out a small lock-blade knife with brass bolsters. Sheldon takes it, feels its weight, and opens it. He rubs his thumb across the edge of the blade, then looks up at Tormod and frowns.

"You should be ashamed of yourself for even owning this, let alone trying to pass it off on an old man. Now give me the real one. Come on now."

What arrives is a Hattori hunting knife with a mahogany handle, brass furniture, and a four-inch blade.

Sheldon nods. "That's right," he says.

Standing on the soft earth, he picks up the largest duffle bag and empties its contents into the truck.

"Oh, come on, man. Please? All we did was give you a ride."

Sheldon takes the bag and a large fishing net he finds inside. He ignores their complaints.

"I need a needle and thread. Who has a needle? You're not leaving until I get one."

With his newly acquired stash of items, which seem quite random to the hunters, Sheldon makes the men promise that they will take Paul and the license-plate number and his own ID to the police.

He looks at Paul, who is still sitting on the truck bed between Mads and Tormod.

Sheldon raises his hand to say goodbye.

Paul does not understand, and begins to cry.

Sheldon tries not to do the same.

He doesn't have the heart to watch the truck drive off. Paul is looking at him. If they can see each other grow smaller, and if Paul is crying, Sheldon will not be able to concentrate.

Not looking is no different, really, from not scratching. The consequences are the same, either way.

In a few moments, the sound of the truck's engine fades and Sheldon is standing alone at the intersection where the main dirt road continues on and around the bend to the right, past the parked cars. The approach to the summer house is to his immediate right, and leads like a darkened medieval trail to the lair of a dragon.

"What do we do now, Donny?" asks Bill.

"You're still here?"

Bill shrugs. "I'm always here."

"That only condemns your inaction even more."

"The police are going to come eventually. Are you sure you want to go up there? I mean, really, what's the point? What can you possibly do?"

Sheldon sighs and does not argue the point. He knows it is true. He is hungry and weary. His head hurts. His arthritis is getting worse, and the only remedy he's found that helps—raisins soaked in gin—isn't available.

He leaves Bill standing at the intersection and walks to the side of the road opposite the Mercedes and the Toyota. He crouches down and looks at the cars more intently.

"What are you doing?" Bill asks, more loudly this time.

"Shut up, Bill."

Sheldon crouches lower and, still unsatisfied with his view, finally succumbs to getting down on his hands and knees, hoping that he'll find a way to get back up.

"Sheldon, seriously . . ."

"Shut up, Bill."

Sheldon crawls slowly to the yellow car and stops when he finds his first footprint. It looks like a sneaker and has a strange symbol: a check mark above what appears to be a small apple. It is in the center of the shoe, and is helpfully distinct from the other footprints he finds.

Another print, on the passenger side, is a workman's boot with its typical diamond-cloved imprint and raised heel. Sheldon names him Logger Boy.

Apple and Logger Boy came from the truck. The footprints are all around the vehicle and facing in every direction. Maybe they were milling around, waiting for something. Both are too big to be a woman's foot. Each looks a little too small to belong to Lars.

On the driver's side of the Mercedes there is one clear set of footprints as well. They are unmistakably military. They have the ubiquitous rectangular tracks edging the front of the boot around five clovers, and a thick, elevated heel. The boots could be from almost any army, or they could have been bought at a surplus store. But Sheldon suspects they weren't.

"Sheldon, what are you doing?"

"I'm learning. I'm an old dog on my hands and knees, and I may very well be nuts, but I'm learning." He rotates, slowly, to a sitting position in the middle of the road, and wipes his hands.

"Three men: Mr. Apple, Logger Boy, and Lucifer. Lucifer got here first. Got out of the car and walked into the woods. At some point, he came back and connected with the other two. Then they all went into the woods."

"How do you know they connected?"

"Here." Sheldon points to the rear of the Toyota. "Lucifer's footprint is superimposed on Logger Boy's. The form of his boot is clear, but the edge of Logger Boy's is deformed. That means he stepped there afterward."

"You came a long way with that boy to say goodbye so easily."

"It wasn't easy. It was necessary. Now help me up."

"Can't."

"Why not? You busy?"

"You know why."

"Oh, I see."

Before the big push to get back on his feet, Sheldon takes the knife from its sheath and proceeds to puncture the two tires on his side of the Mercedes. He then uses the car door to right himself. Once up, and on a whim, he tries the handle, but it's locked. Inside, he sees cracked blue vinyl seats and a gearshift lever with the numbers worn off from long use.

With care, he walks over to the Toyota and punctures its tires, too.

*No one's going anywhere. This ends here.*

When satisfied with his handiwork, he sheaths the knife and puts it back in the satchel. He walks to the middle of the road and collects the other items he'd taken from the hunters, then slips into the woods like an old sniper.

The forest is dense here, and the ground is uneven. There are short mounds and small drops where glacial outcrops have been worn smooth by silent centuries of rain and wind. A blessed cool breeze that started on the Siberian tundra rolls in low and crisp under the thick canopy of the poplars and majestic oaks.

Sheldon walks as silently as possible to a rocky enclave invisible from the two roads, and sets to work as quickly as his poor hands and eyes will allow.

He takes out the knife, jabs it through the duffle bag near its bottom, and slits it open the way an experienced hand disembowels prey. He lays the bag open on the ground, with the bottom facing away from him. Putting the blade down, he takes the large fishing net and places it over the duffle bag. Donny makes allowances for movement and stretch, then cuts away the part of the net that hangs beyond the bag.

He inhales the cool breeze and holds it in his lungs until the pain starts. Then he releases.

At New River, in 1950, he'd spent hours on the firing range. The firing point wasn't covered by the sort of long lean-tos that shelter golfers as they pitch their shots deep into narrow fairways. At the Marine shooting range, the men fired from a small mound and lay in the dirt, or the dust or the mud or the grime, depending on Mother Nature's mood that day. When it was hot, they sweated and itched. When it was wet, they itched more. If they twitched or whined, they risked a rifle butt to the back of the helmet by the rifle master, who was utterly charmless.

*Just breathe.*

They would run ten miles a day, to tone their bodies and slow their metabolism. They cut down on sugar and coffee. Anything to teach the heart not to beat. Slow, slow goes a metronome. Less air, less breath, less life. Anything to keep the sniper still, to keep the scout moving, observing, recording, returning.

This was fifty-eight years ago.

It is all clearer now than it was then. Rhea would say it is the vivid fabrication of an aging mind. More likely, though, it is the clarity that comes from aging—from the natural process of releasing the mind from imagined futures, and allowing the present and the past to take their rightful place at the center of our attention.

The past is palpable to Sheldon now, in the way the future is to the young. It is either a brief curse or a gift before oblivion.

*Just breathe.*

One very rainy day on the firing range, Hank Bishop was on Sheldon's left, trying to hit a two-hundred-meter target in a light fog.

Hank Bishop, bless him, was not very smart.

"I can't tell if I hit it," he'd say after each shot.

"You didn't," said Donny.

"I can't tell if I hit it," he said.

"You didn't," said Donny.

"I can't tell if I hit it," he said.

"You didn't," said Donny.

After more of this sort of conversation—of which Sheldon never tired—an unexplainable and miraculous event took place. Hank somehow reflected on his own actions, thus breaking the cycle and stimulating a question.

"What makes you so sure I didn't hit it, Donny?"

"Because you're shooting at my target, Hank. Yours is over there. Here—I'll find it for you."

In the increasingly heavy downpour, Donny silently unzipped his chest pocket and removed a single red-tipped bullet. He ejected the magazine and laid it down next to him. Then he cleared the chamber of the remaining round and slipped in the tracer bullet.

He took a shallow breath, let it out halfway, took aim, and squeezed the trigger.

The red phosphorus round ripped through the fog like a burning dove through an alpine tunnel, then slammed into Hank's wooden target. It made impact almost dead center, and the line of Marines started whooping and clapping, causing the rifle master to run down the line with his rifle butt clanking on the helmet of every man in the squad.

Tracer bullets are not especially designed for penetration. So the burning round wedged itself in the wooden target, which immediately smoldered and hissed and caught fire from the inside out.

"Horowitz, you numbnuts. What the hell do you think you're doing?"

"Wasn't me, sir."

"It sure as shit wasn't Bishop!"

"All right, it was me. But Hank couldn't hit his target, sir, and mine's already good and dead."

Sheldon is using these same hands to sew. He works as quickly as his fingers allow. He threads the needle with the fishing line, and uses the butt of the knife as a thimble to push it through the duffle bag to sew the net onto it.

He is conscious of the time, but he forces his mind not to imagine what might be happening in the summer house.

It takes him more than half an hour of deep concentration. He is worried that the needle is too thin to withstand the constant abuse of the task. The duffle bag is made of thick cotton, but thankfully it is loosely stitched and Sheldon is able to run the needle between the coarse threads.

When he is finished, he looks at his handiwork. It's reasonably good, given how little he had to work with. Now he needs to complete the gillie suit with brush and branches and tufts of earth. He doesn't want to use only material from his immediate surroundings, and instead wants the camouflage to blend with the widest array of life around him. He wants to become one with the forest—for his suit to be an actual, living part of the world around him.

When he is finished, he digs silently into the soft earth to where it is moist, takes a small handful of dirt, and rubs it over his face and the white backs of his hands. He smears dirt over his shoes and rubs it into the still green sections of the duffle bag. When he is satisfied, he places the ghillie suit over him, with his head in the curved section of the bag's bottom. As a final touch, he punctures the suit to the left and right of his collarbone, and weaves the strap from the duffle bag through the holes. It now rides him like a squire's cape. And, with this, he is ready.

"Now what?" asks Bill.

"Precisely," says Sheldon.

# CHAPTER 20

I T WAS ALWAYS BEST to the keep the number of people involved in an operation as small as possible. Enver had had problems back in Serbia with loose lips. Plans that had been made in darkened rooms after hours were too easily brought into the light and exposed.

"Loose lips sink ships" went the saying.

When he was in his early twenties, it all shocked him. The capacity of the Serbs for horrific violence not only enraged, but confused him. How could people hate strangers so intensely? Enver never fell entirely into that trap, and he prided himself on that. His militia assaulted only those who were connected to the crimes against his people. He was driven to avenge the dead and to restore the honor of his people. He wasn't fulfilling some mad ideology, and he wasn't killing in the name of God. He was content with the justifications for his actions.

The trouble, toward the end, was that almost every Serbian man was a killer and his wife a devilish harpy, offering up foul whisperings to stir his cold blood. How could it have been any other way?

Men kill because they want to. Something makes them want to. But the choice is always theirs, and with that choice lies their fate.

The man who answered the call that Enver placed was well known in the KLA. He was known to Kadri. He was an unremarkable man of average height and no particular strength or speed. There was no special viciousness in his demeanor, or cruelty to his appetites. He did not drink to excess, and he did not justify his actions by wrapping them in lofty words and history and emotion. He did not indulge in conspiracy theories in order to bond with other men.

Those who knew him did not talk to him much, because there was little to say and less to hear. When he was talked about, however, there was one point of common agreement. All believed that he no longer had a soul. He was the living dead. He was called Zezake: the Black.

The Black is Enver's protection. His bodyguard. His soldier. He was sent to Norway to hide Enver from the Serbs, and to stay close to him and be of service.

To be Enver's shadow.

The Black is a model citizen in Oslo. He waits for the light to change before crossing. He signals before he turns. He holds doors open for women with strollers at United Bakeries. He never grumbles about the long checkout lines at the Wine Monopoly.

The Serbs know he is here. It is unlikely that the Norwegians do, though. He travels quietly, with false papers. He rents rooms and moves on. He leaves nothing behind. He is a ghost, and knows how to drift through Europe as only criminals do.

The Kosovars and Albanians are well organized and mobilized in Oslo. They do not constitute a large population, and many of them know each other. They look out for each other, and one way of doing so is to watch out for the Black so that the Black can watch out for Enver.

And now he has a job to do. The Black has received the call from Enver, and has set about doing what Burim and Gjon failed to do. He is to recover the boy, for the simple reason that he's been instructed to, and that is what he does—follow instructions. He has gone to the black market and bought an aged but functional Colt 1911 .45-caliber pistol and an old Winchester repeater with a wooden stock. The stock of the rifle has a swastika etched into it by its former owner. The Black has purchased it, not because of his political leanings, but because of the reduced price and the likelihood that the owner would want to forget the transaction.

The rifle uses an iron sight and holds five rounds. The Black has tested it in the hills outside the city, and found it reliable and accurate.

He has been told to gather the weapons and come alone to the summer house. Enver has given him the address. He will find his own way.

The Black does not know that the hunters have taken the boy. What he does know, however, is what the boy looks like and what his real name is.

His special-operations training has taught him always to fuel a car or truck just before reaching a mission's destination, because it prepares the vehicle for either the return trip or a rushed escape. So when he pulls into the Esso station in Kongsvinger, it surprises him to see the boy through the windshield. He is holding a piece of moose jerky and standing among five young Norwegian men.

The Black sidles up to the pump and drives his Fiat slowly past the mini-market where the boy is standing with the jerky. He opens the glove compartment and removes a bright red plastic folder. Inside the folder is a series of pictures of the boy. His passport photo. A few surveillance shots. Photos of him with and without his mother. With longer and shorter hair. With an ice cream cone.

The Black holds up the photos and compares them to the boy. The boy sees the man in the small car looking at him and stares back. There is no recognition. The two have never met.

The Black realizes immediately that their chance encounter changes the calculus. It rearranges the pieces on the chessboard. The assault on the summer house was to attain a single goal: to find the boy. If the boy has been found, there is no need for any of it.

Considering this, his face remains unchanged.

The Black takes a mobile phone from his jacket pocket and calls Enver. He knows the lines can be traced, which is why he uses only pay-as-you-go cards. He knows his phone can give away his location and can even be used as a microphone by the police, who have the ability to remotely activate the phone without him knowing it—which is why he throws away the SIM card each time he calls to Enver.

The phone rings and is answered.

"What is it?" says Enver.

"I've found the boy."

There is silence for a moment.

"Do you have him?"

"No. But I will soon."

"What about the old man?"

"I don't see an old man."

"Who is the boy with? The police?"

"No. He's with local vacationers. Hunters. Maybe fishermen."

"Take the boy."

"Should I bring him to the house?"

Enver sighs into the phone. If only this call had come last night, the answer would have been no. Enver, Gjon, and Burim could have returned to their vehicles and met the Black at a random location, switched cars, and Enver could have made for the Swedish border on an unguarded side road where Norwegian black marketeers traffic alcohol and cigarettes.

But the call did not take place last night. It is taking place now.

"Yes. Matters have already been set in motion. Bring him here after you finish your business. And bring the weapons. We won't stay long."

There are five of them, plus the boy. All are in their late twenties or early thirties. He watches them leave the mini-market with groceries. Each carries a bag, and the boy walks slightly behind them. He is an odd one, this son of Enver's. It was known that he lived with his mother, and that the mother was odd—a fast-talking liar who, it was said, turned tricks to pay the rent. Whatever she did, though, she did for her son. It is unclear why Enver upset the routine and decided to take the boy from Norway. But the reasons people do what they do is no longer a question that haunts the Black.

So here he is, silently following a group of men about whom he has no information. Why would the boy be here without the old man? He can think of no reason. The old man must be inside buying something, or urinating. It is what old men do. He decides to wait for the pensioner to emerge.

But he does not emerge. Instead, all five men and the boy get into the truck and start it up. Then pull off.

The Black follows the pickup out of the Esso station and onto a secondary road. It is paved and quiet. There are a few cars on the road, but not enough to protect the men. The odds are in his favor.

The forest is thinner here on the outskirts of town. Brown and yellow grasses edge the road and poke through old potholes and cracks. The weather is fine. The surface of the road is dry.

The Black puts the small car into third and overtakes the truck. The driver with the lined face looks at him as the two cars ride parallel for a moment. Then the moment passes. When the Fiat is a full five car lengths in front of the pickup, the Black slams on the brakes and the back of the car spins out.

The truck's driver also slams on his brakes and screeches to a halt just before hitting the Fiat. The Black is already out of the car. The driver's side faces away from the pickup. He stands behind the Fiat, looking over its silver, rusted roof. In a smooth gesture, he swings the Winchester into play, chambers a round by flicking the lever down forty-five degrees, and takes aim at the driver.

The boy is not in the cab; he is sitting in the bed of the truck with three men. The Black knows this—he watched them as he drove behind.

This is better and makes the job easier.

The Black fires the rifle into the window of the truck, shooting the driver in the face. Blood splatters across the windshield. The other man in the cab, obviously unaccustomed to war and its necessary responses, is frozen in place like the animals he undoubtedly hunts. The Black takes aim, flicks the Winchester's lever again, and kills him.

He hears a commotion at the back of the truck, and then footsteps on the steel slats. He crouches to the ground and looks between the wheels of both vehicles to see whether they have come down from the truck and are trying to run. He knows from experience that if they run directly away from the truck, he will be unable to see them, and will have to move to the left or right in order to gain the needed line of sight.

He sees no feet, but believes he soon will.

When he stands again to look over the roof of the car, he sees a chubby man with dirty-blond hair holding a rifle above the truck's cab. His arms are shaking. Before the Black can reacquire a target, the man shoots.

The bullet passes the Black's head closely enough for him to hear it, and it leaves a terrible buzz and ringing in his ear.

He then fixes on his target and shoots the man. His aim is slightly off, as his shot seems to have hit the man lower in the face than he intended. But the target drops from view, and this is all that concerns him at the moment.

He crouches down again, and this time does see their feet.

The boy's smaller feet are to the right and running with one of the men. The other man is making for the woods to the left. There is a chance he might escape, because the Black has to make a choice. If he steps to his right to sight the man with the boy, he will obscure his view of the other man. If, on the other hand, he steps left, he will be able to shoot the one making for the woods, but will then have to chase his targets. And he does not want to chase his targets.

He is sure-footed and moves quickly. Stepping behind the Fiat, he sees the man running with the boy and manages to shoot him. But the shot is low, and catches him in the small of his back. The man writhes and screams on the ground. The boy, on the other hand, stops running and turns to face the Black.

He is crying, but is mercifully silent. Crying upsets the Black, and he has made a concerted effort to stay away from children for that reason. It is the remaining sound—aside from cats howling in the night from hunger—that continues to touch a nerve.

He jogs forward so he clears the truck and has a complete view of the road. The other man has indeed escaped into the woods. In his youth, the Black might have pulled the .45 and peppered the forest with random shots, but he does not do this sort of thing any longer.

The Black now walks slowly. There is no immediate hurry. His concern is that the survivor has a telephone and will call the police. Everyone in Scandinavia has a mobile phone.

He stands beside the boy and looks down. He runs his thumb under the boy's eye, wiping away a tear. When the Black looks into the boy's face, it reminds him of what he no longer sees when he looks in the mirror.

The one who was shot in the back is Mads. He is still alive, though his eyes are already vacant. There is no need to shoot him in the back of the head. He will either die soon or he will not. In either case, his life is not significant compared to the one who fled.

What is significant, however, is the sound coming from the truck behind him.

The Black turns to look at the pickup and is genuinely surprised to see the fat one pointing a rifle at him. He has lost part of his face, but he is evidently able to wield a weapon.

The Black puts down the Winchester and draws out the pistol. As he takes aim, however, he feels a sudden pain in his knee. He looks down and sees that the boy has struck him—forcefully—with some kind of stick that has a handkerchief tied to the end.

And in that instant he hears a rifle shot.

Tormod's bullet hits the Black, ripping out a piece of his upper thigh. But it has missed the femoral artery—which is lucky, because that would have killed him. It was, considering Tormod's condition, a brave effort. It is also his last, because, on one knee, the Black uses the bullets from the pistol that he has not fired into the woods to kill Tormod.

The Black says to the boy in Albanian, "Come with me," but the boy does not move. More strangely, he does not respond at all. It is as though he does not speak Albanian. So the Black says it again, this time in English, and again the boy is immobile. Confused but undeterred, the Black grabs a handful of the boy's shirt between the shoulder blades and drags him back to the car.

Picking up the rifle, he limps into the Fiat, bleeding from the leg. He opens the glove box and uses the needle and thread in his medical kit to stitch himself together. He bandages his leg and takes a long drink of water from a canteen stored under the passenger seat. The boy's tears have stopped flowing. Perhaps he is in shock. It hardly matters either way.

Truly, the Black cannot understand when and why emotions begin and end, morph from one into another. This no longer even prompts speculation in him. There are no more mysteries when the soul is dead. Only problems.

When Enver answers, the Black's report is brief.

"I have the boy. The police are going to find the cabin. I'll be there soon. I'm injured. Be prepared to leave."

"We're ready," says Enver.

The Black removes the SIM card from his mobile phone and snaps it in two. He replaces it with another.

Satisfied, he closes the driver's side door and starts the car. He should be at the road to the summer house in less than ten minutes.

## CHAPTER 21

DONNY MOVES QUIETLY, one small step at a time, further into the woods. His balance is not what it used to be, so it is harder for him to hold himself steady on one foot and to find the right placement for the other. He is still far enough from the road that he thinks it safe to remain upright, but he will crawl and become one with the ground as he gets closer.

He stops abruptly.

Just off the private road that leads to the mews and on to the house itself, he catches a glint of metal off to the side in a gully. He is on level ground now, and instead of moving closer, he moves farther back, onto a small rise, and sinks into the prone position.

Without making any wide movements, he takes the binoculars from his belt and brings them to his eyes. Out of habit, he does not use his trigger finger to adjust the focus, to avoid getting a splinter from the focus wheel.

Sheldon does not know much about motorcycles, but he can recognize the badge on the fuel tank. It is the unmistakable blue-and-white wheel of a BMW, and the bright yellow fuel tank means it is Lars's bike.

It lies inert in the gully, facing the main road and away from the house, as though it were on the way to leaving the property.

He does not see any people near it. No one dead or injured. The wheels are not spinning. He cannot hear the engine knock or whine.

*Whatever is going to happen has already started.*

It is not the exertion that will kill him, but the surge of adrenaline. His heart beats faster, and a thin layer of cold sweat has already formed on his forehead, threatening a chill, pneumonia, or death. The cool breeze that was a blessing only minutes ago ushers in a future without him.

Sheldon keeps the binoculars to his eyes and scans to his left. The forest and light blur until he catches the slightest glimpse of the color red. It is a red that was once the color of a sports car or a vibrant sunset. It is faded now, and pleasing. It makes the summer house at one with, but always apart from, the sheltering wood.

He cannot see any windows from here. He cannot see the sauna. And that is where Moses and Aaron are hiding.

Convinced he is alone, he moves more quickly now. He knows that the human eye is most attuned to movement and only then registers color. We are not hunters. We are designed as prey, and our senses control us like prey. His drill sergeant was clear on the matter.

*When we see movement, our pupils dilate and we stare at it like idiots. Our adrenaline pulses through our heart. We panic and prepare to flee, but we don't flee. Why? Because we aren't fast, and we don't have any teeth worth a damn, and we don't have claws, and we're bad swimmers, and we can barely climb, and we aren't half as clever as we think we are. We are food. But my job is to turn you from food into Marines! You cannot imagine how hard my job is. I might as well turn lead into gold! I might as well turn my wife into Rita Hayworth! The only reason I am not involved in either of those hopeless but potentially gratifying pursuits is that the U.S. Marine Corps is not paying me to pursue those other pursuits. They are paying me twelve cents a week to turn you from prey into predators! And do you know how the running, scared prey becomes the predator? Do you? I'll tell you how! By stopping. And turning around. And deciding to kill. I will now teach you how to do that. You! Horowitz, what did I just say?*

*Sir! Eat or be eaten, sir!*

He needs to cover ground and find the sauna, but not allow the enemy to spot him. He has done it before. But that was almost sixty years ago.

Now his eyes let in only one quarter of the light that a young man can see.

One fall and his bones will break.

The high registers of sound are only a memory.

What can he even hear? Can he hear a leaf crackling under the heels of an enemy? A weapon being cocked? A bird taking flight, signaling that he is not alone?

He is no hunter now. He is a dreamer. A dying specimen. A useless man.

"I'm dressed like a bush."

"Yes, you are, Donny. Wasn't that the idea?"

"Who am I fooling? Is it just myself?"

"Are you sure you were a sniper? Not a file clerk, like you told Mabel?"

"How would I know how to make the ghillie suit?"

"You're very smart, Sheldon. Maybe you figured it out."

"It's more than that. There's muscle memory here. I know how to step. I know how to look. These are memories that are a part of me. But it's not just about what I remember. It's what I don't remember."

"How so?"

"I don't remember filing anything."

"Either way, Sheldon, here you are. And what are you going to do about it? That's the only persistent question in life."

"I'm going to find the rifles."

"Well, if that's what's going to happen, you should get on with it."

The land dips into a long, shallow valley before rising to the house. The earth is moist and cool beneath the leaves, easier to find a sure footing. The light is still strong, and the Nordic sun is high, casting only short shadows. He recognizes the shallow valley as an alluvial rift created by a glacier or river eons ago. It is helpful to know, because it means the valley continues in two directions, and he can use that knowledge of the land to his benefit. It means the sauna will not be where floodwaters gather. It is not here or on the other side of the mews. It will be on higher ground. Drier ground. It will be up and behind the house.

*I'll take it wide and away.*

A younger man might have taken a route closer to the house, which he now approaches from the left and hundreds of meters into the woods. A younger man might have worried about Rhea with such intensity that he would have armed himself only with the short knife and used it as a weapon. But Sheldon is not a younger man. He cannot overpower anyone. From a seated position he can barely push the knife through a canvas duffle bag.

When we look into a forest to find the source of a sound, we look at the spaces in between. Between the trees where the light shines through. Between the branches to glimpse the blue sky, or the gray and silver linings of the heavens. Our eyes look for light, and search for something to carry us from the darkness of the wilderness.

And so Sheldon moves among the shadows. He clings to the base of trees. He lies flat for minutes at a time where the ground is uneven, and he becomes the forest floor. He uses his knees and elbows to steady himself, because there is no longer enough strength in his chest to keep his frail body above the earth for very long.

How much time has passed?

It's been about an hour. Forty minutes to make the ghillie suit and another twenty minutes on the move. Is that possible? It feels like much longer.

He would grow cold here if it were not so hot under the duffle. He should be wearing gloves. They always told him that. Leather is best. Racecar drivers and horseback riders wear gloves to absorb the sweat and keep a grip on the reins. Metalworkers and woodsmiths wear them. Gardeners and mountain climbers use them.

*Such gentle hands,* Mabel had once whispered to him.

*Not anymore. Now they are calloused and scarred. They are bloody and alone. They seldom have each other for company anymore. They have grown indifferent to each other. There isn't so much to clap for any longer.*

Most of the men in his squad took to snipping off the index finger of their gloves and then sliding it back on unattached. It was possible to lose it this way and end up with one cold finger—which happened, but only rarely. Being gloved was important, and all the men knew it. It was the best way to keep their hands supple and warm. The raiders protected their hands the way that surgeons protect theirs. The way that violinists and pianists will not remove hot food from the oven.

The men would remove the leather finger only right before a kill.

Sheldon looks back over the ground he's covered. He is impressed with himself. Clothing does have a way of making the man. A soldier stands taller in his uniform. A doctor acts more authoritatively in his white smock. The sniper creeps lower. Is sneakier. Gets closer.

The red house moves like the sun across the horizon. He has tracked it across this forested sky, and it is now coming to rest at his extreme right. It is larger than he expected. He has always imagined it as a single-room shack of coarse pine with a steep roof. A sort of outhouse or dog shed on a swept tundra that never thaws in the summer. A little photo on the refrigerator on his way to the iced coffee.

In actuality, it is larger than that. Sheldon reckons the house is a one-story, with two bedrooms and an attic. Maybe one hundred and twenty square meters. It is raised slightly off the ground, so there is a crawl space beneath. It is probably designed that way to keep it dry in winter snow and during the spring runoff.

Two steps lead up to the front door. He is much too far away to see footprints, but there is no need to check. Lucifer's tracks came back to the Toyota from the woods, but Mr. Apple and Logger Boy left the scene only once.

There is nowhere else they could have gone. They are inside.

With the bike overturned, Sheldon can only hope that Rhea and Lars are there, too.

A little farther now and . . . is that it? He scans the spot with his binoculars. The edge is straight. Clearly man-made. It is a structure of some kind, about one hundred meters from the house. Sheldon creeps over huckleberry shrubs and fallen birch limbs. He avoids a dead badger, and is grateful there are no crows there to be startled and give away his location.

Yes, there it is, the sauna he has imagined. A single room with a roof—large enough to seat half a dozen people and dry the firewood. A dipping spoon inside to douse the rocks with cold water and build up steam. Where fair bodies simmer to a blistering rouge like a harlot's cheeks after a firm roll.

Sheldon comes at the sauna from the back side, allowing it to eclipse the main house. He stands now for the first time, and feels the pain shoot up his back.

The door is on the far side, facing the house, but there is a small window in the back, where he can see inside if he stands fully erect.

It is dark inside, but not pitch-black. There is a round window on the door that lets in enough light so he can scout the contents of the room. A bench runs around three sides, and on the left wall there is a second, higher bench. The seats are worn, and even though there is no fire, he can smell the wood. It reminds him of being young and full of spunk. The feeling comes as an unwanted diversion. He tries immediately to repress it, but the memories that come from smells are the hardest to send away.

*Is this the kind of place a man would store weapons?* Surely it is not. Ammunition is not likely to ignite at the reasonably low temperatures at which humans bake—otherwise the Middle East wouldn't be armed. But it can warp delicate woods, and force metal to expand just enough to throw off the precision of a fine instrument.

*So where are the rifles?*

Sheldon stares through the rear window some more, but the idea doesn't come to him.

"How's it going?"

"Bill?"

"Yeah."

"I can't find the guns."

"Where have you looked?"

"Well, I've looked through this window here."

"Sounds thorough. Might as well pack it in."

"All right, sunshine, what's your bright idea?"

"Actually, the idea is yours. If the sauna is too hot, then they can't be in the sauna."

"So they're outside the sauna."

"Well reasoned."

*They're with the wood!*

Sheldon walks left and peers around the corner. He can see the house, and is pretty sure the house cannot see him. But there, as Bill suggested, is a second, small shack. It has no windows. It stands about two and a half meters tall and is less than two meters wide and a meter deep. More of a closet than a shack. In these parts, given that the property is not a farm, the little outbuilding could not be mistaken for anything other than a wood-and-tool shed. It is an utterly unremarkable place worth no one's attention.

It is a good place to store a weapon, Sheldon figures. It might grow cold there, but the damage to the gun is far less of a risk than theft from the main house. There is always the risk of accident, too. This is why Sheldon never owned a gun once he got back from Korea, unless you count the old pirate gun that Saul used to play with in the antique shop.

Bill, meanwhile, had a decommissioned musket, so when the two of them started going at it, there was no getting any work done.

The door to the shed is secured with an old-fashioned Master Lock encased in red rubber. What is useful is that the lock is actually open. The inverted U of the lock has been set into place but not pinched closed. There is little point in wondering why this is so. He has to go in. He just hopes that no one has gotten here before him and taken what he needs.

The door hinge is on the right, so it swings toward the house. Sheldon steps into the shed and closes the door behind him. It is dark inside, and warm. It is so confining that for the first time in days he can smell himself. His body reeks, he is smeared with dirt and fungus, and he is streaked with the excrement of birds and worms. Every part of him blends with the soil—everything but his blue eyes, which take in the sharp rays of light from cracks in the roof.

There is a rake, and three shovels of different sizes. There is a paintbrush that is stiff from neglect, and a coil of rope that was once dependable but has been too long near a gas canister and is now suspect. There are archery targets and fishing tackle. And above him, jutting out from a shelf, is a leather case half the length of a rifle.

Sheldon presses up on the case and tries to keep it from scraping as he pulls it off and down. It is heavier than it looks. Or perhaps he has grown weaker.

He wants to leave here immediately, but knows that a rifle without ammunition is useless to him. If he is caught here, he could be killed without a fight. It is too much of a risk, though, to leave and assemble the rifle, only to come back. It needs to be done here.

Trying not to knock anything over, he lays the case gently on the dusty floor, listening intently for any sound from outside. The case is old and has a combination lock on the front, with three numbered dials that can be rotated with the thumb. In the 1960s, a common code was 007, in honor of Sean Connery, and Sheldon tries it, without success. The factory default on most cases is 000, and he tries this as well, without success.

"This could go on all day," says Bill.

"Why's it always Bill? Why not Mabel? Or Saul? Or Mario? Or

someone I passed on a highway. Why do you come here dressed like the drunken Irish pawnbroker from next door?"

"I thought he was dear to you."

"He was, and I miss him. Which is why I resent you dressing up like him. Finished burning bushes, are you? Now you want to be Irish?"

"It's been a long time since we really spoke. I miss our conversations."

"I have no more to say to you than I did before. It's you, if anyone, who has some explaining to do. So piss off, I'm busy."

Sheldon silently turns the case around so the hinges face him. He wedges the knife blade under one of the hinges. By inserting a small stone under the blade, he creates a fulcrum, and he presses down hard on the hilt, successfully prying the hinge off.

He repeats this on the second hinge, and it comes off without a fuss.

He resists looking at his watch.

Knowing it will creak slightly, he lifts the lid of the case. To his surprise, there is only one rifle.

"Which one are you, Moses or Aaron? The damaged one, or the brother who makes it to the Promised Land?"

Sheldon lifts it from the case and feels its weight. It has been decades since he handled a rifle. He never intended to hold one again. But here, in the improvised ghillie suit, on the floor of the dusty shed, he remembers who he once was, with a confidence and clarity that has been missing for years.

The rifle is a Remington Model Seven with a twenty-inch barrel, which Donny wishes were twenty-two inches, for added accuracy. Ammunition is supposed to be stored in a separate location, but Lars obviously trusted the hiding place and the locked case. There are five rounds of .308 Winchester, which look and feel familiar because they are about the same size as a NATO 7.62 mm. They are the sort of rimless bottleneck rounds that he used to squeeze off—at a rate of three hundred a day—back at New River.

The Remington, though, is a single-shot, bolt-action rifle, the kind that a father and son might own. Nothing fancy. Just a good, dense-wood deer hunter with a walnut stock and a Bausch & Lomb scope.

Donny assembles the weapon, opens the bolt, and slides it back. It is smooth and well oiled. With his finger, he checks the chamber to be sure it is empty, then he slides in a round and presses forward, firmly but quietly, on the bolt. He locks the bolt down into its groove.

With the safety on, he takes the remaining four rounds out of the box and puts three of them in the breast pocket of his jacket, under the ghillie suit. He places the final round above his right ear.

Sheldon checks the shed one last time to see whether he might be missing something—a clue, or the other rifle. There are paper targets and duck decoys, a pair of snowshoes and a set of skis, some odd strings dangling from a hook with brightly colored ends, an empty tube that looks as if it may have been used to carry architectural drawings, and two aged tennis rackets.

He debates the merits of closing and replacing the rifle case, and decides it is worth taking the few extra seconds involved. He is not used to working in a crisis like this, not used to the pressures of a hostage situation. As a sniper, he worked alone or with a spotter. He was dropped off someplace and made his way—usually in his own sweet time—to the objective and set up his position. He did not run around like a nervous cop wondering what to do, as he has to do now.

Camouflaged and armed, Donny's countenance changes. He stops sweating, and his back no longer feels pinched in the lumbar region. Even his hands feel looser.

And then the objective changes.

As he advances on the house from the shed, he sees two figures making their way up the mews toward the front door.

There is a tall one and a short one. The tall one is pulling or dragging the small one. They are more than one hundred and fifty meters away, through trees and bushes.

How long has it been since he drank water? Could it be as long ago as this morning? No, it was on the truck.

He stays hunched over as he slips up the path toward the house.

It is a bad angle. A terrible angle. He is moving perpendicular to a possible target, giving the enemy the longest time to detect his movement. They are converging on the same vortex. Donny is closer and may reach the house sooner, but he will have no time to set up. He'll be completely exposed. And he has no idea who the others are.

And then a small gift descends. From the edges of Lapland comes an arctic breeze, carrying with it the scents of juniper and snow. The breeze rustles the trees surrounding Donny in a whirl of protective movement and hum.

At fifty meters from the house, the ground cover begins to thin, and he knows this is it. He drops to his belly and slithers off the path to the left, where the ground has eroded a few inches because the earth is less densely packed here than the dirt on the footpath. He lies low and adjusts his ghillie suit.

Checking the wind and the angle of light, he takes his position.

Donny brings the rifle into play and checks his sight.

It would be good to have a spotter now. Hank never did cut it as a shooter, but they moved him off the rifle to the scope and found him unexpectedly effective. In part this was because he was well meaning and gullible and so did what he was told, but in part because, unlike Mario, he wasn't smart enough to question what he was doing. Hank was good at finding the range and at suggesting where to set up the shot. And despite being a goofball, he was eerily silent when working.

But Hank is not here now, and Donny has to select the shot himself.

The tall one is an unremarkable man in a black leather jacket. He is holding a lever-action rifle at its balance point, just in front of the receiver.

The small one is Paul.

Sheldon closes his eyes tightly. So tightly that the grid of cones and rods casts a mosaic against his retinas and resets his mind.

He blinks, and then blinks again, to be sure. But, yes, the boy is still there.

So now there is a choice, and either choice is a failure. If he shoots the stranger with Paul, he might be able to pull the boy into the thicket and hide him under the ghillie suit long enough for the police to arrive. But if he does, he sacrifices his granddaughter and Lars to whoever is in the house. The other men will hear the shot. They will find the body. They will take their revenge.

Sheldon aims at Paul and studies his face through the scope. Paul has been crying, and his face is red and puffy. The Wellingtons are bright blue against the cool yellow of the mews's summer grass. Paul no longer has his hat and horns. His Star of David is less like a comical act of defiance and more like a target or provocation. There is resistance in his steps and anger on his face, where before there had been none. The boy has been pushed to his limit. And still he doesn't know that his mother is dead.

Sheldon can only wonder what has happened to the hunters.

The shot is getting easier to take. They are walking toward him. Toward the house. Donny eases off the safety and places the cross-hairs between the man's eyes. There is no venom in his look. He is not speaking, and doesn't appear at all frustrated over Paul's resistance. He is dragging the boy where he wants to take him.

Donny lowers the sights to the center of the man's chest. It is an unfamiliar weapon. He does not know how the ammunition responds, how well the scope is aligned, and whether the barrel has been cleaned. The best he can do is shoot for the center of mass and hope that his hands do not twitch, that the gun reacts, and that Paul will come when he is called.

Or, to be more precise, he hopes that Paul will run to him when a name that is not his is called out in a language he does not speak by a man holding a rifle and dressed like a bush.

*This is not a good plan.*

Donny breathes. He takes air deep into his lungs and lets it out slowly. He takes a second breath, shallower than the first, and lets it out halfway. Without Hank, he checks the wind one last time. He measures the gait of his mark, and judges the distance to the target and the time it will take for the bullet to travel that distance so that the round can penetrate his heart at the correct moment of the step.

With Sheldon balanced and in position, time is replaced by eternity.

In finding his form, he gains composure.

There is a moment of calm.

In that moment of calm, Donny pulls the trigger.

## CHAPTER 22

Y OU DRIVE LIKE AN old woman," says Sigrid to Petter as
he passes the Esso station in the middle of Kongsvinger.
Her hand is on her forehead, and she stares at the road as
though willing it to slide faster beneath the wheels of the Volvo.

They have already heard the radio announcement: shots have
been fired on a small side road near the gas station.

"I'm driving as fast as I can. I don't usually do this."

"You had to pass a test."

"They don't retest us."

"That's going in my report."

"There's no need to be rude."

"I'm anxious."

"At least you were right," Petter says.

It is an odd comment, and offers no comfort. The cruisers arrived at the road only five minutes ago. There was one survivor
with a bullet wound in his back who is now in critical condition and
being airlifted to Oslo. A passing motorist stopped, and once the

terror passed she called the local police station. It took only minutes for Sigrid to be notified.

Sigrid takes a blue-tinted bottle of Farris water from under her seat and has a long drink as Petter weaves and bobs through small-town traffic. She imagines the summer house and its surrounding land—the dirt road that leads to the footpath up to the house, and the field stretching in front of it.

"How are they coming?" she asks Petter.

"The troops?"

"Are they coming by air?"

"They've come by helicopter as close as they can get without being heard. They're doing the rest on foot."

"Where are they now?"

Petter does not look at her. His eyes scan the road for errant balls chased by children, and for cars passing through T-intersections while their drivers stare like idiots at their text messages.

"Close," he says.

There is a click—a distant but familiar click. It is the sound of a rifle being dry-fired. The Black has heard this sound before. If done repeatedly, it can damage the firing pin, so he does not do it often. But over the years, with so many weapons around so many inexperienced young men playing with their guns like toys, he has heard this sound countless times.

The sound has come from the woods. It is not the crisp snap of a twig. It is different from the long crunch of a leaf or the muffled bunt of a bone. It is distinct. Metallic. Sharp. It is a sound of war.

He stops and holds the boy firmly in place. He is not paralyzed by fright. He is trying to get a bearing on the sound. He would like to hear it again, to know where it came from.

He is twenty meters from the two steps leading up to the bright red house that rises incongruously from the dusty tones of the late-summer earth.

When he stops, the boy also stops. He is sullen and pulls against his captor, but only as a form of protection, the way an animal might suddenly, and without immediate provocation, turn on its chain and gnaw on it with a low growl. The boy does not care why they have stopped. He wants to be free and to run.

There are sounds, usually but not exclusively spoken sounds, that announce the end of days—when knowledge is shared that all is lost and can never be recovered. The notification of a loved one's death is such a sound.

The sound of a firing pin striking the back of a bullet that does not discharge is also such a sound.

It is the sound of hope lost. A story ended.

To anyone else, the sound of Sheldon's rifle misfiring is a thin, sharp click. To Sheldon, it is as loud as a coin thrown into an empty swimming pool in the dead of night. It travels for miles. It tells the world where he is. What he is doing and why.

His mark has stopped moving. He has clearly heard the gun misfire. The boy does not know this sound and is unmoved by it, but the man knows it. It is on his face. There is no confusion. He has turned and is looking into the woods.

Donny should be silent. He should be still. This is how the sniper survives when running is impossible. He should trust his position. Trust his camouflage and wait for the mark to pass. The goddamned rifle is obviously broken.

*Moses. The flawed one.*

Sheldon, however, does not do this.

As quietly as he can, he lifts the bolt and slides it back until he feels the friction of the bullet. If he pulls too hard, the solid round will be ejected and fly off to his right and land in the leaves, making more sound. So he reaches his left hand over the breech and eases back the bolt handle until the tip of the bullet is angled out.

Putting the failed bullet to ground, he takes the one from behind his ear and reloads. Bolt forward, then down. No safety. He takes aim again and—without the pause, without the memory, without the doubt—fires.

There it is again. The distinct click of a dry-fired rifle. Such a strange thing to hear. Is someone playing with him? The Black looks again into the woods. Deeper now. In the trees, where a sniper might hide. Along the base of the trees. He has done this before. But he sees nothing. No one out there.

He also hears no birds.

"We are walking again," he says to the boy in English.

He pulls the boy forward to the house and walks up the two stairs to the door. He does not knock. He turns the latch and steps into the dark entry, where he makes out the shape of a familiar face as his eyes adjust to the light.

"We are not alone," he says to Enver.

He then steps in fully with the boy and closes the door behind them.

That quickly, Sheldon is alone again. Everyone he cares about is in the red house in front of him. It is as impenetrable as an ancient fortress. He is a flaccid and useless old Jew, covered in shit and lying on the hard Christian earth of a land that has never known him, never known his dreams, never heard his songs.

There is nothing left in these hands, this body. No purpose. No function he can perform.

*I have deluded myself in my final act.*

He remembers the cold water of the Yellow Sea—the golden sands of the Gobi on its surface—seeping into the rowboat as he paddled with the strength of a Hellenic warrior. He remembers his determination then to serve a cause greater than himself. The success he once felt, and the quiet honor of receiving a medal from his country. Now, on this summer day, he has delivered his loved ones into the hands of killers. His granddaughter and her gentle husband. His neighbor. Her son.

*What a fool I was to have believed I could do anything. That I could have proved I was greater than my own destiny. It is this that killed my son. I pretended to be a man of action. But I am a dreamer.*

He remembers a joke. A righteous Jewish man dies and goes to meet God. He approaches Him and says, "May I ask you a question?" God sees the puzzlement on the man's face and takes pity on him. "Yes." So the man asks, "Is it true that the Jews are your chosen people?" God considers the question. "Yes," He says, "it is true." The man nods, opens his arms, and says, "Then would you mind choosing someone else for a change?"

*I am a foolish old man and have caused nothing but harm. I am so sorry. I can never express how sorry I am.*

"Are you talking to me?" asks Bill.

"Why would I be talking to you?"

"I just figured."

"I don't want to talk to you. I have nothing to say to you. The forgiveness I want is not from you."

"OK."

"I'm not comfortable with the notion of God being Irish."

"You aren't the first person to say this."

"I don't want to die alone."

"You won't, Sheldon."

Sheldon crawls on his hands and knees along the path from the sauna to the house. At the corner of the building, he stands up. It feels good to be on his feet. Caked and crushed, he shuffles to the front door where Paul and his captor disappeared. With his right hand, he takes out the knife and grips it tightly. He is not afraid. He knows that behind this door is his own death. Inside is his remaining family. Inside is the glowing woman who had a baby growing in her belly just the other day, promising a new generation to his family. On that day, he sat like a king on his throne in a northern kingdom and prattled on about days gone by.

*It is called dementia, Sheldon*, Mabel had said to him.

And so it is, my queen. So it is.

At the front door, he smiles his last smile and stands as straight and tall as he can muster.

With a deep breath, Sheldon Horowitz turns the latch on the door and pushes it open.

"Here, here, turn here," says Sigrid, her head burning but no longer throbbing.

Petter turns the wheel hard. The Volvo is on the same road that only hours before the hunters had taken in their pickup and negotiated with the old man over fishing line and a needle.

"Turn off the lights," she says in a whisper, as though her voice might be heard over the sound of the diesel engine. "Pull up behind that Mercedes."

She radios in her location. She knows that everyone at the police station is waiting for news. But there is no news. So there is nothing left to say.

"You want me to block the road?"

"I want you to drive up the dirt path as far as the car will go."

"It's not four-wheel drive."

"No. Why would it be?"

"I don't think we should get there first," says Petter.

"I think someone needs to be there now," Sigrid says. "Drive the car up that path until there's no more path or no more car," Sigrid says. "That's an order."

Petter turns onto the path that Lars uses for the motorcycle. He puts the car in low gear and thunders up the path. The car shakes and bounces. He drives it like a rally car. They are making headway, and they are both thinking the same thought. It is Sigrid who says it first.

"If the fucking airbags go off in this Volvo, I am invading Sweden, so help me God!"

"There. Up there. It opens into the field we saw on the map."

"I don't see any action. Do you see any action? Where are those men?"

"There's radio silence. I can't get between those trees."

"That's it, then. We're on foot."


It is dark inside the house. Sheldon holds the broken rifle tucked under his left arm in the way that a British earl cradles a shotgun after a good duck hunt. His right hand holds his knife. In the foyer he sees boots, scarves, hats, jackets, fishing poles, and a box of candles. More than that, he cannot tell. It doesn't matter anyway. It is no longer his physical surroundings that count. He is no longer Donny, the boy soldier from the green hills of western Massachusetts, who would grow up to be a New Yorker, a husband, and a failed father. He is no longer the man he was at war. The man who struggled to find a place. Now, here, dressed like a fool among the mad, he becomes the man he needs to be.

Facing the darkness, he announces loudly and clearly, so that no one in the house can have any doubt about what is being said: "I am General Henrik Horowitz Ibsen. And you are surrounded!"

# CHAPTER 23

IN THE LIVING ROOM, near the kitchen that connects to the foyer, Gjon has been handed the Black's pistol and is checking it when the General announces himself. Burim is sweating and clenching his knife. Enver looks into the kitchen incredulously.

Enver speaks to Zezake in Albanian.

"You said we were not alone."

"I was right."

Enver grunts. The Black is still holding his own rifle. Enver has his knife in his belt.

"Shall I go and take care of him?" the Black asks.

"Stay with the girl. We may need her as leverage."

"What do you want us to do?"

"Me, I'm going to Sweden with my son. You," he says, "and you, and you, are going to stand your ground and make sure that happens."

Burim's sweat drips into his eyes, and when Enver says this, Burim wants to cry like a child into Adrijana's nape and take it all back, take back every argument and stupid objection he has ever made. Tell her she was right about everything. Tell her that it has all gone horribly wrong and that he never understood that none of this was ever a game. It had just seemed . . . surreal. Yes, like a dream or hallucination. He was dabbling in a universe he didn't understand, and he never intended any of this to happen. For any of it to go this far.

"I'll go!" says Burim, and before any of the three men can say anything, he springs for the kitchen.

He is around the kitchen table in five long strides, and when he sees Sheldon he drops to his knees in front of him and looks up, pleading in English, "Let me go. Please. Let me go."

"Give me your gun."

"I don't have one."

"Is the girl OK?"

"Yes. Please let me go."

"Where is she?"

"Shh. She's in the living room. Please. Let me go. Please."

"OK." And Sheldon stands aside.

Burim gets to his feet and takes one look behind him. He has been in the house for a long time. His eyes are adjusted to the light. He sees more than shadows. He sees the evil itself that is around the corner. He will now go home. And he will apologize for all he has done.

He pushes open the door, bounds over the two steps, and runs. He runs with every ounce of energy in his young body. He runs with fear and purpose. He sprints for the dirt road at the end of the mews, where they ran the Norwegian and the American off the motorcycle last night as they tried to escape. He will go to the center of town and announce himself to the police. He will beg forgiveness and take his punishment and try to become the man who Adrijana has always wanted him to be.

Sigrid and Petter are out of the Volvo and making for the house on foot when they see a young man clenching a large knife running toward them with the conviction of the devil. He is coming straight at them, closing fast. Sigrid raises her Glock and takes aim.

She calls out in Norwegian, "Halt or I'll shoot."

But Burim does not speak Norwegian.

"Halt or I'll shoot," she warns a second time.

But Burim, too afraid to stop, does not stop. He does not even know he is holding a knife, so it never occurs to him to drop it. He cannot imagine that he is even here.

Sigrid fires, and Burim falls.

Sheldon checks his watch when he hears the shot from outside. It is twenty past two in the afternoon. This means absolutely nothing to him. What possible difference could it make?

He had this thought one time before, when Saul was twelve. It was the middle of summer, and they were in New York. Something exciting—not to Sheldon, but to Saul and his friends—was about to happen at Union Square, and he had to rush out the door *right now*.

But something caught Sheldon's eye. It was also about twenty past two in the afternoon, and Mabel was starting to get supper organized as Sheldon was polishing all the black shoes in the house.

The something that caught his eye was a watch on Saul's wrist, which was not the wrist it was supposed to be on. Thinking back on it now, as Sheldon turns the corner into the living room of the summer house to see his granddaughter, he can't remember what kind of watch it was. Which is strange, because he had made such a fuss over it.

"Hey. Where are you going?" he had asked Saul.

Saul skidded to a halt and launched into such a rapid slew of words Sheldon knew that whatever he was saying had to be true, and he immediately regretted asking, because, really, what difference did it make?

Interrupting him, he held up his hand and said, "Yeah, yeah. OK. What are you wearing on your wrist?"

Saul looked down as though it were a trick question of some kind.

"A watch."

"My watch."

"Well, yeah. So what? I wear it all the time."

"But you still have to ask."

"I wear it all the time! I always ask, and you always say yes. Can I go now?"

"Not so fast. Asking is important. Every night after dinner, I ask your mother if she wants me to do the dishes. She always says yes, but I still ask."

"That's not the same thing."

"Why not?"

"I don't know. It just isn't. Can I go now?"

*Saul. My son. Outwitted me at age twelve. But he failed to do it when it mattered most.*

Sheldon steps into the living room.

They are waiting for him. Three men—the one he failed to kill, one he has never seen, and the one in the white Mercedes. Sheldon looks at their shoes.

"My men have you surrounded," Sheldon says. "Give up. Let the man, woman, and child go. Maybe you'll live."

Enver studies his face intensely. Sheldon can feel him trying to penetrate his own stare. He is trying to make a connection beneath the layers of fabric and brush and bravado. And as close as Sheldon is to success in his charade, the one quality he cannot mask is his age.

"I recognize you," says Enver.

"And I've recognized you since before you were born."

It is only then that Rhea believes her ears, and only her ears. Though he is standing directly in front of her, she had not recognized him by sight. And she wouldn't have, had he stood there in a bathrobe and slippers with his coffee mug, because it is impossible for him to be here. To exist here, in this world, at this moment.

"Papa?"

"Rhea," he says.

Lars is not here, and Sheldon fears he must be dead.

The boy, physically unharmed, stands in the corner. He is, as ever, too traumatized to speak.

"Papa!" she yells.

Enver is going to leave with the boy now. And before he does, he is going to kill the old man.

Sheldon stumbles back a step as Enver advances. Sheldon drops the rifle and raises the knife for one last attack. He wants to plant the blade in Enver's throat, but he lacks the strength. The arbitrary laws of time have taken away his last defenses.

With valor, he lunges for Enver's chest. But he misses.

Enver's strike is hard and experienced. It cuts Sheldon down the left carotid artery and across the chest.

Sheldon's right hand grasps his throat and he staggers backward into the kitchen and against the table.

The task done, Enver grabs the boy—who screams now—and takes him under his arm and out through the back door. The boy's screams are deafening, and Enver shouts at him in Albanian to shut up. To quit the yelling. To knock it off or he'll smack him. But the boy will not stop.

He does not stop when Enver drags him to the quad runner parked at the back of the house, which is waiting to take them to Sweden.

He does not stop screaming when he catches a glimpse of a man in a black uniform holding a small black rifle.

And he does not stop screaming when he sees Lars Bjørnsson emerge like a ghost from behind a mighty beech with a compound bow, and release a carbon-composite arrow into the heart of the monster.

Sheldon cannot be certain of what he sees or hears anymore.

Life—whatever this life may be—is draining from him. It may be that Rhea leapt to her feet and shoved the man that Sheldon failed to shoot into a window, and somehow, as she did this, his chest exploded as though silent bullets had penetrated his thorax from outside the window. And without a sound, the remaining man — who had stood quietly in the corner holding a pistol — fell lifeless to the floor.

It may be that she ran to him and held him up, pulling him to the front door, calling him, "Papa, Papa."

It may be that together they fell out the front door, their bodies tumbling down to the cool ground, his blood flowing to the earth.

It was certain, though, that the light around him was radiant and wonderful.

A woman appears. She is in uniform and has a kind face. A nurse, he presumes. He sees men in dark outfits scurrying around him. Perhaps they are hospital orderlies. This nurse is smiling at him. It is the warm and loving smile of someone with good news.

*Mabel must have given birth. It must all be over now.*

Sheldon reaches up his hand and touches Sigrid gently on the cheek.

"My son. Is he OK? Is he well?"

"Your boy is fine, Mr. Horowitz. He is just fine."

# Acknowledgments

This book was written in 2008 in Geneva, Oslo, and Fornalux. The ending came to me in the moments before my son, Julian, was born that April.

I am not sure how much of this book was written by me and how much was written by Sheldon himself. So I extend, here, my thanks to him for all his assistance. Which isn't to say he was easy to work with . . .

I lifted the definitions of "snarf" and "twerp" from Kurt Vonnegut's 1977 interview with the *Paris Review*. I suspect he'd be delighted.

The lighthouse at Palmi-do at Inchon, Korea, was built in 1903. In 2006 it was made obsolete and replaced by a modern one. But the diminutive eight-meter tower still stands in the shadow of its big brother.

Unusually, this book was first published in Norway in 2011, in Norwegian, despite its having been written in English. The story has undergone additional revisions since then. I consider the English-language publication definitive.

In 2012, sixty-seven years after the end of World War II, the Norwegian government formally apologized to the Jewish population for its actions during the occupation.

My special thanks to Henry Rosenbloom and Lauren Wein for their editorial assistance.

Deepest thanks of all to my wife, Camilla, who makes everything possible and gives it meaning. And to my daughter, Clara, you are already an inspiration.